Prai

"The most enduring aspec   —absolute, complete, and unflin   even as
they endure hardship and   ₅ greater.
Cast Away, another fine novel from an author whose imagination and
unflagging empathy bring about stories that stick to the ribs like the
best meals."

—CRAIG LANCASTER, *600 Hours of Edward*

"A big-hearted, funny, beautiful novel about the dreams we chase,
Cast Away bridges generations and countries to remind us that no matter what, however unexpected, we may be sustained by love. A wonderful book."

—TESSA FONTAINE, *The Electric Woman*

"A terrific read."

—TANYA PARKER MILLS, The Book Bungalow

"Johnstun navigates the complicated intersection of a broken immigration system and the ever-shifting American dream with a sharp wit
and deep historical awareness that makes *Cast Away* impossible to put
down. This novel is a continual feast for the senses and exploration of
the heart."

—PATRICK RAMSAY, Happy Magpie Book & Quill

"A deeply human tale about what it means to struggle, overcome and
thrive. This is a moving, impactful novel that's chock full of heart."

—ADRIAN TODD ZUNIGA, *Collision Theory*

"A family saga spanning almost a century, *Cast Away* presents the universal immigrant experience while in search of a better life for future
generations. A well written and delightful story. Couldn't put it down."

—MICHELE SHAUL, founder and editor of Label Me Latina/o

"*Cast Away* explores our ideals of a better life, be they on the far side of a TV screen or a border, and the people and places sacrificed to get there. Johnstun has written a delectable, humorous, heartwarming read not to be missed."

—HEATHER MATEUS SAPPENFIELD, *The River Between Hearts*

"Johnstun conveys human emotion and experience and the entangled dynamics of border policies with poignancy and power—a complex and rich read that restores our faith in the human spirit. *Cast Away* enriches the mind and heart!"

—DAWN WINK, *Meadowlark*

"Expansive in its scope as it connects the past to the present, heart-breaking but hopeful as it chronicles the ways we find connection to each other, *Cast Away* is a masterfully woven story from Johnstun, a writer to watch."

—RUBÉN DEGOLLADO, *The Family Izquierdo*

Praise for Kase Johnstun's
Let the Wild Grasses Grow

"Johnstun knows his terrain well, creating a palpable sense of the sky and soil, grasses and wildlife of the mesa—and the winds of change that swept through the nation for two tumultuous decades. A tender evocation of grief, hope, and dignity."

—*KIRKUS REVIEWS*

"The characters in *Let the Wild Grasses Grow* are connected by a deep-rooted bond to the land and their shared Mexican heritage. Johnstun's rich writing style pays homage to what it means to be a westerner, and to the intensity of true love."

—*BOOKLIST*

"Unflinching and beautiful, Johnstun's novel *Let the Wild Grasses Grow* is easy to fall into and hard to shake. It is at once lyrical and cinematic."

—LEIGH CAMACHO ROURKS, author of
Moon Trees and Other Orphans

"*Let the Wild Grasses Grow* is a propulsive read."

—SEAN PRENTISS, *Finding Abbey*

"Johnstun's prose is immediately relatable to any reader through its humor and the small, sacred, and compassionate moments that make all of us want to be a part of these characters' families. The conflicts that are overcome in this book, even though in an earlier time period, can give us hope, and let us know that we can get through the terrible problems of today."

—SEAN DAVIS, *The Wax Bullet War*

Cast Away

CAST AWAY

a novel

Kase Johnstun

TORREY HOUSE PRESS

Salt Lake City • Torrey

First Torrey House Press Edition, May 2024

Published by Torrey House Press
Salt Lake City, Utah
www.torreyhouse.org

International Standard Book Number: 978-1-948814-92-8
E-book ISBN: 978-1-948814-93-5
Library of Congress Control Number: 2023933988

Cover design by Kathleen Metcalf
Interior design by Gray Buck-Cockayne
Distributed to the trade by Consortium Book Sales and Distribution

Torrey House Press offices in Salt Lake City sit on the homelands of Ute, Goshute, Shoshone, and Paiute nations. Offices in Torrey are on the homelands of Southern Paiute, Ute, and Navajo nations.

To my father

PART ONE

Chapter One

VERONICA

MÉRIDA, YUCATÁN, MEXICO 1923

VERONICA CHAVEZ WATCHED THE SOON-TO-BE DIVORCEES AS THEY NAV-
igated the streets of Mérida. She followed them and hoped one of the
men, covered in a beige linen suit and recently purchased Mayan hat,
would leave the courthouse, see her standing there, and fall in love
with her, swept up in the ecstasy of leaving his puta of a wife. The
ex-wives must be putas to lose the love of their beautiful, rich, white
husbands.

She followed one soon-to-be-divorced couple from the town
square, where their trolley dropped them at the courthouse. They stood
and waited for a moment after the trolley left; the man unfolded a map,
and the woman peered over his shoulder and pointed. With a nod, he
agreed. His eyes were blue and his hair was dusty blonde. He wore
the same thin, beige linen suit that all the men who came to Mérida in
the 1920s to get divorced wore. Veronica imagined a store gigante in
los Estados Unidos. It was at the port, and men, ready to board a ship
to cross the Gulf of Mexico and get a divorce, stood outside in a line,
wearing heavy blue suits. They entered one by one, and when they
came out, they all wore the divorce suit—beige linen—and boarded
the ship.

Veronica was the oldest of four girls, but her father never felt the loss
of not having a boy. She got up early every summer morning and
packed up his fishing boat. By the age of six, she was the best deck-

hand her father had ever known, and with her help, he made a good living hauling in fish and selling them at the fish market.

Veronica and her father would rumble from the dock into the Gulf of Mexico, his three-horsepower Evinrude spitting tar-thick exhaust into the air. The little motor pushed against the swells of the morning tide, and once they were out over the reef, the water cleared up. Thousands of fish swam in and out of the Yucatán reef, and every morning, as the sun rose up over the ocean, her father would nod at her and she would smile and jump in feet first to swim with the fish as the water rose and fell around her. She felt more alive when surrounded by water than at any other time in her life, like her skin was made to soak it in. He let her swim as long as she wanted, until her hands grasped the side of the boat and he lifted her up and onto the deck. He would give her a hug, kiss her wet head, and say, "Cast away, mija, cast away." Then the work for the day began.

Ten lines and two nets were always in the water. Veronica worked five lines and one net while her father worked the others. When a fish got on, she yanked at the pole to set the hook. When she was younger, she would miss the fish or yank at nothing, mistaking the swell of the ocean tugging on the rod for a bite, but as she got older, she rarely missed. The yank had to be perfect: not so tough that the hook ripped the lip of the fish, but not so soft that the fish spit it out. She raised and lowered the rod to let the fish run a little bit and keep the line from snapping. She gave a little and took a little. Too much pull or too little give would rip the mouth right through, and a big portion of the day's or even the week's catch could swim away from the boat.

Every once in a while, Veronica and her father would float over a school of tuna, mackerel, grouper, or sea bass. Three, four, or five lines would drop hard, and one of the dragging nets would fill up and pull the boat one way or the other. Dragging into a big school of snapper could line her father's pockets and feed his family for a month. He could keep half of the catch and sell the rest. When the rods dropped down together, Veronica's eyes lit up with fear, excitement, and adrenaline. She jumped to her feet and ran to each rod that had a fish on it.

She yanked to set the hooks and placed the rods back down into their holders. She did this while her father wrestled with the net that hung on the side of the boat. He was small, but he had the strength of a man twice his size. He grabbed one end of the net and hooked it onto a latch on the inside of the boat and then pulled the rest of the net in, fish flopping and jumping and hopping around his legs. A larger fish could snap a leg if it hit it right, so he had to avoid the largest of them as they tried to flop back into the sea. Veronica's father had to wrangle all these fish into the live storage box filled with seawater before he could help her.

But she needed little help. Once she set the hooks, she ran back to the first rod and reeled it in. She threw the big fish into the open live storage box, cut the head off their bait fish, baited the hook, and dropped it back down into the school of fish before moving on to the next rod. "Fish on, fish in, bait out," she repeated to herself. By the time they made it through a school of fish, the live storage box was full, and they could fit nothing more on the boat, so they were free to head home for the day. Most of the time they didn't. Instead, they pulled in all the rods, except for two, and sat and talked and waited leisurely for a fish to bite. With smaller bait, they hoped to catch more of the beautiful fish that swam along the reef's edge. The angelfish. The butterfly fish. The surgeonfish. They wanted to reel them in, hold the brightest things that the ocean and life had to offer, and throw them back.

"Okay," her dad would say when the sun began to bake their backs.

"Okay," Veronica would say. She'd strip down to her bathing suit and jump into the ocean to swim above the reef until she got tired.

But much sooner than her dad wanted, Veronica started to disappear on Saturday mornings. She was out the door, with her hair primped and wearing her prettiest dress, in search of an American divorcee.

—

Veronica twirled her dark Mayan hair and sat in one of the famous concrete loveseats of Mérida alone, acting as if she were there to watch the men paint the bottom of the trees white to protect them from the appetites of bugs. She placed one hand on her leg and patted her knee with her fingers until the couples began to move across the stone streets of the great Yucatán city. She felt graceful and invisible. The soon-to-be-divorced couples didn't notice the stunningly beautiful Mayan girl following them around corners and yelling out, "Tu esposa es una puta! Soy princesa Maya!" hoping to plant an early seed in the man's mind. She hoped that when he exited the courthouse, he would be happy to get rid of his wife and, more importantly, be looking for a Mayan princess to sweep off her feet and take home with him to los Estados Unidos.

The man and his wife of unremarkable features stopped at the courthouse steps. Its pillars jetted up beside them and made them look small in comparison. They stayed there for a moment, as if second-guessing themselves, as if the busy street, filled with vendors and tradesmen, became quiet for their last moment of marriage.

"Tu esposa es una puta!" broke the silence and their gaze into each other's eyes. They entered the courthouse frowning and separated. While they were inside, Veronica pulled her hair from her ponytail and brushed it out. It flowed down onto her shoulders and lay like a piece of silk on her back. She smiled and batted her eyelids at the courthouse exit, hoping the handsome man would exit and see her going about the business of being breathtaking, graceful, and seductive all at once. When he didn't come out after the first thirty or forty snaps of her head and eyelids—the process was usually a couple minutes long—Veronica's neck started to kink up, and the soft, elegant movement of her head turned to a quick, jerking movement like a rubber band being snapped from her right shoulder to her left. But she was determined to catch his eye with her elegance. After the fiftieth or sixtieth snap, she looked more like a drunken peacock than a beautiful Mayan princess, and that was when the man and his wife walked out of the courthouse. She did not catch his eye. She didn't even see his eyes.

The man and his wife held each other and cried when they walked out, and the tall columns of the courthouse seemed to curve in to embrace them. Tears dripped from the man's chin, and the couple walked down the stairs past Veronica. She glanced down at their hands and saw their wedding rings shining below the knuckles of their ring fingers.

"Mierda," Veronica said. She walked away, back toward the empty S-shaped loveseat in the city center.

Chapter Two

Chuy
Salt Lake City, UT, USA 1990

RESEARCHERS HAVE PRESENTED STUDY AFTER STUDY ABOUT THE SAD shape of Americans' views of financial success. More than one third of the people in this great country of ours believe that winning the lottery is the only way they will be rich and change their lives, and more than that, they believe that playing the lottery is a solid investment in their future.

I'm not one of those idiots.

I know the lottery is a scam. I know that anyone who believes that the lottery is a legitimate option for fulfilling their dreams should have his head examined. I'm no dummy. From a young age, I knew exactly how I would get rich and save my family—I would be the winner of the reality TV show *CastAway Island.*

We walked off the plane in Salt Lake City, Utah, to a world painted white. White attendants, white families with white hair on the tops of all their white heads, and white temples with tall white spires that shot up into the air. My great-aunt Veronica, my grandma Rosa's oldest sister—who had always told us stories about her oldest sister who lived in Salt Lake City and had taught her to make flour tortillas when she was little—met my mom, my brother Hector, and me outside of security. To pick us up, she wore her best day robe and rolled up to us in her red, motorized wheelchair.

Aunt Veronica was old, really old, and her hair had been sprayed so firmly in place that air got trapped between the sticky strands of the aerosol net. My mom told me that mi tia came to the United States in 1923. The US Border Patrol hadn't been created yet, and immigrants from Mexico, with no proper paperwork, weren't considered aliens by the US. I tried to talk to her in Spanish, but she acted like she couldn't hear me, tilting her head toward me and cupping her ear. The three of us walked beside her on the way to her car, like secret servicemen accompanying an old, deaf, robed diplomat through the airport.

My mom, dressed in her most formal dress—flower hat, flower dress, high-heeled shoes with a flower on each toe—held her Green Card in the air like a shield, although we had all been cleared through customs. If a white kid so much as looked at her, she put the Green Card in his face and said, "Legal!" She'd worked hard to get it, begged my aunt to sponsor her, walked down to the consulate every week, jumped through every hoop, and even used some of the money my father had sent back from the states last summer to grease the hand of a consulate official to push the paperwork through a little faster. To her, the Green Card she flashed in the faces of white Utahns at the airport was a small representation of everything my father had done for us over the last four years. The crossing back and forth over the border, the giving up of his blacksmith job, the back-breaking work, and the rooming with five other men in a studio apartment downtown.

"Gracias, Tia," I said to my aunt. She cupped her ear and rolled on.

As we walked, my mom placed her hand on my shoulder and whispered, "Use your English words."

"Thank you, Tia Veronica," I said as loudly as I could.

She slammed on her brakes. Her hair did not move. She looked up at me and said, "You're welcome, Chuy. You are a handsome young boy. You will do fine here." She patted my arm and gunned it.

Hector slugged me on the arm, "Ooh, señor guapo." He slugged me again. "Guapo, guapo, guapo." Hector's left eyebrow dropped down as if to wink, but he didn't. I'd picked up a few words in English faster than him. I'd been able to memorize all the cities in Utah, and now I was our aunt's handsome young nephew. Now, I know that he was jealous, but then, I thought he was just a dick of an older brother. He was good at that.

In my aunt's boat-like Lincoln Town Car, we drove out of the Salt Lake City Airport and through the west side of the city, through the neighborhoods that sat west of Interstate 15. On the east side, big, fancy houses crawled up the slope of the Wasatch Mountains, and the bright green, perfectly manicured lawns of the University of Utah campus loomed above the east side like money perched up above, looking down on the concrete-grey west side of the city.

Rose Park. El Parque de Rosas, that's where my aunt lived. Hector and I sat in the back of the car and let Rose Park swallow us up. The red, green, and white of the Mexican flag and the emblem of the eagle clutching the serpent between its teeth decorated the Rose Park landscape—peeling Mexican flag bumper stickers hung from the rusty backs of cars, knitted red, green, and white blankets sat on couches in the windows of homes, and mailboxes shone with the national colors of my home. My aunt rolled down the windows with the automatic window button. We stared, wide-eyed, in an effort to see as much of our new country as we possibly could, a country that at that point didn't look much different from the one we'd left. Traditional Yucatán and Michoacán and Jalisco music twanging with violins, guitars and double bass wiggled through the air, mixing with the deep thud of Chicano rap. We were flooded with sounds old and new; sounds of Mexico.

When we pulled into the driveway, had our eyes not been stuck on the sights and sounds of Rose Park, we might have noticed the car pull into my aunt's driveway behind us and come to a stop, and we might have noticed my father standing near the garage with his arms and hands already extended into the air, ready to squeeze us as long as he could.

Since my dad had packed his bags in the middle of the night four years earlier, our reunions had become the end all and be all of my year.

Summer work would dry up in the Estados Unidos, and the hiring managers would walk up to him on his last day of work, hand him his final paycheck for the season, and give him a few extra dollars for his journey back to Yucatán—to Chelem. He would arrive near the end of October. We never knew exactly when, so when the front door of our one-level home opened and he walked through, my world also opened again. He would throw off his cowboy hat, and by the time I got to him, coming toward him at a full sprint, he'd have his hands and arms extended so far out to reach me that his embrace began three feet away from his body and continued until I had long lost my breath from the tightness of his squeeze.

Hector always hung back and waited for me to let go, waited for Dad to come to him, waited for my father's return to seem less heroic. When my father wrapped his arms around his eldest son, Hector leaned into him and shrugged, pushing tears to the edges of my father's eyes.

At the beginning of every October, I started to talk about Dad's return home, about the stories he would tell us about the mansions he built, about the pools that he dug, about the bathrooms the size of our entire house. Hector would not say a word. He shrugged and locked me out of our bedroom. Mom and I would talk about Dad coming home and play the guessing game of what day we thought he'd come through the door.

"The seventh!" I'd say. I was ten years old, the seventh was a few days away, and I hoped snow would close the job sites early.

"Oh, mijo, not that early," my mom would say. "Even if it does snow early, they'll wait for it to come every day before they close up for the winter. He'll be home the eighteenth. That's my guess." Every year she nailed the date. Now, I think she knew all along, and liked to keep me guessing, as her way of keeping me yearning for him. When my bedtime came, Mom would walk with me to our room and stand with me outside the door. She knocked on it with her wedding ring and asked Hector to open up. When he didn't—and he never did—she started to ask questions about the girls in his class.

"What about Marta Martinez? I bet she would make a good kisser.

She has such full lips. Or what about Lina Juárez? She would make a good wife. She has a little extra meat on her. I bet she is a good cook. What would you rather have, Hector? A good kisser or a good cook? Both are good. I suggest the good cook because she has eyes for you. The good kisser..."

When Mom started to talk about how Francisca Franco looked at his butt during Mass, Hector's walls fell down around him. He'd open the door enough for me to slide my hand in the gap and walk through.

Mom would smile and walk to the kitchen to start separating the good beans from the bad. She covered our kitchen table with pinto beans and sipped on a beer. Her lips pursed with each sip, as if kissing a lover, and with a butter knife, she'd push the good beans into a large bowl on the left-hand side of the table and the bad beans and pebbles into the garbage on the right hand side, never missing her mark, all while she hummed an Abajeño tune. Like me, she waited for my father to walk through the door, even if it would be another month before he did.

"Mis hijos," my dad yelled in my aunt's driveway in Rose Park. I turned and saw his arms stretched out toward the sky. He threw his hat in the air and waited for us to jump out of the car and run to him. The lock on my door jammed when I tried to open it, so I rolled down the window and jumped through. I had turned fourteen a week earlier, but I wasn't too cool to run to my dad and wrap my arms around his Mexican-cowboy shirt. He squeezed me until my lungs held no more breath.

Hector, slow and patient, stepped out of his side of the car. He held his hand over his eyes as if to shade them from the sun and peered at Dad and me. He had no bedroom to escape to and nowhere to hide, so he turned his back on us and walked toward the neighborhood park. Mom, although weary from all that went into leaving our home in Chelem, jumped out of my grandma's car and chased after Hector, but my father yelled for her to stop, so she did, her long flowery dress continuing after Hector in the late afternoon breeze.

"Let him go," my father said. "He will find his way home."

She turned back toward my dad and ran to his arms.

Hector walked toward the entrance of the park. His short gait carried him across the street, over the curb, and into the park's entrance. He walked across the grass and made his way past a group of boys who huddled in the shade of a tall oak tree. After he passed the group, one boy flew from the huddle like a used shell popping from a revolver and tapped on Hector's shoulder.

Mom and Dad stayed long in their embrace.

Chapter Three

Veronica

Mérida, Yucatán 1923

Veronica watched a quiet man with a shaved head and a cap to cover it sit on a bench in front of a stone table and write. The bench's legs beneath him were carved in the shapes of lion's paws, and tiny ceramic pieces of red, blue, yellow, green, and purple, pieced and glued together, illuminated a Mexican sunrise on the tabletop beneath his tablet and pen. For a man with thin eyes, a wide nose, and a long forehead, he was handsome. All the imperfections came together to create an attractive face. In his mid-twenties, his eyes bore extra wrinkles and his lips seemed to sag with a prematurely pessimistic grin. Sitting alone at the ornate park table, the whiteness of his skin shone.

The man pulled a large, rubber eraser from his pocket and erased something with the lead-stained end. He pulled his hat from his head, threw it on the table in front of him, and cussed aloud, his bright-white scalp glowing in the sunlight.

He laid his head down on the table, his upper body covered in a thick leather jacket with perspiration gathering between the leather and skin. The devastatingly hot and humid air that blew in from the Gulf of Mexico squeezed him like a wet rag.

Veronica, quietly and with confidence, walked up behind him, tapped him on the shoulder, and spoke.

"Su chaqueta," she said. "Su chaqueta. Hace demasiado calor aquí." Her voice was quiet and patient and fell out of her mouth like light rain falling from a cloudless sky. He lifted his head to her but said nothing. Because he said nothing, Veronica turned and walked toward home. With purpose, she swished her hair back and forth but did not turn back to him.

His chin dropped to his chest as she walked away; she knew this. Her dress revealed her lean, dark ankles. She was beautiful; she knew this also. He jumped up from the bench, grabbed his notebook, and followed Veronica home.

Veronica saw him from the window and waited for him to knock, but he didn't, so she knew that this one needed a little help. There he stood on her doorstep, nervous and exhausted because of his intolerance to strong sunlight, obviously. He pulled his hat off his head, and the rich sun reflected off his whiter-than-white scalp. He clutched the hat tightly with both hands and then turned around to leave.

At eighteen years old, she knew she had more balls than he did, so she opened the door behind him and yelled out, "Señor. Necesitas mantener tu sombrero en tu cabeza. Hay mucho calor." She pointed to his hat, his head, and then the sun.

He, again, sat awestruck. He looked at her like one of those children who wanted toys while their mother shopped, their eyes pinned to the colorful, spinning thing on the shelf, so Veronica stood in front of him and snapped her fingers, and he finally spoke, "Buenos dias, my name is Jason," he said. His Spanish was very basic.

Veronica stood there and wondered what made this young American man so different from all the others that she had seen. He was not confident. He did not look like he had money. He was not in Mérida to shed a bad marriage. He did not wear the standard beige, linen suit that most American men wore. A leather jacket, a thick cap, denim jeans? She felt like he wore these clothes to torture himself, to see what the heat of hell would really feel like, but here on earth. At first, she wanted to think he was some kind of idiot that didn't know when to take his dumb ass out of the sun or, at least when he was in the sun, to wear clothes that might not pull every last ounce of heat from the air and trap it next to his skin, but her disdain turned to admiration. His eyes sank into his face, and they seemed to stretch forever into his soul. At the end of his jacket, his fingers held his pen and pad of paper, so she knew immediately that this young man was not in Mérida to cleanse his life of a woman but to gain something powerful. This attracted her more than any man who tried to avoid sweating in his suit.

Veronica walked up close to Jason, and she turned him back toward the park with a glance of her eyes. They strolled beneath the stone overreaches of the buildings, through courtyards and outdoor hallways encircling them and stretching upward toward the light of day that fell into the buildings' centers through an open-air archway at the top. These buildings with inner courtyards stretched out on the streets of Mérida, and Veronica walked Jason through them. She pointed toward the sculptures that sat at the tops of the interior columns, but Jason's view stopped at her fingertips.

The sun had set, and the walk had to end. Veronica sat down in the middle of the historical park in the center of the city. She looked up at the giant cross that stretched from the top of the Cathedral and prayed to God to keep this young man in her life.

Jason sat down next to her. He placed his hands on the stone wall and straightened his elbows. He sat stiff and timid. Veronica reached to him and pushed on his inner elbow, and his entire body drooped and relaxed, the scrunched wrinkles in his forehead becoming smooth. He extended his arm to touch the soft skin of her forearm, but before he could, a small, dark, leathery hand grasped Veronica's arm with force.

Veronica tried to jerk her wrist free, but her father held on tightly. She writhed in place and screamed for him to let her go, but he held on to her like a fisherman holds onto a trophy fish. When Jason pushed off from the wall in an attempt to stand, Veronica's father—much shorter but much stronger than Jason—shoved the poet back down on his butt and walked away, towing his daughter behind him and shouting, "Pinche puto pendejo gabacho!" The poet did nothing behind her.

Veronica's father dragged her all the way home. She fought every inch.

She yelled out that she had found the man she was going to marry, and her father popped her mouth with his fingers every time she opened it. At their house, he managed to open the front gate, the front door, and her bedroom door with one hand and toss her into her room, locking the door on the inside and pulling the lock pin on the outside, shutting Veronica in.

Like a jailer, Ricardo Luis Chavez kept his daughter in her room for a week. Her father popped his head in sporadically and shouted, "No daughter of mine will fall in love with a gabacho, especially a gabacho who is so stupid to wear leather in this heat! Hay tonto!" He'd slam the door behind him and sit in the hallway and pray to Mother Mary and all the angels and saints that they would save Veronica's heart from the gabacho tonto. At night, Veronica fell asleep to her father murmuring, "No daughter of mine. Gabacho. No daughter of mine. Gabacho tonto."

The week stretched on and on and on until Sunday came around and her father opened the door, handed her clothes for Mass, took her by the hand, and walked with her to the Cathedral to confess her sins and receive communion. Veronica hoped for the gabacho poet in the square, but Jason was not to be seen.

Chapter Four

CHUY
SALT LAKE CITY, UT 1990

I STARED AND STARED, AND MY GREAT-AUNT VERONICA LET ME STARE. She spent her whole day wrapped up in a knitted blanket, knitting and knitting and knitting some more, like she'd been given the ass of a silkworm and had to make sure to clean it out, spinning layer after layer after layer of a new blanket onto the floor. Her Aquanet hairspray held the shape of her hair so tightly that I wondered if I could break it off her head, but other than my father's saws—all of which he had taken with him to work that morning—I couldn't think of anything else in the house that might disrupt the cotton ball-shaped hairdo.

"Mi tia," I said. My stomach grumbled beneath my t-shirt. "Tengo hambre."

She lifted her eyes above the top edge of her glasses and dropped them back down again. "You may not understand this, Chuy, but in this place, in this town, with these people, English will protect you. You can frown at me all you want. I don't care."

My mom left early that morning to register with the state. My dad went to clean the large, industrialized barn of a local dairy farmer. Hector disappeared.

The night before, Dad carried an old mattress from the bed of his 1971 Ford pickup truck, hauled it into my aunt's kitchen, dropped it on the floor, and flattened it out with his boots. He pointed to it and told me to lie down. I did and fell asleep fast.

Hector came home after my parents went to bed and left before they got up that morning. He rolled over the top of me, slept for a few hours, rolled back over the top of me and walked out the back door of the house.

Mom and Dad talked loudly about him that morning. The sound of Mom's sobbing leaked out through the bottom of the bedroom door, and the sound of Dad's mellowing voice followed it. The crying stopped but the soft sound of my father's voice continued until they both left. His voice followed her through the kitchen and into the shower and left with her when she got into the car to head off to her first matriculation meeting at the city-county building downtown.

"We're gonna lose Hector to those boys if we don't get him out of here," Mom whispered to Dad from the driver's seat of Aunt Veronica's car that took up the whole driveway.

"I'll figure something out," my father said.

Her tears dried, but the wrinkled lines around her eyes remained as she pulled out of the driveway and blew me an air kiss. I caught it and wished they wouldn't leave me alone with Aunt Veronica.

She looked down at me, finished a red row of knots, and asked me something in English. Dark liver spots covered her hands and face. After each finished row, she would pause in thought and click her dentures together like two snapping turtles fighting in her mouth. She snapped them together so hard that the impact would have busted out real teeth. As if the end of her thought traveled to the muscles in her jaw and back to her hands, she stopped clanking her dentures and returned to knitting.

The two of us sat in that room for hours on that first full day in Utah. She knitted. I starved. After breakfast time passed and the sun rose high into the sky, my great-aunt pushed on one arm of her rocking chair and stood, her legs and arms seeming to work against each other. On used-up legs and old feet that she stuffed into stiff-edged shoes, she shuffled into the kitchen. She wobbled one way and then the other and then back again the other way until she placed her hand on the stove and steadied herself. With her right hand, she took flour, baking powder, salt, and shortening from the cupboard, and all of a sudden her movements had purpose—her legs steadied, her hands no

---

longer shook, and her arms moved faster and faster, combining the salt, flour, and a bucket full of saved lard and grease into a giant bowl that had appeared on the stove seemingly out of nowhere. Hands that resembled a skeleton's moments earlier became strong as she kneaded the ball of dough. Her thumbs punched into the doughy glob, and her fingers made the inside of the glob the outside, and the outside of the glob, the inside.

She threw a frying pan on a burner, separated the big glob of dough into twenty pieces, and snagged a rolling pin from some mysterious place. She rolled out a circle, threw a cup of lard and grease into the pan, slapped the dough into the pan, fried it up, and placed it in a tortilla warmer that, like everything else, appeared seemingly out of nowhere. Within twenty minutes, a large batch of flour tortillas sat in front of me on the kitchen table. Under the dim kitchen lights, my aunt returned to her old self and struggled to sit down in her chair at the table.

I jumped up to help her, placing one hand on her elbow and the other around her waist, but she tapped me across the back with the rolling pin that she had managed to grab from the edge of the stove.

"You can help me when you can tell me what you're doing en Ingles," she said. I had no idea what she had said to me, so I continued to lower her down into her seat while she continued to tap me over and over with the rolling pin. By the time I got her nuzzled into her chair, she had landed taps to my back, my arms, and my ass. I figured she was being stubborn and didn't want anyone to think she needed help. She'd been alone a long time and had done fine without a fourteen-year-old boy helping her in and out of her chair. But my dad taught me to be chivalrous and to help old people, even if they protested, because, "Los viejos necesitan nuestra ayuda."

"Porque no tortillas de maiz?" I muttered. We never ate flour tortillas in Chelem.

"Sit there, estupido," she said to me. Her shaky finger waved toward the chair in front of the steaming batch of fresh tortillas. I understood that. She was finally going to let me eat, and my stomach jumped in ecstasy, my mouth started salivating, and my eyes grew bigger than the tortillas themselves. I'd never seen my mom make flour tortillas—corn was a staple in Yucatán—but these smelled so good that I slid my hand beneath the lid of the tortilla warmer and snatched a fresh, hot pillow of dough.

She tapped me with the thick middle of the rolling pin, and the tortilla fell to the ground.

"I am hungry," she said. "Can you say 'I am hungry,' estupido?"

My fingers felt tingly from the tap to the top of my hand, my knuckles turned pink, and she expected me to speak English?

"I'm hungry," she said. "Tengo hambre?" She held the rolling pin high into the air with that same Hulk-like strength she used to fling pots and pans and dough all around the kitchen.

"I hungry," I said. Few places on my body hadn't been tapped with the roller, and I wanted to save them.

"That's good enough for a tortilla," she said. I reached down and grabbed the tortilla, and placed it on the plate in front of me. My great-aunt moved the beans, butter, and salsa across the table and lay the rolling pin down between the food and me. I'd seen and felt what she could do with it, her old and weak arms becoming strong with a fiery determination, and I was not going to tempt fate by reaching for the beans and butter.

Digging down deep into my mind, I pulled "I hungry" out again, thinking I could at least get some butter from my mastery of English. I repeated myself, and she looked at me and didn't say a word, so I figured her silence to be the go-ahead. With confidence, I reached for the butter, and with the speed and agility of a hummingbird's wing, mi tia snatched up the tortillas, wrapped them in foil, and placed them in the fridge for dinner.

"I hungry, I hungry, I hungry," she said. "Hablas lo mismo que un bebé!" She raised her fisted hands to her eyes and rubbed them as if she were crying like a baby.

My eyes burned and the words "*I AM HUNGRY*" screeched from my mouth and hung in the air. I knew I had said what she wanted me to say. I knew the words were right. I knew that since I said them she would give me the butter, beans, and salsa, so I reached toward the fridge, took a tortilla from the foil, and stuffed it in my mouth.

That night, Mom and Dad would come home, we would eat dinner together, and mi tia and I would stare at each other across the dining room table. She'd squint her eyes at me and mouth the word bebé when my parents weren't looking. I would chomp on my food, feeling victorious with every swallow.

Mom and Dad had no idea what happened that day. They didn't notice the showdown happening right in front of them. They looked at each other and mouthed the word *Hector*, their oldest son not returning home for dinner for the second night in a row, and the second night in a new country. My father's confidence that Hector would turn it around quickly fell from his eyes to his mouth and neck, and as dinner ended that night, his head drooped with fear and guilt.

"Chuy, stop chomping," my aunt said to me.

"Mama!" I yelled out. I'd hoped the chomping would lead to a reaction from my aunt that would lead to a reaction from my parents. My dad lifted his head and began to speak. I knew that he wouldn't let this continue, that he wouldn't stand for my starving to death, and that I would no longer have to give into my aunt's torturous persuasion to speak English.

"We can't stay in Rose Park," my father said. "We must move somewhere that will be better for Hector." He shook his head and placed his hand on my mother's hand. He squeezed it and looked across the table at me.

"I know we just got here, but we have to find somewhere else to live. Sorry, hijo," he said, running his hand back through his thick mass of wet hair.

"No problemo, señor," I said. "No problemo." I smirked at my crazy aunt and smiled so big that my ears moved up and back.

Chapter Five

VERONICA

MÉRIDA, YUCATÁN 1923

VERONICA SNEAKED AWAY FROM HER HOUSE AND MET JASON EVERY DAY for three weeks. Not one to sit idly and wonder, she began bringing a notebook to the park and writing her own poetry. Jason looked over at her when she wrote and dropped his head down, giving her a good-job-for-a-child kind of smile. But she *was* a child. Eighteen years old, wrapped up in love with an American poet who didn't speak her language. Some days she wrote lists for school or described what she saw around her—*the park trees stretched toward the sky like a dead man's arm coming out of his grave, and the branches stretched out like his fingers, grasping for his last bit of air—the stone walls lay on the ground like shackles on the earth's wrists, they wind through the park, and trap the soul of the ground beneath them.* Veronica had been reading a gifted and re-gifted copy of Pablo Neruda's *Crepusculario*, and she loved the young poet's voice. At the time, Neruda was a few years older than Veronica, and this fueled her love for the young American poet who sat next to her and removed his hat every few seconds, dragged a hand across his damp head, and scribbled a few lines on the page. She knew she had found her gabacho Pablo Neruda, and she gave into the rush of emotion that caught her every time he placed pen to paper.

Veronica didn't want to admit it, but every time she walked down the brick-covered streets of old town Mérida, she started to tremble from the inside until her fingertips twitched. She knew no English. He knew little Spanish. Their first few meetings in the town square were quiet, quiet enough to make the silence comfortable. They both knew why they were there, and they didn't need words to muck it up. Most of the time, Veronica would sit next to Jason while he wrote. Mérida was a town for lovers, for romantics—S-shaped loveseats filled the parks and squares, and bolero-singing trios roamed the streets looking for young lovers to unite with their lyrics of lost loves and dark hearts.

Veronica and Jason had yet to touch or meet at night because of the watchful eye and strict hand of Veronica's father, but Jason would trace the edges of his notebook like he was stroking her thigh, and Veronica would run her fingers along her knees as if they were his. She sat beneath the Mérida Cathedral and thought about ways they could touch each other. Her mind dove into places it had never been. She did not question how or why she had these thoughts. She did not delve into her own sexual psychology or wonder if she was normal. In Yucatán in 1923, young girls not much older than her walked the streets with new husbands and protruding bellies full of new Catholic babies, even though the state was currently under the rule of the Mexican Revolutionaries and General Salvador Alvarado, who had shut down all the churches. But that's not why she wanted Jason. She loved his white skin and shaved, long, thin head. The men in Mérida all had dark, Mayan skin. The European influence could be seen in the massive cathedrals and resemblance to a great Spanish city, but did not extend to the blood of the Yucatán people. The light-skinned Spaniards stuck to themselves in the early centuries of colonization and pushed the Mayans into the poor barrios of the outer city. Veronica had a love-hate relationship with white men long before Jason walked into the Zocolo with his paper and pen.

Jason sat next to her, and she could feel him glance at her every few minutes. They sat and smiled and wrote, her descriptions beginning to take the form of stanzas. They had yet to kiss, grope, or caress, but she wanted to so badly. She knew he feared her father. She knew this was why he stayed away from her physically. Veronica, on the other hand, got frustrated. She took his not kissing her as a bad sign. *Does this man have no cajones?* she thought to herself, and one day decided to see if he had a big enough sack to go after what he wanted.

Veronica did not show up at the park the next day, but instead sat in her room and looked out the window to see if her poet would come and find her. Veronica sat and looked out the window that morning, but the bald, white poet in his cap did not come. Stray dogs roamed the dirt road in front of her white stone home in the outer barrios of Mérida. Shirtless children played in the heavy sunlight of summer, and men swung long pickaxes into the ground, chipping away at the limestone shelf that lay beneath Mérida and the entire peninsula. The square stone houses stretched out for miles to El Centro de Mérida, and Veronica followed the many different pathways to her home from the center like a hawk hunting mice through weeds in a field. Her mouse didn't come, and she didn't know it, but Jason sat alone in the city center writing poetry, thinking about his work, and thanking Veronica for hating him.

Chapter Six

I COULDN'T GET AWAY FROM MY AUNT FAST ENOUGH. IT TOOK MY DAD two weeks to find another permanent, non-green card, and citizenship-unnecessary job, and it became the worst two weeks of my life. Mom ran to the bus every morning. With previously unrealized dexterity, she wrapped a hairnet around her hair, put on eyeliner, and tied on the waitressing apron that read, "If you haven't had pig today, it's not a good day," all while sprinting toward the bus and hurdling abandoned tricycles, basketballs, and neighborhood dogs. I stood on the porch and watched her leap into the open mouth of el autobus giganto. Before it carried my mom off toward the city, my aunt had already begun to yell at me through the open door.

Since the night my father decided to move us away from Rose Park, my parents and my aunt asked me to go to my room right after dinner so they could pour beer after beer into tiny plastic cups, play cards, and throw out the names of cities they believed would take us (but mainly Hector) away from all the temptations on the west side of I-15 in downtown Salt Lake City. I lay in my bed and listened to the ups and downs of their conversations. Laughter swelled like a wave and crashed down onto a shore of what sounded like sobs. The one word repeated was Hector's name. It usually came after a wave of laughter and brought on the crying.

The shadows from the street danced across the ceiling. I dreamed of a place without my aunt, her lectures, or her snide comments about my English. I dreamed of a bedroom of my own and school at the end of the summer. I dreamed of las rubias sitting next to me in class. I imagined I could smell their perfume when I picked up their dropped pencils, leaning close enough to hopefully rub a shoulder or place my cheek beneath their golden strands of hair. Part of me believed that I might be the cool new kid in school, and the girls would flock to me because they were dying to find out what mysterious secrets I held beneath my skin. I could be a bullfighting prodigy who left Mexico because I was bored of the spotlight. Or I could be a cattle rancher who spent my early years (the years between eight and fourteen), on the back of my trusty horse, Old Spice. I had no idea what Old Spice meant, but I'd seen the name flashed across the TV screen and accompanied by manly men who always seemed to get their women. I could tell great stories to woo them. Old Spice and I pranced across the high desert plains of the Mexican frontiers; Old Spice and I wrestled steer to the ground, and Old Spice and I spent our days and nights with some of the toughest, yet loving, men that the rancheros could hire.

But every morning before the day my father pulled into the driveway and screamed out that he had found a job in Provo, Utah, I had to spend my days staring at my aunt and pleading to be fed. Most days mimicked our first day on our own—she'd whip up some food and make me say, "I am hungry." She would give me one tortilla with no beans, salsa, or butter.

"Por favor!" I yelled out in anger.

"Please pass me the beans," she said. It took four days to get beans with my tortillas. I'd say "pleece" instead of "please." I'd say "may" instead of "me," and she'd tap me with the rolling pin, tossing spoonfuls of beans into the air, which I would have to clean up later for accidentally letting the words "que rico" slip from my mouth after I actually got a few on my tortilla.

The importance of tradition and respecting your elders aside—I was so ready to get rid of that old bag. She'd taken to haunting my dreams as a giant walking rolling pin chasing me down the hallway yelling, "Pleece, pleece, idioto." I also awoke to my nightmare and lived with her alone all day while Dad hammered nails, Mom dished out pork bellies, and Hector, who disappeared in the middle of each night, dropped through his window during the day to sleep.

The day after Dad announced that we'd be leaving Rose Park, I got up before anyone else in the house. I packed my bag with the few things I owned, placed a blanket down on the grass next to the truck, and slept until the sun came up over the Rocky Mountains. I planned to leave my aunt's house and say nothing to her so she wouldn't have a chance to whack me with some solid household appliance for saying, "Adios."

But as the sun rose higher into the sky and the dry Utah air choked down its rays, bringing more and more water from my body, no one came out of the house. I'd expected them to be ready to go early, to be out the door and on the road, to be driving away toward what I understood to be whitest, cleanest city in los Estados Unidos, so I waited until the chili pepper thermometer that sat outside the kitchen window registered 100 degrees. Earlier that Saturday morning cats and dogs and kids roamed the streets. Hector and his friends drifted on the edge of the park beneath the tall maple trees. Hard-working men—those the bobbing heads on television forget about when they talked about immigration—mowed their lawns in their tall ranchero hats and Wrangler jeans. But as the red mercury in the chili pepper rose, children disappeared into houses, lawnmowers were put away in sheds, and Hector and his friends disappeared.

A ring of salty perspiration hung on my shirt around my neck. When the mirage on the blacktop began to look refreshing, I knew it was time to head inside. Since my mom and dad were home, my aunt wouldn't lecture me for using Spanish, but I knew I would be forced to thank her for her hospitality.

I threw my bag of clothes and magazines beneath the front tire of my dad's truck and headed back inside. I opened the door to silence. I'd expected my aunt to yell at me to close the goddamned door because she wasn't paying to air-condition the neighborhood, but no one greeted me. I'd been gone all morning, and no one waited to ask where I'd been. The house lay silent and empty—the swaying of the sphere in the center of my aunt's grandfather clock ticking softly. Before that day, I didn't know it made a noise, the sway and tick hidden beneath the shouts of my aunt yelling, "It's called a couch, and you can't sit on it until you know how to say it in English."

Whispers and shushes came from Hector's bedroom and mine. I turned toward the door to the room and saw the door cracked open an inch wide and three sets of eyes stacked on top of each other staring at me.

"It's not him. It's just Chuy," my aunt said, for once in Spanish.

"It's not *just* Chuy," my father corrected, raising his whisper a tad to tell my aunt that he disapproved of her use of the *just*.

"She meant it's just *not* Hector," my mother replied, hoping to tamper down any potential argument.

"Nope, I meant it's *just* Chuy," my aunt repeated.

"Chuy, get in here," my father said. "We're going to trap Hector." He stuck two fingers through the crack of the door and waved them for me to come into the room. "It's hot out there, and he's gonna have to come in soon. Then we're going to jump him, tie him up, and put him in the car," my father said. I waited for him to laugh or roll his eyes or do anything to show that he was kidding, but he did none of those things, keeping his eyes focused and squinting past me and toward the door.

"Get in here before you blow it, estupido," my aunt said.

"Tia," my father growled, "cállate."

"Look how skinny he is," she said. "If he could learn English a little faster, he'd be a little fatter, but he refuses to try. If he's not estupido, he's terco, and it's stupid to be so terco when you're hungry."

My father's eyes disappeared from the stack, and his voice grew loud, but all he could get out was "He..." when the doorknob on the front door started to turn. It was Hector, home for his afternoon nap, and I stood between him and the SWAT team that lurked inside our bedroom door.

"Run, estupido," my aunt hissed, and my parents added, "rápido, rápido."

I ran as fast as I could and hurled my body toward the door, my father opening it enough for me to turn my body sideways and fly through. He closed the door but left a crack so we could see Hector walk toward the kitchen, lift the tortilla towel, and snatch a cold but moist tortilla from beneath it. He scanned the kitchen for family and reached into the refrigerator to pull out some beans and chili verde. His shoulders relaxed and his newly-acquired tough guy attitude left him for a moment, revealing the sixteen-year-old brother I'd grown up with, my brother with the soft eyes who waited with me for our father to come home. My brother, who had talked with me all night until we fell asleep. That brother appeared in front of us with my aunt's food in his hand.

"He deserves to eat less than estupido," my aunt said. "At least tonto here isn't out all day with his bandanna friends." My aunt, full of frustration over Hector eating what he didn't deserve, flung open the door, blowing our plan and our cover, and limped and sagged her old body toward Hector. She pointed her cane at him as she walked.

"Put that goddamned burrito down," she yelled at him.

Hector's eyes widened. He threw the tortilla, the beans, and the leftover chili verde into the sink, and, at first, he held up his hands like he was under arrest, but when he saw the rest of us perched in the doorway, his machismo came back to him, knowing that we felt like we had to gang up on him and trap to make him do anything. This gave him a sense of dominance over the rest of his family. He dropped his hands back down to his waist and told his aunt Veronica to leave him alone because she didn't scare him like she scared Chuy, that he wasn't some kind of niña like Chuy, and that she should mind her own business.

Hector took another tortilla from beneath the towel, scooped up some more beans, and dumped a bunch of chili verde onto his plate. My parents and I stood shocked at the edge of our bedroom, knowing that something had changed in Hector that might not change back.

When Hector lifted his bean and chili verde-filled tortilla to his mouth, Aunt Veronica, in her rage, shed the limp and shuffle and became the nimble ninja I had met my first day in los Estados Unidos. She swung her cane toward his face so quickly that he had no time to dodge it. Hector fell to the floor next to his unfinished burrito. We would tie Hector's hands and feet and carry him to the truck that day. He would wake up on our drive out of town. He would yell and scream, but no one would answer him. We all knew that the way to keep Hector out of trouble and keep him as a member of our family was to kidnap him and take him to Provo: the city where no one had sex; the city of Brigham Young University; the city where you couldn't buy alcohol; and the city where it would be difficult to find any friends who drank or smoked or hung out on the all-white, returned-missionary streets of the Mecca of the Mormon Church.

I would live anywhere my father didn't have to leave for most of the year and I didn't have to live under the fascist roof of my crazy, sadistic aunt. Plus, I would be the new guy, the brave former cattle rancher who sadly had to kill his trusty Old Spice to escape the rough and tumble life and the tough men who circle their horses around the campfire every night. I would be the new guy, the mysterious guy, the guy everyone wanted to know—Chuy Luis Chavez.

Chapter Seven

VERONICA

MÉRIDA, YUCATÁN 1923

VERONICA FINALLY GAVE IN AND WALKED DOWN TO THE MARKET THE Sunday after she left her poet sitting alone with his skinny pencil in his hand. He was there, smiling as he scribbled away with his pencil, and did not look up to find her. She continued walking alongside the stone walls of the market and stopped for a bowl of sopa de lima, a fragrant chicken soup with tortilla strips swirling in a bath of lime juice. The poet's pencil moved across the page like a sprinkler dropping water on a thirsty lawn. Every once in a while, he would look up, run his fingers across his chin, and start scribbling again. The stone bench had become dark beneath him.

She realized that he didn't miss her. She saw that the shade-dropping trees, the smell of the vendors, and the sweat on his back and skull gave him all he needed, so she turned away to walk back home and leave the poet alone for good. She thought about how he never came to find her, how he never followed her home again, and how he never stood up to her father and asked him properly if he could see his daughter. This was not the man for her, she thought. She lifted her hand in his direction, touched her index finger and thumb together to create an "O," and raised the other three fingers in the air, to call Jason an asshole. She derided the sexuality of a man who was unable to chase a woman or stand up to her father—and who broke her heart, making her feel as worthless as the garbage tossed in the basura. At that moment, her anus gesture high in the air, Jason looked up and saw the beautiful woman who had left him with unbearable pain—a pain that could only be salved by seeing her now giving him the "okay" sign with an index finger to thumb and her other three fingers sticking straight up into the air.

He jumped up from the ornate table in the middle of the park and ran to her. He took her by the arms and pulled her close to him and kissed her like she had wanted the wimp to kiss her for weeks. "Losing you created my best work," he told her. "I had to lose you to find the muse. Real work. Full of pain and love and heartbreak and anger."

She had no idea what he said, but not taking the chance that he might lose his cajones after this one kiss, she reached up and put her hand around his neck and pulled his face and lips to hers. They kissed for hours, as new lovers do. They walked for a minute and stopped, pulling and tugging at each other. If she could, she would have pulled him so close that they became one. It took them nearly an hour to fumble to the table where his notebook lay. They sat down together and kissed and kissed and kissed.

He stopped to pick up his notebook. He read his poetry aloud to her—page after page after page. Veronica knew very few of the words, but she felt the beauty of their rhythm. They bounced and flowed and weaved and fell and hollowed and filled. Jason's eyes read through the pages. At times, they closed, but she could see them move around beneath his eyelids, as if he were seeing the words come to life in the darkness that lay beneath the thin skin that separated him from the sun of the Yucatán.

Two hours later, two blocks from the center of Mérida, the two of them walked through the center square of Jason's hotel. The hotel lobby, like many buildings in the city, was hollow and squared in; the rooms shot up, adorned with balconies covered in hanging plants and flowers, and ornate railings that framed the open air and basked in the sunlight. White pillars of wood rose from the ground to the top of the hotel, and Jason and Veronica used them as a place to stop and kiss and smile and laugh. They laughed and cuddled and ran their hands across each other's skin as they walked up the stairs to Jason's hotel room. He fumbled with his key and the door handle, doing his best to keep one hand on Veronica at all times, and she kept her arms wrapped around his waist beneath his thick and heavy leather jacket.

The door opened into a small but lovely room. It was a simple room with a bed, a nightstand, a reading desk, a toilet, and a small shower. A white drape hung from a circular frame above the bed and fell onto it like a blanket of clouds rolling over mountains and down into a valley, and the two of them tumbled through the drape and onto the covers. Soon, their clothes were on the floor, and they lay naked together.

Veronica stopped for a moment and sat up.

"Mi primera vez," she said, and she could see he understood.

"I'll be gentle, tranquila," he said.

At home three weeks later, after days and days of personal poetry readings and lovemaking beneath the white drape, Veronica waited for su regla, but it didn't come. She knew why. She'd seen it before. Eighteen-year-old girls disappear with a lover during the day or are married off by their fathers, and three or four weeks later la regla does not come like it usually did, but a baby does, nine months later. She knew. She did not try to fool herself or to convince herself that it would come in a couple of days; she sat back on her bed and let the fear of her father's anger sweep through her because he was the one who could hurt her with his disappointment.

"Americano?" she imagined him asking, his voice trailing into a whisper at the end as if he were praying for it not to be true. "Veronica, mija, por qué?" he would ask but not really want the answer. He would forbid her to marry the American. He would bar her in her room until the baby came, and he would make her confess to the priest and live in his home forever. She would never marry. She would be one of those women that would live in her father's home, in her younger sister's home, and in her son's home (if the child was a son as she hoped), until she died. Her deadening future lay before her like a map of the inner city, with no room for more roads or outlets or alleyways—it was all settled. So she stood, walked down the stairs, found her father sitting at the table drinking coffee, and leaned over to give him a hug and a kiss on the cheek. "I love you," she told him. "I'm leaving, but I'll be back soon." He patted her arm with his hand and kissed her on the cheek, and as if he knew that he would never see his daughter again he said, "I love you, hija. You are my heart and wherever you go, you will always be my special hija."

She walked out the front door, tears falling freely from her eyes, and headed to Jason's hotel room, scanning the walls of the city and pressing leaves between her fingers to remember her home. At the top of the stairs of his hotel, she knocked on the door. He opened it and welcomed her with a hug.

"Un bebé," she said. Her hand rubbed an imaginary belly above her waist.

Jason's eyes grew wide and he went red.

"Okay," was all he could say.

"Okay?" she repeated.

"Okay, I think it's time we went to my home," he said. "Seattle. Before you get too sick. We should go. Enfermos."

The next day they traveled to Puerto Progresso, walked out onto one of the three long piers that prevented boats from coming any closer than three miles from the shore, and boarded a cruise ship to Veracruz. On board, they passed tiny cabin after tiny cabin until their guide opened a door on the top deck. It was huge. Jason had purchased the nicest room for their night on the Gulf of Mexico. There was a queen bed, a bathroom, a sink, and a place to get dressed. It was bigger than her room at home, and Veronica felt like royalty sleeping above all the rest of the travelers in five-foot by five-foot cabins lined with bunks and filled with the smell of four bodies crammed together in an unventilated room. Her room had windows that opened to let in the breeze from the sea.

"The best for you and my baby," Jason said. He led her to the bed, and they made love while the ship departed.

From their bed, she could see the Yucatán float away, and she waved goodbye to her family and the sequestered life of a young mother with no husband. This time she did not cry but turned toward the open sea and smiled at the future that lay ahead of her.

The next day, they docked in Veracruz and boarded a train to Mexico City. As he had for the ship, he reserved the nicest room on the train. The next day they arrived in Mexico City. He bought a room with a view, and they stayed up all night long, the city rumbling beneath their balcony. He bought champagne and convinced Veronica that it wouldn't hurt the baby, so she drank the bottle with him. They fell asleep in each other's arms and woke to board another train to Ciudad Juarez and cross the US border.

The border in El Paso in 1923 was a shack with a guard and a line of Mexican workers waiting to cross the border and work on the railroads. With Jason at her side, they walked past the line of Mexican men and their families. Jason held up his passport, and they gave Veronica a piece of paper and a stamp. They boarded another train that would take them from El Paso to Denver to Salt Lake City to Portland and into Seattle. Jason chuckled when he told her that she would have to sit in another compartment all the way, so she thought he was joking. But when she followed him to the sleeping cars, he chuckled again and said, "Sorry, but my dollar doesn't stretch as far here." The train conductor punched his ticket and escorted Veronica back to the economy car, where she had to sleep sitting up for the next three nights.

When the train pulled into Seattle, Jason came to her car and yelled for her to, "Come on out." She was tired, but he had paid the attendee to make sure she had enough food for the trip. They walked together from the train station up Alaskan Way, along the Seattle Pier. They stopped at the entrance of a run-down apartment building, where

Jason took out his keys, opened the door, and led her up five flights of stairs to her new home. He opened the door and showed her around the damp, musky, and tiny one-bedroom apartment.

"Here we are," he said. He closed the door behind her.

Chapter Eight

Chuy
Provo, UT 1990

OUR FAMILY WAS ABLE TO STUFF EVERYTHING WE OWNED, INCLUDING A tied-up Hector, into the crew cab and bed of my father's truck. We headed south along I-15, and the urban sprawl of Salt Lake City followed us, circling the state prison that at one time was built miles away from civilization and southward toward Provo. I didn't care about the road or the big homes or anything like that. I just watched the peaks of the Wasatch Range. They shot like a row of jagged teeth into the sky. I knew very little about Provo except for what I learned by listening through the seam in the doorway when my parents and aunt sat up late into the night drinking cerveza and searching desperately for an answer for Hector, knowing that they'd been in the States a short time and hoping he had not already gotten a taste of what he could become if left to his own devices.

"Provo, blah, blah, blah, muy blanco," my aunt would say over and over and my dad would answer with si, si.

"Mormones blancos son diferente," my aunt would say over and over again.

In Rose Park, during those first few weeks, I didn't see too many white people—mostly people like me, with Mexican flags waving in their front yards and pork grilling on their outdoor grills. There were a couple of white families scattered throughout the neighborhood. One white guy lived next door to us. From what I understood, he was a brilliant scientist whose wife left him for another man. He wound up on his porch every night after driving home from the university, drinking beer, and practicing his Spanish with everyone else out at night. People liked him. They could see the sadness in his eyes, and men, though tired from a day of hard labor in the sun, would walk up his steps to talk to him for a few minutes, maybe even have a beer with him, and nod their heads as he told them in his broken Spanish about how his wife was "greasing some other guy's pole" while he was at work. His Spanish didn't have to be good for every man to understand his pain, so before each of them left, they patted his shoulder, tipped their caps, and gave him a, "Lo siento, lo siento." By the time enough men stopped by at night, he had gotten plenty drunk and would yell into the night, screaming to himself, telling the sky and the stars the same story about his wife until he passed out in his chair. I expected my aunt to get pissed and yell at him to shut up or go over and hit him with something, but she didn't. All she did was close her window when the vulgarities started to fly from his mouth and whisper, "Lo siento, lo siento." She'd look at me, call me estupido, and tell me to go to bed. So when we drove past the Point of the Mountain, I vowed to forget about the way that old bag treated me during my first few weeks in Utah and move on to my new and exciting life in Provo.

When the truck stopped in front of the Charity Gifts Apartment Complex, when my dad stepped out of the truck and placed his cowboy hat on his head, and when my mom leaned into the back seat and told me to untie my older brother, I knew we were home. Hector had given in to his kidnappers and jumped out of the truck beside me to scope out our new home. The world, as if dropped in the washer with a cup of bleach, had been scrubbed clean and bleached white. Sidewalks had no cracks and were clear of any litter or dirt or scuff marks. Young family after young family walked by the complex. Each of the parents pushed double-decker or side-by-side strollers, and babies that looked to be exactly nine months apart in age popped their heads in and out of the stroller visors. But what surprised us most was the white-blonde color of their hair. Thick heads of blonde hair swayed in the afternoon breeze that breathed out of Provo Canyon. Moms with blonde hair and lightly tanned skin, and dads with blonde, or, at the darkest, dirty blonde hair, pushed babies with hair so white and frail it looked like thin threads of silk sitting on top of their cream-colored foreheads, all of them walking toward a giant white building with a golden man holding a gigantic trumpet on top. Spires stuck straight into the sky, mimicking the Rocky Mountain peaks behind them.

I held all my possessions in one box and a duffle bag as the procession of whiteness walked toward the giant white building. I was not estupido. Even I knew that the parade of baby strollers was heading to the Mormon temple. They did not go inside, but rather roamed around the outside. They talked and ate from picnic baskets and, eventually, greeted a newly married couple who walked out of the temple doors and onto the edge of the temple stairs. They waved to their family and friends who waited outside to congratulate them on their recent nuptials.

One family, noticing us moving into the apartment complex, shouted out, "Hola, nuevos amigos."

"Hola," I shouted back. The father waved, so I waved. The man spoke perfect Spanish and invited us to join his family for lunch on the lawn of the temple.

"Bueno," I said back and waved for my family to follow the blanco family for our first friend-making experience in our new city. But when my dad caught sight of me walking toward the young, blonde man with a blonde wife and four blonde children—all the kids under the age of five—he shouted to the man in Spanish.

"Gracias, señor, pero no hoy, gracias!"

He thanked him for his hospitality and told him that we needed to get ourselves settled in because it had been a long few weeks and a long day and that it was about time we had some family time to regroup. My father thanked him again and with a subtle wave of his hand and a not-so-subtle look in his eyes, he asked Hector and me to hurry on inside and help him start setting up.

The apartment was small—one bedroom, one bathroom—much smaller than our home in Chelem. It had no garage, no handcrafted stone walkway, and no veranda for my parents to sip sweet tequila and laugh on summer nights like they did before Dad left for los Estados Unidos. "A better life," he'd said when he left. "More secure," he'd said. "A place where the government isn't corrupt," he'd said. "A place where money meant something," he'd said. But in Mérida, he was a good blacksmith who entertained tourists with his craft, someone everyone looked up to. I didn't get it. I didn't get how this dingy, dark, and empty one-bedroom apartment—where I would have to follow Hector's smell into the bathroom every morning, where rich white people would walk by the window every day, and where I'd have to sleep on the floor for months before we could afford furniture—was the better life he talked about.

After we had set up blankets on the floors in the bedrooms and unfolded our futon in the living room, the apartment setup that kept us from joining the nice blancos was complete.

My dad, covered in denim, yelled out goodbye and slammed the apartment door behind him. Mom laid out the Help Wanted section of the Provo Herald and searched for a replacement job. Hector lay on the futon and slept. There was nothing for him outside the apartment except clean streets, white people, and their love for Jesus and Joseph Smith. He might as well hang out with me, and wish, like me, that we were falling asleep in our beds in Mexico.

The giant gold man with his giant horn reflected golden sunlight into our dark and breeze-free apartment. Whiteness surrounded us— white sidewalks, white temples, white hair. The sky, although cloudless that day, turned white in the reflection of the window.

The strangest thing about Provo was its smell, or, more accurately, its lack of smell. The smells of baking bread, frying pork, and roasting giblets wove through my neighborhood in Chelem, and those same rich aromas found us on Friday nights and Sunday mornings in Rose Park—the smell of the food in the summer air turned neighborhoods into communities, into very large families sharing in a communal love. Local restaurants, packed wall to wall to wall, filled full city blocks with the deep and strong scent of baking poblanos and broiling bistec. They saturated the air with hours of sweating and marinating and basting that, along with the heat in the summer months, made the block smell, taste, and feel like the inside of a roasting oven.

But Provo had no smell. The restaurants that surrounded our apartment were perfectly erected to match every other restaurant in the chain in every other Provo-like city in the country. And what amazed me the most was that although we lived steps from the doors of the nearest chain restaurant—with its flashy sign and hostess that opened the front doors for its guests—I couldn't smell anything. No remnants of cooking blew outward onto the streets when the hostess opened the door for customers, and, somehow, all the food smells remained in the kitchen.

The white people pushed strollers and drank from juice bottles and smiled in the sunlight. Even in the heat, they wore long shorts and long-sleeve shirts that revealed hints of white flesh. Women covered their upper arms with what looked like two layers of blouses, and all their thighs and knees with long, skinny-legged jeans. None of the men wore tank tops or even v-neck shirts to help cool them down during the hottest time of the day. But, all covered up, they smiled and smiled and smiled.

And when I couldn't handle looking at their smiles and perfectly white teeth any longer, when I wanted to yell out the window and tell them that they shouldn't wear so much clothing, when I wanted to run outside naked except for my underwear and show them how cool my body felt with fewer clothes on—wiggling my cool and breezy backside in front of them and dancing on the grass barefoot—my dad backed into the apartment with a giant, square television and yelled for the whole family to help get it set up.

Dad stacked one moving crate on top of another and set the TV down on top of them. Hector stood up from the futon and snatched the shiny, metal rabbit ears from my dad's back pocket, scanned the back of the TV for their socket, and stuck the antenna in place. Hector and I stood behind him, and his hand reached for the antiquated knob to turn on the TV. All we could see was white static and the occasional wave of color that moved across the screen from the left and disappeared when it hit the right edge.

"It's broken," Hector said. The rare smile that we had all missed and that had been resurrected when my father brought the TV into the apartment flashed and faded away like the wave of color that moved across the screen and disappeared.

"It's not broken, hijo," my father said. "We had satellite TV in Mexico. We got to find some channels." He took one rabbit ear in each of his hands and waved them around the room that was purposeful chaos, one rabbit ear waving left and the other waving right. And then it happened. The flash of color held steady on the screen, instead of whooshing away. I saw people on a beach, beautiful people on a beach, all fighting to stay on a greased-up log. Some fell and disappointment covered their faces along with sand that stuck to the sweat on their skin. The beautiful, nearly naked people who managed to hang on to the slippery log did whatever they could to not let go. One man with hair that covered his entire back dropped onto his balls and screamed out in pain before sliding sideways off the greasy log that hung five or six feet above the beach. Another man dropped to his belly and hugged the log as tightly as he could before the TV host cranked a lever that spun the log to make the belly man slide off onto the beach. Two people remained. One woman wore a pink bikini that had slid so far down her ass that the TV station had to blur it out. She wrapped her legs around the log and squeezed—her calf muscles and quadriceps bulged from her legs—and the look on her face was as determined as I'd ever seen. Behind her, a short man, who did not seem to be that strong, did not have the same crazed look in his eye but instead had one of peace, wrapped his legs around the log. He didn't squeeze, he relaxed his body and gazed off into the ocean and breathed deep breaths until the woman in the pink bikini tried to adjust her grip and fell.

I didn't know English. I couldn't understand what the host said when he placed a necklace of bones around the calm man's neck. Hector's eyes bulged out in anticipation and that fading smile came back. My father held the rabbit ears for the next twenty minutes so we didn't miss anything. Mom joined us and tried to ask questions, but all three of us shushed her. All she could do was smile because her men, her family, had come together to watch twelve people sit and yell at each other during a ceremony of sorts, what I would find out later to be a juried event. At the end of the bickering, each player voted and someone went home.

I didn't need to know English to know that these people were playing a game on an island in the middle of nowhere for a prize. Their skinny faces and dirty skin showed that they had been there for a while.

"$1,000,000. Un millón," my father said. After the credits rolled and my father dropped the rabbit ears, he told us all about the show, the money, the challenges.

"Un millón en pesos?" I asked.

"Un millón en dolares," he said.

We sat and talked for hours after the show ended. We dreamed of the money. We imagined what it could do for us. We pulled together wishes and placed them in an imaginary bowl of hope that someday we could beat the system, that my dad wouldn't have to hide, that my mom wouldn't have to work, that Hector could be Hector again.

Huddled on the futon, with Mom and Dad cuddling up and Hector fighting me for more space, it felt like home for the first time since I packed my large duffel bag and walked out of our beautiful home in Chelem. But every few minutes, I would glance around our empty apartment at the white fuzz on the TV and the moonlight shining off the giant-horn-tooting man on the temple, and wonder why my dad wanted this life for us instead of the one we had. He would have to go to work the next morning in Wranglers, a long shirt, and a hard hat, and he would have to stand beneath the hot sun and shovel gravel or smooth-burning blacktop. Mom would have to search for a job. She would hope to be a waitress, but with her limited English, she would more likely find a bussing gig. Their lives got so much harder by moving here. I didn't get it.

Chapter Nine

VERONICA

SEATTLE, WA 1923

JASON COULDN'T WRITE A DAMN THING SINCE HE AND VERONICA
found each other for the second time—not in Mexico, not on the boat
ride back, not anywhere—and he started to get angry. He tore up paper
and slammed his fists and turned and glared at her. In Mexico, and
when they first arrived in Seattle, his anger disappeared the second he
crawled into bed with her, folded his legs in behind hers, and pushed
his nose into the crease between her neck and shoulder. They lay in
their bed under three blankets; each blanket tossed a different way. He
would try to write, get angry, and give up and climb into bed again.

Veronica waited for his screams to fill the air because it meant
they would be close again, warm together in the blankets. They had
no money, except for a bit of savings left from what Jason had built up
for his Mexico trip. But they were happy. He could try to write while
she cooked the foods of the Yucatán for him: the panuchos and flautas
and fried squid.

Until Veronica got sick. She had been lucky on the boat. She made
it through the months when she was supposed to be sick from nau-
sea. She made it nearly two months before the queasiness and exhaustion of late afternoon set in, but when it came, it came on strong. It
wasn't morning sickness. It was something else that rose inside of her
and stabbed at her stomach. By the time three in the afternoon came
around, Veronica felt too tired to cook. She couldn't stand the smell
of food or be in the kitchen long enough to drizzle the squid with
oil and lemon and push them around the frying pan with her wooden

spoon. She couldn't roll the tortillas with her roller. The back-and-forth movement shook her balance off, and she would run to the bathroom and vomit in the toilet.

But they were happy, even when Veronica smelled of vomit and got too hot to have Jason behind her. His body, his erection, made her even more queasy.

They were happy until the first time he hurt her. He couldn't write more than a couple of verses that day. He climbed into bed with her in the late afternoon, pulled her dress up, and moved his body into hers. Veronica tried. She held still for him. She even moaned a bit to make it seem like she wanted him there, but she didn't feel well. The movement, the heat against her back, and the swirling in her belly like her uterus and stomach had begun to wrestle, made her vomit on the wooden floor next to the bed. Some of it splashed back and up onto them.

"I'm sorry," Veronica said. "I've been sick."

Jason pulled away from her and knelt on the bed, his lower body exposed in the sunlight that came through the ashen window. He kneed Veronica in the back, hard. She fell off the bed and into her own vomit. Her dress sucked in the bile. Her hair became stringy in its wetness. She cried. Jason shook his head, put on his pants, walked out of the room, and slammed the front door to the apartment on his way out into the hollowed-out streets of Seattle.

She had seen who he really was, and it was time to go, but she felt scared and alone and thousands of miles from home. Finding her way back to Mexico seemed impossible as she lay there on the floor. No money. Very little English.

Chapter Ten

CHUY
PROVO, UT 1990

I STOOD OUTSIDE OUR APARTMENT DOOR. GRAY ASTROTURF COVERED the exterior walkway that wrapped around the complex. One propped-open green door with yellow numbers after another propped-open green door with yellow numbers lined the walkway, and spinning fan blades in dirty white fan casings stood in the entrances of the open doorways, pulling air from the open window on the other side of the un-air-conditioned apartments. Like me, neighbors stood outside under the awning that put off a three-foot cover of shade from the one-hundred-degree sun. For the most part, everyone who stood on the walkway was some kind of brown. Some were really brown, some were mostly brown like me, while others were kind of brown. Sharp elbows and hands hung over the balcony railing and tossed cigarette ashes into the dry, yellow patches of grass beneath them. I stood and waited for my dad to come home. Our favorite show, *CastAway Island*, was on that night, and I couldn't wait to get our evening started—an evening full of tortillas and beans and salsa verde and juried predictions. I had already started to guess who would be voted off the island, and I knew I had to pick a girl. The previous week, my dad accused me of guessing that men would be voted off because I wanted, deep down, for all the women in the bikinis to stay on the show. I protested adamantly, but I had to take an honest look at my track record and admit that I liked the challenges more when women in bikinis were a part of them. I was fourteen, and my dad had recognized my love of skinny white women running around in bikinis and called me out on it. Self-assessment can be enlightening. I chastised myself for not committing to memory all the butt cheeks and boob curves that Mexican television so happily flashed at me. While I drifted back and forth in my head and thought about all my favorite castaways, I recognized they were all beautiful women and tried my hardest to rank them from one to ten for the sake of being thorough.

One of those dropping cigarette ashes fell from the sharp hands of one of the people and lit a piece of grass on fire. Within seconds, the entire patch of dead grass had turned from dying yellow to burning orange, and the heat from the flames circled the apartment complex, switching a miserably hot day into a miserably hot and smoky day.

The people who walked around our complex to get to the temple or the Chili's held their hands over their mouths and pointed at the flame that erupted from the center of the complex, but they did nothing to help. More than anything, I think the fact that none of us got even the slightest bit excited about the burning patch of grass shocked them the most. After the fire burned for a few minutes, one of the smokers walked to the edge of the balcony with a bucket and dropped water over the flames, dousing them instantaneously. She went back to smoke over the edge above the grass. I went back to thinking about the bikini-clad women of *CastAway Island*. Women continued to smoke. Fans circulated the air, and my dad pulled up in his pickup.

Children played on the lawn of the temple. They danced around and played tag and picked up grass and blew it into the air. They seemed so innocent, and their clothes were immaculately clean, undeniably new, and obviously fashionable. I knew that if I were to become the cool, new kid at school whom girls would follow around, I would have to blend in, dress more like the locals.

Dad walked up the stairs, pushing away the spiraling smoke from his face, and reached out his arms for me. He smelled like sweat, but I didn't mind because that's how I remembered him during the long summers when he first left to come to the States to work. I lay in my bed in Chelem and tried to recreate his scent in my nose. I wished that he would come home and be a blacksmith again—that way I wouldn't have to miss him and think of his sweat anymore.

When he dropped me back down to the ground, I asked him if we could go buy me some clothes before school started.

"We have enough money to eat and pay rent for this apartment, hijo," my father said. He pulled his ranchero hat from his head and wiped the salt that sat between the wrinkles in his brow and hair, enough water to douse the fire that had been extinguished.

"Okay," I said. What else could I say? My asking seemed almost stupid. "Well, can I cut my jeans up to my knee?" I had noticed that all the beautiful women in Provo wore their jeans all the way down to their knees. I didn't notice what the men wore, so I figured it was the same. If clothes in Provo were the *CastAway Island* producer's blur marks, the women of Provo would be blurred from elbow to knee and all in between.

"Sure, hijo," he answered. He leaned back against the railing of the balcony and looked toward the mountains. The sun had bleached them white as it began to set above Utah Lake. He placed his hands on his hips, and he looked tired from the day, but with a quick push off the balcony railing and lunge toward me, he acted like he had all the energy in the world to hang out that night. Mom would be gone. Hector would be the asshole that he had been practicing to be, and Dad and I would begin to cook, talk, and get ready to guess at *CastAway Island*.

"Come on over, Chuy," he'd say. He slid Mom's apron over his head and tossed flour into a bowl. "Grab the Crisco can." He pointed to the cupboard next to the stained-yellow fridge that looked like it could have been all white at one time.

"Okay," I said. I reached down, opened the cupboard door, slid my hands around the large, round, metal canister that read CRISCO on the side, but it didn't have Crisco in it. When we bought it, it did, but not since. We used the slimy, slick, gelatinous goo of condensed vegetable oil, but once it was done, we filled it with grease leftovers from anything we cooked. Grease from fried chicharrones. Grease from bacon.

Grease from sopapillas. Grease from Crisco. I placed the Crisco jar on the counter, opened the lid, dug out a big spoonful of hardened grease, and dropped it into my dad's pan. It sizzled and popped and smelled like memories of all the other nights my dad and I cooked together since we got to Provo.

He took a handful of pork trimmings from a bucket of them we got from a friend up the street and dropped them into the pan. They danced on the surface of it, white and pink and rubbery cuts of fat and skin that most people would discard, and they spread a smell of home.

I pulled out a bowl, he tossed in some flour, and he took another can of Crisco from the cabinet above him—to make sure we didn't mix the fat with vegetable oil—scooped up some new Crisco, put it into the bowl, and began to roll it together with his hands for the tortillas.

I used our special ladle with holes in it to dip into the sizzling pan, pull out the frying pork parts and drop them on a paper towel next to the oven. As I'd been taught since I was little, I picked up the pan and dripped the excess grease back into the first Crisco jar to be used later, while my dad rolled the tortilla dough. He gave me a squeeze with one arm and dropped the first tortilla into the pan to fry.

Seven o'clock approached, and Dad had already put together a spread of tortillas and fried pork chicharrones. Hector sat behind us and yelled weird English words while listening to his portable CD player that magically appeared out of nowhere. I'd asked him when he bought it, and he laughed at me and said, "Bought it? Yeah, right. I found it."

"When were you in somebody's car who owned a portable CD player?" I asked him. I couldn't think of anyone who had one.

"Be quiet," he answered.

The contestants on *CastAway* ran through a maze while blindfolded and had to collect trinkets along the way. When they got to the end, they took off their blindfolds and arranged the trinkets in a way that spelled out "Winner." My dad and I didn't always cheer for the same person to win (my favorites always being those in bikinis), but we always cheered loudly enough to push Hector out onto the front porch. He would make sure to grab the biggest sopapilla, slather it with the remaining butter, and slam the door to be a dick. For a moment, the smile on my dad's face would drop off, but Dad would slap me on the back, cheer for his favorite contestant, and smile again. When the jury began, Dad and I shouted out our guesses. We had one rule that we had to abide by. We had to shout out our first guess before the tribe spoke, and we had ten seconds after the tribe had spoken to revise our guess. If one of us were to guess the same person both times and get the answer correct, we got an honorable congratulations, and that was awesome. The jury began. To prove my dad wrong, I chose the prettiest girl who provided the most blurred areas during challenges and shouted out her name. My dad shouted out the same name.

The tribe spoke. They accused. They backstabbed. They grumbled. When the host shut down the discussion, my dad looked at me for my final guess. I looked up at the screen and saw the beautiful woman who always promised blurred body areas because she tried so hard at challenges by jumping, crawling, and sliding. She didn't care if the motions gave her a wedgie or pulled her swim top halfway down, and, to me, that effort deserved another couple of days on the island. She showed true grit and conviction. Since I didn't answer immediately, my dad shouted his guess out—the same as before, the woman I felt had given such heart. When I opened my mouth to shout out my vote, I couldn't help but say the name of the old man with gray hair that covered his entire gordo body. He too provided blurry spots but not the type I ever wanted to imagine. The fat, hairy man survived. My big-hearted player went home. I don't think the tribe could have been more wrong.

Chapter Eleven

VERONICA

SEATTLE, WA 1924

WHEN VERONICA CAME HOME FROM THE MARKET, THE DOOR WAS cracked open. She looked back into her memory and saw herself closing and locking the door through her tears, so she hesitated before she went inside, knowing that Jason would have to have gotten up from bed, walked to the door, purposely unlocked it, and left it open. A frigid Seattle breeze ran up the staircase of the old apartment complex, whistling as it came, and pushed the door open slightly more, revealing Jason's naked backside in the kitchen.

Veronica held her breath. The naked man went about his day as if he had clothes on. He poured a cup of coffee. He added heavy cream. He added honey. He carefully slid his fingers through the mug's handle and walked into the bathroom between the kitchen and the bedroom. The sound of his teeth scratching against his toothbrush gave Veronica a chance to exhale and inhale another deep breath. But she could not bring herself to move from the doorway. The *pmphh* of the shower being turned on gave her another chance to breathe.

Knowing that he stood behind a fabric curtain, she moved past the kitchen and bathroom into the bedroom and hid in the tiny closet opposite the two twin beds. She shut the folding doors and sank back into the piles of Jason's dirty black pants and black shirts, the smell of smoke circling up around her. The shower's low hum took her home. The heavy Caribbean rains drenched the hard, red dirt of the Yucatán shelf. Inch-wide raindrops fell to the ground and splayed outward until the dirt became mud. Children ran through the muddy streets and slid to a stop. Real laughter, not like any laugh she has laughed since she left home, came from the bellies of her mother and father and sisters and brothers. The boisterous, havoc-wreaking winds from the irreconcilable hatred between the Atlantic Ocean's coolness and the Caribbean's warmth slammed against the adobe and cement walls of her childhood home. SLAM.

SLAM again. It was not the SLAM of memory, but the SLAM of the front door of the apartment and the SLAM of the bathroom door. The hum of the shower was dwarfed by the unmistakable sounds of lovemaking against the wall between the bathroom and the bedroom. The voices came: the howls of orgasm and the gasps of shortened breath. Then the hum of the shower again and laughter.

Chapter Twelve

Chuy

Provo, UT 1990

IT WAS SUMMER. WE LIVED IN A SMALL APARTMENT. THERE WAS LITTLE to do, so Dad and Mom let Hector and I sleep in as long as we got our chores done, the few that there were, before they got home from work. Most mornings, Dad rattled around in his room, collecting his tools and drinking his coffee for about ten minutes before he and his tool belt clanked their way out the apartment's front door and started up his truck with a rumble and a loud spurt of noise. I would wake, then close my eyes again until a few hours later when the sound, or smell, of Hector's farts would wake me again.

That next morning, my dad stood at the end of my bed and wiggled my feet with his hand.

"Get up, hijo," he said. "Let's go buy you some new clothes for school."

He had changed his mind. At night, in a dream, he must have seen the light—I needed new clothes to be the mysterious and cool new guy I wanted to be. Wasn't that why he did everything to bring us to los Estados Unidos? I jumped out of bed, threw on my newly cut-to-the-knee-Mormon-style jean shorts and a t-shirt, and ran outside toward his truck, deciding that all other hygiene would be pointless until I wore cool, new, hip clothes. There was no need to brush my teeth if I was going to pair them with old clothes.

Before my dad could get a glass of water and meet me at the truck, I ran down the stairs and jumped in the cab. He walked out of the apartment and stopped at the passenger-side window and tapped on it. He whistled and pointed to the bed of the truck.

"Your clothes are back there," he said.

I looked into the rearview mirror. His tools, big and small, lay on the bed of the truck. Smaller tools were harnessed in horizontal, wooden slots that he had built for organization. Larger tools like saws, awls, and power hammers sat in wooden slots around a large compartment that held his air compressor. He had saved a little bit of money after every job to buy his own equipment, professing that with his own well-maintained tools, contractors and subcontractors were more likely to hire him. Amongst his tools, in the center of the truck bed that was usually left open for hauling materials, sat a lawnmower, but no clothes that I could see.

"Get out, mijo," he said. He walked around to the back of the truck, dropped the tailgate, wheeled the lawnmower to the edge, and lowered it to the ground. He found my eyes in the rearview mirror, pointed downward toward the lawnmower, and mouthed, "Tu ropa, hijo."

"Are they under the mower?" I asked.

"No, hijo. If you want new clothes, you're going to go mow some lawns, pay me rent for the mower, and go to the store yourself," he said. "Now help get this mower on the ground."

I got out of the truck and joined my dad at the back.

"If I help you get it on the ground, does that mean I agree to your terms?" I asked. My dad had repeated the words saying, "Boys make promises; men make commitments," to Hector and me since we were old enough to break promises, so I knew that if I agreed to mow lawns, I could not break that commitment. The man standing next to me couldn't have given two shits about what I spent my money on but, more than anything, wanted me to earn it. The lawnmower lay at the end of the bed. He had obviously bought it used but had to take some time to fix it up for me so I wouldn't have to worry about maintenance. Shiny new nuts and bolts popped out from every joint, the edges of the blades had been sharpened and shone like polished silver, and all of the levers and pulleys and belts had either been replaced or cleared of gunk. If I helped him take the mower off the truck, he would expect me to get after it immediately. If I didn't take it off the truck, he would be disappointed in me. The weight of my dad's disappointment would be a lot heavier than heaving around some trash bags of grass a few days a week before school. I reached for the mower. We took it off together. He showed me how to mix the gas and oil, how to avoid flooding the small engine, and how to let the machine do most of the work. He patted me on the back and left for work. Standing with my mower in the middle of the parking lot, I knew I had better get started if I wanted to buy the clothes necessary to convince the ladies in my eighth grade class that I came from a long history of rich rancheros.

I scanned the horizon for an untrimmed lawn, but saw row upon row upon row of clean-edged, manicured lawns. For a desert state, Utah couldn't have been brighter green. Like Astroturf on a futbol field, grass sprang out of the ground. No brown or empty patches existed— just thousands upon thousands of sprigs of grass cut to three-quarters of an inch. It had been trimmed along the sidewalk edges like a military cut along the ears, high and tight and even, an edge of brown dirt separating sidewalk gray from grass green. Sprinklers doused the grass in the early morning and created hundreds of little rainbows along the side of the road. These green markings of property lines seemed as natural as the white spire and the golden Moroni that shot up from the top of the Mormon temple next to our apartment complex.

In our tiny town in Mexico, lawns didn't exist. White concrete houses lined the road, and behind them, more white concrete houses stretched toward the gulf on the north end of town and toward Mérida on the south end. Weeds lived there, not Scotts Miracle-Gro. Giant iguanas swam through those weeds. Infertile dirt sat on top of a giant limestone shelf that made up the Yucatán Peninsula. Beneath that shelf lay death—the crater of the asteroid that killed the dinosaurs and shifted the earth's climate for millions of years to come. Our little town, however, had become something. It had built itself up as a getaway for Méridians to come and play on the beach.

For a couple months each year, Hector and I would set up a make-shift stand on the corner of the town square. Merry-go-rounds and carnival booths whirred around us. Vendors came from all the tiny towns that lined the poverty-stricken coast and the world seemed to center around us during the months of July and August. Money traveled in the pockets of visitors, some Mexican, some American, some Canadian, all wealthier than us.

"Iguana Tail Key Chains" was scribbled across the top board of our stand. "Authentic and Battle Scarred" was written beneath us on the front board of a rickety, converted coco de pay stand we rented from my cousin. We would string a line from one edge of the sign to the other and hang five or six iguana key chains on it, making the line droop down and tickle our heads when we stood beneath it. That was all the marketing we had to do—two cute entrepreneurs giggling beneath rare iguana tails. Black spiny-tailed iguanas dominated the rocky, dry terra of the northern, coastal Yucatán. Their thick necks and striped backs blended into the gray limestone that jutted out of the earth, and their quick feet, known as the biggest and fastest of their species, shuttled them across the dirt and launched them from the ground to an adjacent wall. They could get big, three feet big, but rarely lived that long, mostly growing to about two feet from head to tail and living their days on flat, cement ledges basking in the dominant Yucatán sun. Their spines scared children and people from the US and Canada. Once the reptiles escaped their younger, smaller years as well as the hawks and owls that roamed the sky in search of baby iguanas, they had few natural predators and lived up to sixty years. Unlike tinier lizards and geckos, these fast bastards didn't have biologically replaceable tails, so when they lost them, they lost them for good. They would hang out in gangs, kind of like Hector and his dumb friends in Rose Park. And exactly like Hector and his dumb friends, they'd do pushups, nod their heads rapidly, and inflate their bodies to try and intimidate their opponents. The long, black iguanas thrashed their tails around in aggressive strikes. To stop a strike, they would clamp down on the aggressor's tail and not let go. The vertebrae that connected the tail to the body, unlike their smaller kin, weren't made to break off easily, as their predators were less abundant. When the iguana retreated, the tearing flesh and scales left a bloody mess of carnage and victory.

We looked for border fights. They were rare and so cool. We looked all year round and hoped to find five or six long tails to inject with the strong local rum to stiffen them up and keep them together. We sold them to Méridians more than we sold them to foreigners. Americans and Canadians liked to look at the tails, hold them in their hands, and practice their Spanish by asking questions using the common verbs hacer (to make or do) to ask us if we made the key chains ourselves and comer (to eat) to ask if we ate the rest of the iguana, which is a stupid question, but we'd play along and tell them "por supuesto" because that is what they wanted to hear and probably the explanation most of them would understand. They would pat our heads and move on.

I had no practice in mowing lawns. At home in Mexico, I'd never even seen a lawnmower before, but it seemed like a simple enough machine to operate. Put gas in. Pull the cord. Mow.

Dad had left me a gallon of gas, a jug of oil, and an empty milk carton next to the mower. A note on the red gallon told me to mix them up and make sure and use the squishy primer to get it started. I filled the milk carton with gasoline, leaving room for the oil to top it off, put the lid on, and shook it until it was mixed. The little squishy primer stuck out from the side of the mower like a nipple, and since no one was around when I pushed it and squeezed it, I giggled and smiled. I'd never been anywhere near a woman's nipple, so I could only guess what they felt like. I thought about old, hairy men to stop thinking dirty thoughts, and then I tugged on the rope a couple of times to get the mower started, but nothing happened.

After one good pull, it rumbled to a start, the wind from the blades pushing outward from beneath the blade cover, and a rock from the parking lot of the apartment shot out and tore an inch of skin off my left shin. Blood shot out, and a purple bruise rose beneath it. I shouted "shit" into the air and hopped around the parking lot with my bleeding shin in my hand. The blood covered my fingers and "shit, shit, shit" bounced through the air. Nice Mormon moms covered their children's ears and ushered them quickly down the street. People yelled from cars for me to quiet down, while the old ladies with the cigarettes looked down at me from the outdoor hallways and laughed during puffs. Pain pushed "shit, shit, shit" from my mouth. I rambled off another round of cusses, enough for a police car to pull into the parking lot and stop. Two officers got out. Somehow, the pain seemed to disappear. The officers walked up to me, looked down at my leg, and began to talk in Spanish, asking, "Are you okay, young man? Is this your mower? That looks like a bad cut." I nodded. One officer explained to me that he had done something called a "mission" in Mexico. He had to have done something there because he had no gringo accent. He spoke with a fluency that I had never heard from the mouths of those tourists back in the Yucatán.

"Is your mom home?" he asked.

"No," I said.

"Your dad?"

"No."

"Anyone we can talk to?"

Last I knew, Hector was asleep in his room, farting and cussing in his sleep, but when I looked toward our apartment, I saw Hector's eyes between the slits in the blinds.

"No," I said.

One officer opened the door to the back seat of the squad car, peered in, and waved his hand for me to get in.

"Your language is a problem," the officer said in his perfect Spanish.

I felt extremely confused. He spoke my language perfectly, how could it have been a problem?

"Que?" I asked.

"Your cussing," he told me. He waved me toward the other officer and the open squad door. In this new, strange land, I saw women in knee-length jeans, giant golden men on tops of churches, and more blonde hair than I imagined there to be in the entire world, so when the officer motioned for me to get into the car because of my "shit, shit, shit," I didn't question him. I walked slowly toward the open door with my head down, the other officer put his hand on my head to push me through, and he laughed out loud.

"Es un chiste," the Spanish-speaking officer said and waved me back over to him. "You should watch your mouth, but by looking at the cut on your shin, you had a good reason to swear. Get something on that so it doesn't get infected," he said. His eyes were very kind. "Is this your mower?" He pointed down toward the machine that took a chunk out of my leg.

"Si," I said.

"It's an oldie but a goodie. It will do you fine," he said. He reached down, picked up the handle, placed his other hand on the top of the machine, and yanked hard. Dark grey smoke puffed from beneath the slotted, metal hood, and it began to rumble to life, kicking out clearer and clearer smoke until there was no more smoke coming from it.

"When will your father be home?" He asked. I told him. He patted me on the head, got in his car, waved back to me, and yelled, "We'll be back then."

Dad walked into the apartment at exactly 5:05 pm. Utah summers can be brutally hot, and that day it had reached 104 degrees outside. On the blacktop where my dad spent his day in Wranglers, a long-sleeved shirt, and a hat, the heat sank into the black surface, and like the surface of a pan, it kept the heat and cooked whatever sat on top, reaching upward of 108 or 109 degrees on those days. He threw his hat down on the sofa. Dry, white lines of sweat covered his head and face, the salt clinging to his skin. He kicked off his work boots in front of the door, asked about when mom left for work, and began to take off his pants for his nightly shower before he had even left the welcome mat. His shirt followed. Standing alone and nearly naked except for his undershirt and boxers, his skin stopped steaming.

I searched his eyes for clues. I wondered if the news of my cussing and run-in with the law had reached the work site. Had the cops stopped by or had someone seen the incident and called over to tell him about his son's mouth. When he walked away from the door, I looked for evidence in his steps. Did he know that the cops were coming back to talk to him about me?

"How come you're not talking?" he asked as he walked to the bathroom. "You usually can't shut up when I get home, telling me about Ms. Matsumoto, rambling on about the white girls on the church lawn. What gives, Chuy?"

He shut the bathroom door behind him. The shower curtain rings scraped along the metal shower rod and the water splashed down against my dad. The shower curtain slid across the bar, and he got out, grabbed a towel, wrapped it around his waist, and continued his interrogation. "How's the mower work? Did you get it running? Find any lawns?" He dried off his hair, brushed his teeth, and walked across the hallway to his bedroom. "Someone told me something today that I found really interesting," he said. I knew I had to confess. He knew. He obviously knew. The cops would be there any minute. I should tell my side of the story. He pulled his clean underwear up beneath his towel and let it drop to the floor. He threw on a new undershirt, some clean jeans, and some socks and headed out toward the kitchen to start up the burners on the oven.

"Come on, Chuy," he said. What he meant was, "Come on Chuy, let's start dinner." But my mind thought he was pushing for a confession with his sly, calming, "Come on, Chuy."

"Fine!" I yelled. "I did it! I almost went to jail! The cops will be back in ten minutes to tell you!"

My father stopped moving for the first time since he'd been home. He placed the pan down on the wrong burner and wiped his brow.

"I was swearing because of the lawnmower. It wouldn't start. A rock hit my shin so hard it bled. Who wouldn't swear?" I asked. But now, my father had become quiet, silent except for his breathing, which had become pretty darn loud in my opinion.

"When are they coming back?" he asked.

"Now!" I said. My voice trembled. I didn't know what they did with people who cussed in Provo city limits. The cops were nice, they started my mower, and they didn't lock me up, but I'd seen this strategy of niceness before. *CastAway* winners used it all the time. They stoked the fire. They gathered wood. They went fishing. They were everyone's best friend. They backstabbed their way to a million dollars.

"Chuy, this might be big trouble," he said. He grasped one shaking hand with the other.

"Big trouble?" I asked. "How big?" News headlines of basketball players being dropped from the BYU men's team and kicked out of school for breaking the honor code, losing their scholarships, and having to pay the school back moved across my mind in the form of an ESPN ticker. The night before, a city official had lost his position because he was caught having a beer after a meeting in Salt Lake City. I cussed in public next to a Mormon church. What were they going to do with me?

In my mind, the police came to the door and knocked. They slid their hands onto the guns in the holsters around their waists and warned us of their possible use. My father fought them, but they overpowered him and chased me down the hallway of the apartment. They pulled at my legs as I tried to crawl out of the bathroom window, and I shouted into the late afternoon air that they needed a warrant. "We got a warrant!" One of them yelled right before I felt the butt of a gun against the back of my head. I woke up in the back of a police car on the side of the I-15. The police car walled off the oncoming traffic. Behind it, cars buzzed by, heading north toward Salt Lake City, and behind them, the point of the mountain fell toward us from the summit toward the Great Salt Lake and the State Prison that sat behind me. The fences and gates and wandering dots of bright orange waved and swayed in the summer heat. I knew that would be my home for a while.

"You have a choice, Mr. Potty Mouth," the Spanish-speaking officer said. "You are now outside county lines. You can change your ways, or you can end up in one of those orange jumpers at the state prison, rotting away in a cell with the walls to cuss at." I pleaded, told them I would watch my mouth, and in this version of the story that had played out in my head all afternoon, the officers put me back in the car and drove me home, but before they let me out of the car, they burned the underside of my tongue with the cigarette lighter from the squad car, searing a reminder of my sins for me to carry with me forever.

The knock at the door brought me back to the kitchen with my dad. The knock came again, and a third time before we both moved toward the door. My father's steps were slow and even until he stood a foot from the apartment door. His hand extended outward toward the handle and his fingers grasped it, but he didn't turn it. When I looked up at his eyes, he stared as intently at his hand as I had been staring at it. The knock came again. And he turned the knob and pulled.

The two officers from earlier that day stood on the other side of threshold. They smiled politely. The sun reflected off their golden badges and into my eyes.

"Good afternoon, officers," my father said in a heavy accent.

"I'm Officer Smith and this is Officer Young," the Spanish-speaking officer said.

"Manuel Chavez," my father said in response to their introductions.

"It's good to meet you, Mr. Chavez. We'd like to talk to you about Chuy," the Spanish-speaking officer said.

The sweat on my father's shirt had made it down past his chest and saturated the white cloth so fully that the expanding line of excretion made a distinct border between dry and wet cotton. The tensed muscles on my father's face made me more nervous than I had ever been, and the fear and anxiety grew inside of my chest like it was a balloon and the officers' presence was a mouth pushing air into it. I broke.

"Don't hurt my family! I won't cuss again! I hate orange jumpers!"

I yelled and fell to my knees. I placed my hands behind my back and waited for the cold metal of the cuffs to clamp down on them.

"Chuy, get up," my father said. "They're not going to arrest you because you swore in public." He turned back to the officers. "Are you?"

"Of course not," the Spanish-speaking officer said. "Quite the opposite. We're here to ask your permission for Chuy to mow the lawns at the precinct." A gasp of air came from my father's mouth, and the cramps that had taken hold of my belly had loosened their grip.

"Chuy, would you like to come mow the lawn every week for us? We pay well," the officer said.

My father's hands began to shake again. Now that we knew they weren't going to arrest me, I didn't understand why they shook.

"Dad, why are you shaking still?" I asked, forgetting that one of the officers knew the language.

The officers glanced at my father's shaking hand, and their expressions turned from smiles to concerned gazes.

"Quiet, Chuy," my father said. He placed his hand on my shoulder. Moisture dampened my shirt, and the ends of his fingers massaged the end of my collarbone.

"Do you mind if we come in? Hay mucha calor," the officer said.

"Si, por supeusto," my father said and waved the officers in.

They took off their hats and slid into the living room.

"Thank you. It's really hot out there," the other officer said.

"Great, all we need now is proof of Chuy's right to work in the US. Do you have his papers available? We figured we'd make sure here before we brought him to the courthouse to fill out paperwork."

My father's fingers dug into my shoulder blades deeper. I took it as a sign that I needed to do or say something, so I did. "I can grab them. They're in a box in the kitchen." I shrugged my father's hand off my shoulder and ran to the kitchen.

"Chuy," my father yelled to me. I turned back to him before I passed under the door jam. He looked scared, nervous. Sweat began to drip from his hair like a sponge that had absorbed too much water.

One officer glanced over at the sweat on my father's shirt and neck, more visible inside the house where the light had become even beneath the bulbs and away from the bright sun.

"Nada, hijo, nada," he said, his voice soft and trailing off before saying the second nada. His hands fell to the side of his body. He looked at the officers and gave them a half smile. They returned a slight, conservative one.

Our box of immigration papers sat on top of the cabinets over the microwave. I took the step stool I used for extra height when asked to flip the tortillas and grabbed the box from the top of the cabinets, jumped off the stool, and ran back to the three men standing by the doorway.

My dad reached for the box, but I figured I would open it up and help him out. As I lifted the lid, he lunged for the box in a jerky motion, slamming his hands against my forearm in an attempt to grab the box from my hands. I lost my grip and the papers dropped to the floor at the officers' feet. The men bent down to help us pick them up. One officer found my papers immediately. They clearly stated my legal immigration, the day we got into the States, and the stamp from the immigration officer at the airport. The other officer held a social security card and my father's ID card in his hand.

He read the name from the social security card, "Francisco Garcia." He read the name printed next to my father's face on the photo ID, "Francisco Garcia."

The officers glanced at each other and down at me. They placed all the papers back in the box on the floor.

"Chuy, it looks like you're good to go. We'd be happy to have you mow our lawns," he paused for a few seconds, "no matter what." The Spanish-speaking officer waived his partner out the door and followed him. Before the door shut, he glanced back at my father, whose face had fallen flat with no expression—no movement of the eyes, no upturned lips, no dimples—like someone had shaken an Etch A Sketch and blanked him out. The officer didn't smile or frown. His eyes remained soft and he pursed his lips and dropped his head like he was telling my father, "Lo siento."

He shut the door behind him. My father leaned down and closed the box.

"Don't tell your mother about the officers and the box. Okay, hijo?" he hugged me and walked back into the kitchen to make dinner.

Mom worked late. Hector stayed in his room throughout the night, even after my father had asked him to come out. Hector was unhappy. He didn't say much. He wanted to be back in Mexico. We all knew it. We let him be. We hoped he would come around soon. I missed his teasing, his laughter that came at my expense, and his punches to the arm when he approved of something I did, like spitting really far or reciting lyrics to Control Machete, or belching. My father missed him, too. Sometimes, he sat outside his room and talked to him. Hector never talked back, but my dad would talk about his day and the crazy people he encountered, and how well his new tools worked compared to the junkers he had before. When he got tired, he would walk back into the living room, open a Budweiser and sit quietly for a while before gathering enough strength to talk to my mom and me.

That night after the officers came, my father stood outside Hector's door again.

I knew Hector was in there because of the pure smell of him. I don't know if I had special Hector-odor senses, but I could smell my brother through the walls. He'd recently turned sixteen years old, and his body odor seemed to hug him. If I got too close, it hugged me too. I couldn't get it off me. I think it was his hormones growing. They had nowhere else to go, so I think he sweated them out, but they clung to his skin like barnacles on a boat called "Stinky Hermano."

After we had eaten dinner, a spread of Kraft macaroni and cheese and tuna fish and mayo on Saltine crackers, my dad tried to force his way into our room, which had become, for ninety percent of the day, Hector's House of Sour Stenches. But Hector had become as strong as my dad over the last four years, something I think my dad had forgotten.

My mom had taken the locks out of the doors when we moved to Provo so Hector couldn't lock them out, but as soon as dad turned the knob and pushed the door open, making a slim crack between the door frame and thin, hollow door, Hector slammed it shut, nearly crushing my father's fingers in the jam.

"Hector," my father said. He waved me over to him and pointed for me to sit down on the shag carpet in the hallway that, because of its age, rivaled Hector's odor if you got your nose too close to it. He began speaking loud enough for both of us to hear him. Hector, I knew, would remain quiet, acting like he wasn't stinking up our room behind the door with his breath and flatulence.

"Boys, those men are going to come for me. They know that I don't have the papers they want me to have. Now that they know, they can do nothing else but send me home to Chelem," he said. "I will not cry, and I do not want you to cry because it is the crying that makes it sad, not the moment."

He took a long breath. He leaned against the door. When his whole body weight rested against the thin outer frame of particle board, Hector slowly opened it up, bracing my father's body so he would not fall into the room.

My dad gained his balanced, pointed to the floor, and asked Hector to join me on the shag, brown carpet that looked more like the hair of a shaggy, dirty, brown dog than something we should be sitting on.

"Can we sit on the couch for this?" I asked.

Hector slid down next to me and slugged me on the arm.

My dad put his back against the opposite wall and slid down toward the floor, his back never leaving the stained, discolored wall behind him, until he sat on the ground in front of us and placed one foot next to mine and one foot next to Hector's. From my left foot to Hector's right foot, we had created a chain of Chavez men.

Hector's breath stunk, and I couldn't breathe until my dad started to talk again.

"Hijos, they're gonna come back and take me home, understand? It was a matter of time," he said. "Before, when I was here for the summer to work, I could remain invisible. Me and the other men, we all lived in a small apartment together. We slept side by side on ugly, brown carpets like this."

"Was it stinky like Hector?" I asked, losing focus because Hector sat next to me with his knees in the air and his feet on the ground. His shorts were so baggy that they created two large tunnels right to his ass, and I knew his gastrointestinal system was on a timer, and there would be nothing we could do about it.

Hector slugged me in the arm.

"Shut up, Chuy, for once, hermano," he said. I can't remember any time before that when Hector had called me hermano. I felt so proud at that moment.

"I'm chill, so chill, hermano," I said. I closed my eyes and nodded my head up and down and imagined how cool I looked, like the older brother from La Bamba, the tough one who always did well with the ladies and wore great jackets all the time.

Hector slugged me again.

"Stop acting like you sucked a lemon, man, and listen," Hector said.

My father smiled a half smile and continued.

"Me and the other men, ya know, we went to work, we went shopping for food, we crammed into the same car, and we went back to the apartment, ten or so of us working through the summer and sending money home and counting every day until we could go home ourselves to be with our families. We had no intentions of staying here. And law enforcement knew that. We worked hard, we spent our grocery money here, mostly on beer and sandwich stuff, and we never got in trouble. So they left us alone," my dad said.

He reached out and placed one hand on my knee and the other hand on Hector's knee, and I wondered if I wanted to giggle because of how much his rough hands tickled my skin. Hector didn't giggle, so I didn't giggle.

"Now that I'm here, now that I'm trying to live here with my family, to them, I am no longer summer labor. To them, I am now illegal. I am now trying to skim off their system, entienden, mis hijos?" he asked.

"Entiendo," we said in unison.

He nodded. He pulled his hands off our knees. Thank God. I almost couldn't handle it anymore.

"When they come, if you are here, they will be looking for any reason to send you back too, so I need you to remain calm, si?" he said.

"But they can't take you. We're here now," I said.

"They can do whatever the hell they want to do, Chuy," Hector said. "And there's nothing we can fucking do about it."

"Yes, we can," I said. I couldn't believe that we lived in a world where they could take our dad away.

The moment was over.

Hector flew back into his room.

My father stood up. He pulled me up from the floor. He wrapped his arms around me and said, "Only white, rich people get lucky. And we're not rich. And we'll never be white. And don't ever give them a reason to deport you. Because they'll find one if they want to. No matter what papers you have."

Chapter Thirteen

VERONICA

SEATTLE, WA 1924

FOR A MINUTE, VERONICA SAT BACK INTO JASON'S SMOKE-SATURATED clothing. She moved her hands along the back of the closet door and followed the natural wood patterns with her fingers. The steam from the shower had made its way into the bedroom and leaked into the closet, making the air in her box thick and moist with the smell of soap. Perspiration built up between the door and her fingers. And she felt a tear drop from her eye onto her chest. She didn't know she had begun to cry. It had become such a part of her daily life in the last few weeks that now it happened with no forewarning, physically or emotionally. She felt like she could sit there forever and die. Her lover was having sex with someone else in the bathroom. Her family would never take her back. And the feisty eighteen-year-old girl that walked the streets of Mérida months earlier felt like she had been left in Mexico. The dimly lit closet was small but comfortable, and decisions waited for her outside of it. She knew that what she did in the next five minutes of her life would set her down her path for the rest of it. It would decide who she was and who she would become.

In a parade of giddiness, Jason and a woman stumbled out of the bathroom. They walked a couple of steps before they stopped, tickled each other, and giggled in the fun and erotic cloud of a new sexual relationship. They fell to the floor on the way to the bed and into Veronica's view between the closet and the wall.

Jason kissed the woman's neck.

"Veronica," Jason mumbled under his breath.

"Veronica?" The woman yelled. Her moans stopped even though Jason continued to rock back and forth.

"Nothing," he said. He continued to grind his hips into hers. "I don't even know a Veronica. I don't know where that came from." The words came from his mouth in between soft grunts.

Veronica sat inches from them. He murmured her name. Knowing that she was still in his mind—still wriggling somewhere in his emotions—pulled her up from the crumpled mess of herself and his clothes in the closet. If the thought of her still lingered with him then she could still hurt him, too. She stood, opened the closet door, and looked down at the two naked, wet bodies on the floor. The woman's eyes opened wide at Veronica. Veronica wanted to hurt her, but shook her head back and forth quickly and pursed her lips, her eyelids closing as if to say, "Get away from this man! He's not a good man!"

Jason rolled off the woman. Once on his back, he pushed up off the floor and jumped to his feet. He looked like a cartoon character standing nude in the light of the morning: his bald head seemed like it was half the size of his chest and his skinny legs shot downward from his waist like two toothpicks stuck in a pear. He reached out to Veronica. She turned away toward the kitchen. The young woman dove onto the bed and covered herself with blankets. Shame manifested itself on her face in a rush of tears that fell over her cheeks and onto her paling lips.

Veronica ran to the kitchen while Jason reached for his pants. She flung the door beneath the sink wide open and began tossing pans and bowls onto the kitchen floor. The bangs of metal and steel on the tile floor sent more tears from the eyes of the woman huddled up in the blankets on the bed.

Jason fell into the room like he'd been pushed from behind. He grabbed the countertop to steady himself.

"Stop what you're doing," he said, nearly breathless.

Veronica continued to toss cooking utensils onto the floor.

"I'm sorry," he said. He placed his hands on his bald head and pulled the skin on his forehead up and back like he was trying to stretch it across his skull.

Veronica stopped tossing things.

"For what?" she asked.

"For the woman," he said.

Veronica dug back into the cabinet.

"I mean, I'm sorry for the women," he said.

Veronica stopped again and began to stand, her right arm and hand following the rest of her body. In it, she held her tortilla roller. She walked closer to Jason until she was at arm's length, plus the length of the roller.

She pulled her right arm behind her like a professional softball pitcher beginning her wind-up. When the tortilla roller was parallel with her shoulder, she swung it forward with every muscle in her tiny arm. She aimed it for his balls and connected with more force than she knew she had. Jason did not scream. Instead, trying to decrease the contact, he lifted himself onto his tippy toes, but it did him no good. Veronica swung the roller with the aim of splitting him in half. His cartoon eyes bulged from his cartoon head, and Veronica held the roller in place for five seconds before pulling it slowly backward, hoping a few splinters might find their way into his nuts.

Chapter Fourteen

Chuy
Provo, UT 1990

Dad and I had a tradition. Mom worked the afternoon shift at the local IHOP, so after Dad got home from working construction, we would sit down and watch our show together. He would cook tortillas in the kitchen and place a pile of them on the floor next to me right after the clips from the upcoming show finished. We would talk about the politics, the backstabbing, and all the efforts of some of the cast members to win the million dollars. We would finish by eating our last tortilla and guessing what would happen next, who was in trouble, who was mean and vicious, and who wouldn't survive another jury.

The immigration officers showed up at our house to take my dad back to Mexico during the opening credits of *CastAway*. At first, all there was, was a loud thud against the door, like someone had forgotten how to turn the handle and decided to run into it with their shoulder. The thud turned into two or three more thuds, and then the thuds stopped. There was nothing left to thud against. Three men plowed through the door, dropped it onto the ground, and yelled my father's name: "Manuel Luis Chavez!"

It seemed rude to me. I would have answered the door for them and yelled for my dad if they would have knocked. I did it all the time. Someone would knock. I would push myself up from the brown, shag carpet on the living room floor and hope that a commercial would come on TV so I wouldn't miss a moment of the challenge for immunity. I'd walk backward toward the door, reach for the knob with my right hand, open the door, and call for my dad or mom. I could have answered the door for the men if they'd knocked. I sat in shock and my mind became numb with the realization that my dad would be taken away for good.

The light from the TV shone out the window onto the brick wall of the adjacent apartment complex and reflected off the men's gold badges, momentarily blinding me. Dust from outside flew in the air, and the distinct smell of a burned tortilla traveled from the kitchen to the living room. Dad had forgotten to flip the tortillas before he ran from the kitchen, stopped in front of me, kissed me gently on the forehead, and said, "I'll see you soon, hijo."

The tortilla smoke drifted from the kitchen, passed my father, and passed the big men who stood in the open doorway with their guns pointed at my dad. Dad raised his hands in the air and placed them on the back of his head before kneeling on the brown, shag carpet and whispering to me, "Write me and tell me about every challenge, backstab, and vote. I love you, hijo."

A large man with hands the size of my father's dark brown forearm cuffed my father's hands. He lifted my dad up by his forearms, moved him toward the door, and waved for a beautiful woman to come in to sit with me until my mom got home from work. Her blonde hair, tied in a ponytail, sat on her left shoulder, and she smelled like vanilla lotion. She knelt next to me on the carpet and put her soft hand on mine.

"Las tortillas," I told her. "En fuego."

I was so angry, but all I could say was that the tortillas were burning, their smoke stinging my soul with the truth of why they were left unattended.

"Would you like me to take them off the stove?" she asked in perfect Spanish.

"I'll get them," I said. The opening score of *CastAway* played from the TV speakers. "Stay tuned for scenes from the next episode of *CastAway Island*. You'll never believe what happens next." I ran to the kitchen to turn off the burner and move the frying pan from the heat of the electric coil. Two tortillas sat on a plate next to the oven.

"Do you know what happened and what will happen next?" she asked.

"I didn't get to see the vote, so I will have to wait for next week to see the recap, and since I don't know who got voted off, I really can't guess what's gonna happen next," I said.

"No," she said. "Not with *CastAway*, with your father. Do you know what happened and what will happen next? I'm here to answer any questions."

Of course, I knew what was going to happen next. My dad, his work status, and his travel to make a better life for us had been a part of our lives for four years.

"Yes," I said.

We waited in silence for ten minutes before my mom walked through the doorway. Like every night, sticky stuff covered her IHOP apron. She stood next to what was left of our front door. Wood chunks and dangling splinters hung from the door jamb. My mother's face showed no surprise. Her hair had streaks of gray above her ears that ran back through her long black hair, and while her thin, wiry body looked weak, she could haul a car up the street on her back if anyone tried to hurt her children.

"Listen, blondie. Entiendo why my husband is gone. Entiendo why the door is broken down and why you are here, but I will give you menos de dos segundos to get away from my hijo, comprendes?"

The blonde woman stood, walked toward my mother, handed her a business card, told her she could call if she needed any help with the boys, and walked away.

On the screen, right before the credits rolled and the screen flashed to the next show, the host of *CastAway* placed his hands on an urn and said, "Next week, before our season finale, we'll show you where our past winners are now and how winning a million dollars has changed their lives."

That's when the idea came to me. That's when I knew what I had to do to get my father back. I may never be white (unless I got that thing Michael Jackson got), but I could be rich.

PART TWO

Chapter Fifteen

Veronica

Seattle, WA, 1924

OVER THE NEXT FEW WEEKS, VERONICA'S BELLY GREW, A SMALL MOUND on the front of her body. She spent most of her days cooking and sleeping, doing her best to avoid the man who roamed the house. But all she cared about was the little person growing inside of her. Since the morning when Jason kneed her back and pushed her out of bed, she was scared to death that she had lost the baby, so when she saw her belly round slightly, she smiled for the first time in a very long time. Jason had taken over the bed. She made a pile of clothes every night and slept on the floor. He'd forbidden her from coming out of the bathroom naked, telling her that he didn't want to see her "expanding ugliness of flesh gestation."

She knew she had to get out as soon as she could. She had to avoid him hurting her. But she knew so little English. Outside, on the brick Seattle streets, she could talk to no one, so she stayed in the apartment all day, trapped between Jason and the walls of the city that could not speak to her, imprisoned. But, once her belly began to round out, she felt good inside and started to dream about her family again. She dreamed of birthday parties and celebrations and dinners and laughter. She dreamed of the noisy market in downtown Mérida on Sunday afternoons, street vendors, and the bells of the cathedral ringing above her, and she dreamed of her father's eyes, deep and soft, and at the same time, angry. As if she had joined her child in her womb, she went to a world of warmth, even though she lived in a country where she didn't leave the house because she didn't speak the language and lived like a servant and a ghost within her home's walls.

Jason looked at her and her growing belly with disgust. He liked her food. He liked her cleaning, but he didn't talk to her. If she tried to leave, he stood at the door with his arm stretched out to block her from the hallway. He wrote every day until he hit a wall, and then he would head out to the local tavern to drink while she planned her getaway.

On his way out the door, he turned and scowled at her, "You used to be my muse. Now, you are a freeloader in my home. You used to inspire poetry. Now, you take up space. You used to love me, and now, I see, you hate me with everything in you. I see it." He would slam the door behind him. The sound of his boots walking away was comforting during those days.

Sometimes he would drink the cheap stuff bought from the dock-hands. It was dyed brown and a little watered down, but it was strong. With no way to regulate it, bootleggers could sell paint thinner and no one would say a word. He'd disappeared the night before and came home surly drunk and passed out on the bed. Veronica had her best night of sleep in weeks as the alcohol passing through Jason's blood knocked him out cold for six or seven hours.

When she woke up, he was mid-swig. Half the bottle had been finished. His lips barely kept it in his mouth. Drizzles of the thin, brown liquid fell from his chin and onto his bare chest. He didn't wipe himself clean. He typed away, poem after poem after poem. She even saw him smile once or twice, but the smile disappeared with the ripping and crumpling of paper.

With quiet movements, a slow push up from the floor, and a breath instead of a grunt to get to her feet, she walked toward the kitchen to fry up some eggs and potatoes for their breakfast. She hoped to feed him that day, let him drink and pass out, and then run.

Chapter Sixteen

CHUY

PROVO, UT, 1990

MARRIOTT ELEMENTARY SCHOOL STOOD NEXT TO MARRIOTT MIDDLE School, and Marriott Middle School stood next the Marriott Hotel and Suites. Everything was named Marriott. Hector and I walked down the apartment stairs and across the road toward school. In the last month, we moved from Rose Park, were introduced to *CastAway*, and lost our father to La Migra. But the early morning light, with the purple mountains on our left, the Great Salt Lake on our right, and the smell of ripening salt in the air, made everything seem okay. It was the first day of school, and I was ready to ride in on Old Spice and woo las rubias of my eighth-grade class. In my pocket I carried a notebook full of all my *CastAway* notes. I'd interacted so little with the people of my new country that I knew I needed some kind of manual to navigate their social maze. *CastAway Island* was the most popular new series on television—the TV told me so twice a day—so I figured that if I acted like the people on the island, I would probably fit in fine. On *CastAway*, it didn't matter if you were white, black, Mexican, or Asian. Everyone acted the same. They all stood in groups and talked about what they would do next, touching each other's shoulders and shaking hands before walking to another group of people on the beach and touching shoulders and shaking hands.

I had pages of notes. At first, my notes were organized, sentences staying on the lines of the paper and letters perfectly decipherable, but as the season went on and as the gameplay got more intense, so did my note-taking. Words, like players, started to weave in and out of each other. Long, lean sentences made their way into groups of other long, lean sentences while short, clunky sentences huddled together at the edge of the page. Alone, those sentences would seem weak, but together they were bulky and took up a lot of space.

I followed the numbers on my printout. They led me to my home-room classroom. A girl with a twisted left eye sat alone in the middle of the classroom of empty seats, so I walked toward the seat next to her and sat down. Students filed in behind me. Some came in together and found seats together, and the rest filled in the other seats. The school didn't have a uniform policy like mine did in Yucatán, but it might as well have. All the girls wore those long jean shorts down to their knees with a cuff on the end and a collared shirt with long sleeves and stripes. The boys wore long shorts down to one-half inch past the top of their knee and a polo golf shirt, tucked into a braided belt. All the students, in one form or another, wore a blue accessory or carried a sweatshirt or hat that had the stitching BYU on it, big and white and bold. My multicolored, long-sleeved satin shirt clashed against the room of blue jeans and blue shirts.

"I'm Charity," the girl with the twisted eye said.

I looked down at my notes and found the easiest, shortest phrase I had written down.

"I slay bulls," I said. I winked and looked out the classroom win-dow like a man staring into his destiny.

"What?" a beautiful girl asked. "You slay bulls?" The skin between her eyes wrinkled up. The golden blonde hair on her head moved forward on her forehead like a hat.

I kept my gaze out the window and did my best to look serious: I squinted, nodded my head, and pursed my lips as if remembering my most treacherous bullfight. I imagined a bull coming at me, the flag in one hand and a spear raised high in the other, and stabbing downward into its back as I twisted my torso away from him and he whooshed by me, the tranquilizer beginning to take effect and his gate starting to loosen and stumble. The better image in my head, I figured, the more convincing I would look staring out the window.

"Yes, but I stop," I said, still staring out the window. "My name is Gee-sus." I pronounced the "J" to say it as they say it, "Gee-sus, bull slayer."

The beautiful girl put her hand on the edge of her hair and pulled backward until she tugged nervously on her ponytail. "No, I think your name is 'weirdo.'" She snatched the books on her desk and walked to the farthest desk from me in the room and sat down. She did not mock me. She did not whisper things to other people around. Instead, she folded her arms, dropped her head, and began to pray. She stopped when the teacher came into the room and ushered a tall, white-haired kid down the aisle of chairs and sat him next to me.

At the front of the room, the teacher began to talk, most of it completely incomprehensible to me. I picked up verbs and nouns here and there, but when she started to speak faster, she lost me. I looked at the girl who sat as far away from me as she could and wondered why bull slaying made her move. I mean, in Yucatán, there was really no matador tradition like Mexico City, but the matadors of old were cool and got all the ladies.

The fall had not yet come and summer's heat beat against the windows, but the cool, air-conditioned room made me feel rich, like a man sitting on a hill looking down at peasants digging around in shit.

"Hans and Gee-sus," the teacher said. "Can you both stand up and tell us a bit about yourselves?" She pointed down the aisle toward me and the tall kid next to me. His English was excellent, so excellent that, again, I lost track once he started talking quickly. I picked up "moved" "parents" and "Utah" and "beer," which made everyone in the room blush. He sat down next to me and exhaled.

"Gee-sus, it's your turn," she said.

I'd memorized so little English for the day. I had "I slay bulls" down pat, but that obviously was not as cool as I thought it would be, so I began to ramble off whatever I could. I was so flustered and embarrassed.

"Dad, Mom, Hector, we come to los Estados Unidos together," I said. It seemed like enough to me.

"Can you tell us any more?" She waved her hands in front of her. I sat down. "Yes," I said.

She walked behind her long wooden desk and sat down in her chair. With a pencil, she started to scribble on a small, pink piece of paper. Her pale hand slid back and forth on the desk. The class sat quietly until she stood up, walked down the aisle, and handed me the piece of paper. She put her hand on my hand and pointed to the door.

"Secretary," she said. She pointed toward the door and tilted her hand and said, "Left." She straightened it out again and said, "Last door." Her hand moved from mine and landed on my shoulder. With very little force, she nudged me out of my chair and walked me to the door, hand still placed on my shoulder. She repeated her directions with her hand and said, "Left, then straight, through the last door."

I walked out of the class full of shame, but not knowing why I felt so ashamed and embarrassed. My feet followed her directions until I made the left and they stopped. The hallway was empty. Clean, blue lockers lined the edges of it. There was no art or colors to break up the white and blue. The smell of fresh bleach sat in the air, and the vents kicked out freezing cold air onto the back of my neck, giving me chills from my hairline to my fingers where the note sat.

In meticulous and neat cursive, the note said, "No English."

I never made it to the secretary's office. Instead, I ran through the hallways of the school, out the swinging doors, and along the clean sidewalks of my new home until I got to our apartment. I held "No English" in my hands and plopped down onto the parking curb in front of our apartment. I sat there for more than an hour as cars flew by me on their way to I-15. I stood up to climb the stairs and face my mother, and a long Lincoln Town car pulled into the parking lot. It moved across the blacktop like a person looking for a contact, each wheel spinning and turning in what looked like separate motions. It pulled right in front of me, and the engine shut off. The thick, metal door, heavy enough to dent the blacktop if it fell, opened up, and a leg covered in a white circulation sock followed.

"What in the hell are you doing here?" she yelled. She unfolded her walker and placed its wheels on the ground. "Get the hell over here and shut my door." She pointed to the door and pretended to shut it. "Now, tonto." I jumped up and ran to shut the door and help her old bag of bones toward the apartment.

"I asked you a question," she said. But I didn't have the answer to it. So I stood quietly next to her and waited for her to hit me with something. Instead, I felt course wrinkly skin folds rub beneath my fingers and pull the note from them. I tried to hold onto it, but she hit me on the back of my head with her big stone ring.

"No English," she read. I braced for another hit to the back of my skull. "No English," she repeated.

Instead of the hard, pointy, skin-piercing pop, I felt her fingers run over my left ear from front to back and settle on my neck. She kept them there as we walked up the apartment stairs and through the door. She kept them there as she threw flour into a bowl and started her tortillas.

"It's time you learned, tonto," she said. "No more Spanish around me. And since I'll be living here, that's a lot of English."

Chapter Seventeen

Veronica

Seattle, WA 1924

Months earlier, she roamed the streets of Mérida with her sisters and picked flowers from the dirt that lined her home. She put them in her hair and walked to the market and pretended to flirt with men. The sun would shine down on her skin, and the smell of clean skin and the warming heat smelled like home. It was a home the size of a city that embraced her with arms of art, pillars, and statues of her Mayan heroes that fought back against the conquistadors for centuries. They fell last of all other indigenous empires, surviving the Spanish for one hundred and seventy years, until the seventeenth century. Her forefathers created the first known full form of written communication in Mesoamerica, dating back nearly 3,000 years BC, and their leaps forward into astrology, math, and science were unrivaled by other Mesoamerican empires. Their knowledge shined bright on the land before there was light. They were a strong, smart people, and Veronica sat in this apartment with this horrible man waiting for her moment to leap home to her family. The thing she wanted to avoid was him hitting her again and hurting the baby, so she stayed—she knew it--longer than she should have.

She had to get out, but she was so sick that she could barely move.

One night, she suffered painful contractions that rose from her core to her neck. She had to spend the night in the bathroom on the cold wooden floor. Every five to ten minutes she woke up and leaned over the toilet, but nothing came out. After three or four times, her body continued to lurch forward and jerk inside, and a sharp pain in her back consumed her.

When she finally made it to bed, dehydrated and exhausted, Veronica fell asleep under the covers. She drifted off into a dream. She was back in Mérida. Her father, mother, and sisters were all around the dinner table. They talked to Veronica's baby. Her mom sewed a pair of booties for the new arrival, and her father ran through a list of family names that he felt the boy should have, even though he had no idea if it would be a boy or not. Her little sisters ran up to her and placed their hands on her belly and rubbed and rubbed until the skin was raw.

"Jesús," her father said. "Chuy. That's what you should name your boy. We have generations of Chuys in our family. That should be his name."

Her son danced along the stars. His face took shape in her mind. It was her father's face but soft and innocent and beautiful. The boy dropped down from the night sky and into her arms, and he rested his cheek against her breast. He turned his head toward her and began to cry.

Veronica woke up and then closed her eyes and imagined the curves of the Mérida loveseats beneath her. The cool and smooth carved stone ran beneath her thighs, and the smell of the market air, for one brief second, killed the smells of whiskey and smoke that hovered around her until she did what she needed to do.

The typing and chanting of words continued through the night. She thought he had drunk and eaten enough to pass out, but he sat and typed and drank while she drifted off again, her back aching like she had been stabbed with a dull knife. Her dreams, this time, took her forward in time. She saw a great lake and her boy standing near the lake's edge. His face was sullen, lips dropping downward and eyes closed. She saw him wipe tears from his eyes and throw them down into the water. The sun dropped behind a range of mountains behind the lake and a bright yellow and red line outlined the downward curve of his nose—it was her father's nose. She ran to him to wrap her arms around him, but she could barely move forward and went nowhere though her legs turned. She dropped her hands to the ground like an animal and dug in to move forward, and with her nails tearing in the dirt and her feet pushing behind her, she lunged forward toward the boy. When she reached for him, he shrugged and walked into the water, creating a wake at his knees. She followed him in. The water was warm, gritty, grey and nearly opaque. The boy turned to her. She saw her father's eyes and his nose, but his lips were round and full, unlike any one of her siblings or parents. He reached out his hand, turned his palm upward toward the red sky, and pulled his fingers toward his palm, beckoning her to follow him farther into the water. As she walked deeper into the lake, the warm and gritty water squeezed her until it hurt. The young man stood and looked toward the sun.

Veronica woke up. Orange and brown blood saturated her clothes, and a thick layer of white and pink mucus surrounded them. It took nearly a minute for her to separate herself from her dream and realize that the gritty, thick liquid that swam around her was not lake water, but blood, urine, and mucus that covered her from the waist down. In a panic, she ran her hands through the blood and tried to cup it to put it back inside of her. She screamed and pounded on the door until Jason pushed it open and looked down on the saturated clothing and carpet beneath. His eyes swam in sockets filled with whiskey. His legs struggled to keep him straight, and his head bobbed back and forth on the back of his head. When he tried to kneel, his legs didn't work well enough to ease him to the ground but instead gave out altogether, and he dropped to the ground. He threw up, and the stench of whiskey and bile filled the room.

   She gathered strength enough to pull herself up. She left him there in his vomit and hoped he would choke on it and die.

Chapter Eighteen

Chuy

Provo, UT 1990

THE DAY BILLY OBLITERATED ME ON THE TETHERBALL COURT WAS THE day I realized I would have to train, and train hard, to become a reality TV show champion. Billy owned the court and relinquished the ball to no one. It was true that the athletes in our class gave up on mastering the skills, challenges, and intricacies of tetherball and moved on to playing less intelligent games like basketball, football, and soccer, but I knew in the depths of my heart that if I could beat Billy at tetherball, I could stake a claim at greatness in my eighth-grade class.

During P.E., Billy ended a game against Hans Muller, the German student who moved to town at the same time I did, by slamming the tetherball into Hans's face so hard that it almost slapped the "kraut," as Billy referred to him, right out of him.

Billy, the tetherball champion, was a short kid with no real athletic ability. He had no hair on the left side of his head due to a cosmetic experiment. His mom, an esthetician, used the left side of Billy's head as a hair-removal guinea pig one too many times, and one time, after applying a mixture of paint thinner and avocado to his hair, it never grew back. She stopped experimenting on his head after that, but I noticed that when all the rest of the boys in the class started to grow hair on their lips and chins, Billy did not.

Hans, broken and bewildered after being beaten by Billy, walked away from the tetherball court. Billy rubbed his hand against the bare skin on the left side of his head like his absent hair gave off the feeling of a phantom limb. His pant legs stopped two inches above his ankles, and rips decorated the denim that barely covered his thighs. He owned very few things in his life. The tetherball court was one of them, and he would fight to keep ownership of it.

I stepped into the space that Hans vacated. I'd never played tetherball before. Billy intimidated me, but I'd seen less skilled players beat champions before. On *CastAway*, the stronger and more talented competitor didn't always get the victory. Hubris often got the best of them. The stronger player would puff up his chest and look, with serious eyes, into the camera. Sometimes he would smile before the host explained the nature of the challenge. His brawn would do nothing to help him complete a puzzle or hit a target, and the smaller competitor would concentrate, ignore the onslaught of insults that came from the other team, and put the puzzle together or hit the target. I did not think of Billy when I thought of the brawny men who dominated physical challenges on *CastAway*. When I thought of Billy, the word that came to my mind was "asshole." He did not deserve to be compared to even the beefiest and dumbest cast members on my favorite show.

Girls gathered around the court. At first, during our warm-up—we stretched and ran in place and did jumping jacks—the girls stood in a circle and giggled and pointed at the boys playing football, but when Billy stepped over the white line painted on the concrete, the group of girls turned toward the court. They stood so close together that they formed a wall between us and the teachers who roamed the grounds. Their giggles came to a stop when Billy tossed me the ball. Tetherball followed the rules of every schoolyard game: the victor chooses who begins. Billy told me to start and laughed. It was a known fact that if you are a great tetherball server then you could practically win the game on your serve turn alone. Billy was being a dick on purpose. He tossed the ball around to my side of the court, and when I caught it, the hairs on my prematurely hairy arms stood up on end.

Billy didn't know that I had done two things to prepare for our match that morning. First, I studied the tactics of a sure tetherball win and knew that if I hit the ball hard enough and fast enough that I could win the game before he ever touched it. Second, I concentrated more on the victors of challenges than the women of *CastAway* that week, and brought what I learned with me that day to the tetherball court. I stared at Billy with closed eyelids and a tiny twitch in my left eye—I added the twitch for effect. When Billy continued to laugh and rub his hand along the bald side of his head, the twitch in my eye got bigger and more pronounced. But Billy peered at the crowd and waited for me to serve. Like an NBA point guard shoveling a no-look pass to a teammate, his posture and disregard told me he thought I had no chance of beating him. I got frustrated, lost my gaze and twitch, and hit the ball toward the bald side of his head. In my mind, I had hit it hard enough to knock the covering off—and knock Billy off his feet. In reality, in my anger, my fingers barely nicked the edge of the ball, and it wobbled at the end of the tether until it dropped near Billy's feet. He laughed, bent down, and hit the ball so hard that it flew over my head twenty times and came to a stop when it had fully wrapped itself around the base of the pole. I didn't have another chance to hit it. My research on tactics and my steely gaze did me no good.

"You're banned from the court until you can give me a challenge," Billy shouted. He walked toward the line of admiring girls, knelt before them, and gave a thumbs-up. They circled him and giggled and reached down toward him. He had all the fame and admiration that I wanted—that and the chance to be the next reality TV star, win a million dollars, and buy my father's way back into this country.

I walked away from the court with my head down and my shoulders slumped. The tiny concrete pebbles nearly tripped up my surface-skimming feet. I parked my butt on a bench next to Hans, who sniffled between breaths. His long, blonde hair fell over his face in his hands.

"I'm a good swimmer," he said. His hand muffled his voice.

"Que?" I asked.

"What are you good at?" Hans asked. He lifted his head from his hands and looked up into my eyes. He, like me, knew the power of a steely glare.

I rambled in Spanish, "I'm good at predicting who's going to be voted off the island next," I said. "I get it right almost half the time. When the tribes go to jury, I have a feeling in my gut who's going to get kicked off." Hans looked at me as if he understood and responded in broken Spanish.

"Quantos correcto?" Hans said.

"Dos," I said. "But I didn't get the third one right because my dad got arrested and sent back to Mexico right during the jury."

"I understand," Hans said.

"You're a foreigner too, Hans. I would be careful. They might take you away or your parents away some day," I warned him. His Spanish was much better than my English.

"What?!" Hans said.

"Yep, they do it all the time. If you weren't born here, they can take you away. You should make a plan like mine in case they take your dad away," I said. I began to see Hans as a friend, and I wanted to warn him about the authorities. "I'm training to be the next reality TV star so I can bring my dad back."

Hans became quiet and looked at all the boys playing football and shook his head. He moved his gaze toward Billy and the crowd of girls that surrounded him and looked back at me.

"I want to do that too," he said. "What do I have to do first?"

"Do you have a TV?" I asked.

"Yes," he answered.

"Do you watch it?" I asked.

"Yes," he said.

"Do you watch reality shows?" I asked.

"No," he answered. "We mostly watch *Baywatch* and *Knight Rider* reruns. My dad loves David Hasselfhof."

"Okay," I said. I couldn't fault the kid for bad taste. At least he had stopped crying.

My dad taught me not to cry early on in life. When he left us the first time, I cried all night long, slinking into my mom's arms and asking why he had to go. Hector and I were little then, about eight- and ten-years-old, and scared of life without our father.

Before he left, my dad hammered on metal over a hot fire. Tourists, mostly college students from los Estados Unidos, would jump out of huge air-conditioned busses and gather around to watch my father and other men's sweat drop onto a cast iron circle and sizzle and pop on the hot surface. The students would point and take pictures and place pesos in the tip jar that was set nicely on the adobe wall that separated the students from the Mexican metal workers on the other side. My father could not stop talking about those students. He went on and on about their white tennis shoes and their hair.

The students started joining us—through his stories—at our dinner table at night. Their stories served to us with our fried plantains. As if they had pulled up a chair and begun to talk about the day with us, they were there too. They were tall, with hair that wrapped neatly around their ears.

You'd think that he would grow to hate the students who shuffled off their bus, lined up to look at him like he was a trained monkey, dropped pesos into the "gracias" jar, and shuffled back onto their air-conditioned bus and drove away, most of them plugged into their portable CD players and bobbing their heads to their music in the windows. But he didn't. He'd look forward to the days the busses pulled up. Yes, he liked the extra pesos, but that wasn't why.

Hector and I, and even my mother after initial reluctance, loved to hear the stories of the students. One day my father started talking to the students as they stood on the other side of the adobe wall. Two young girls, neither one of them much taller than the thick mud wall, watched him as he pounded a giant cast iron skillet into shape. Sparks shot from his hammer with every swing and pound, and the two girls jumped back a bit after a particularly large spark shot toward them. My father smiled and laughed at the two of them.

In Spanish, he said, "Don't worry, those sparks don't carry any heat with them." He didn't think the girls would understand him, but when they started to talk back to him, started to ask him questions about the molding, the bending, and the pounding, all in nearly perfect Spanish, his eyes opened wide. While he continued to send sparks into the air, he answered them, telling them all about the precision, focus, and talent needed to shape a rigid piece of cast iron into the pots and pans that are pulled from kitchen cupboards and placed on stoves.

Until that time, the students would shuffle by, chat, flirt, chuckle, and move on, long before the bus returned to pick them up. But on that day, the bus driver had to honk three times—it became four, five, six times, with each retelling of the story—before the students left my father's workshop and headed off to their hotels. At dinner that night, my father's eyes became starrier than ever before. He waved his arms in the air and made Hector and me ask him questions—we'd become stand-ins for the two college-age students.

That story kept fuel in my father's tank until the next set of students rumbled into town months later, and he'd talk to them too. Hector and I would act out the scene at night, drifting off to sleep in our bed together, feeling as if we were visitors in their lives to the north.

One morning, after a group of students came through our town, my father woke Hector and me early. He swung our feet off the bed, pulled our blankets over our shoulders, and hugged us goodbye.

"I'm leaving, hijos," he said. "But I'll be back for Christmas."

I felt the tears well up in my eyes, my eyelashes catching the first one before it could fall.

I managed to muster up a, "What?"

"Don't cry, hijo. This is not a sad day," he said.

"How can this not be sad?" Hector asked.

"Because I'm going to make it so you will be tourists in this land someday," he said. "Tears make this moment sad, not the moment itself. So if you don't cry, and if you smile, you will see this as a good thing."

My dad gave us one more hug, wrapped his rough hands around ours, and gave them a squeeze. When he left, he stood in the doorway. His short, muscular silhouette waved goodbye, and I smiled.

Hans sat next to me on the playground and tried to hold back tears, but so far he'd been unsuccessful at two things that day: tetherball and manhood. When Billy and the girls stopped looking at us, I turned to Hans and yanked his head up by pulling on his curly blonde hair. He yelled "Ouch!" but that didn't matter. He needed to learn that crying on the playground would do nothing to make his situation at this school and in this country any better, and he needed to learn it before Billy, the girls huddled in the group, or the boys playing football saw the tears that ran like tributaries across the plains of his palms.

"Crying makes this a bad thing," I said to him. "Now wipe your tears off and stop it before anyone sees you." I reached into my pocket and took out a replica *CastAway* bandanna, one my father brought home for me one day after work. He knew he couldn't say he bought it for me because Hector would get jealous, and Mom would get pissed because we didn't have the money for gifts outside of those bought for Christmas or our birthdays, but I knew he bought it. The stamped-on *CastAway* emblem had no creases, cracks, or wrinkles, and the edges were still perfectly sewn.

Hans took it and wiped his tears on the now soft *CastAway* bandanna. He looked down at it. His eyes widened, and his tears dried up. He held the bandanna in his hand and examined it with his thumb and index finger, running them over the reality TV show's bright emblem.

"What's this?" he asked.

"What do you mean what's this?" I couldn't believe that he didn't know what he held in his hand. Since it started running more than a year earlier, the show had become a focal point of my young life and the center of my relationship with my father.

Part of me wanted to smack Hans until he started crying again, but the other part of me wanted to educate him, to bring him into my world, and to show him what he had been missing while his family stared at either a bare-chested David Hasselhoff or a leather-covered David Hasselhoff.

"It's the best show on TV," I said, "and the ticket to my future happiness."

"What's it about?" Hans asked.

"It's about wit. They drop these people off on this island and they have to survive for forty-five days on their own," I told him. There was no way to keep my hands from flailing around in front of me. "They have to figure out how to make fire and hunt their own food and avoid deadly bugs and, most importantly, they have to learn how to survive each other. The *CastAway* world opened up around me. I could taste the salty beach air, smell the body odor of other contestants, and hear the cries of the foreign birds all around me.

"You mean they try to kill each other?" Hans said. His eyes lit up maniacally. It scared me a little how excited he got about that prospect.

"No, they try to vote each other off the island. They play with each other's minds!" I yelled loud enough to catch Hector's attention. He sat alone in the corner of the field. His head moved up when he heard my voice, and then it lowered again. He stared at his feet. Alone.

"You mean they don't get to hunt other players?" Hans asked one more time, for clarity.

"No," I said. "It's even better this way because, trust me, someone always gets stabbed in the back." I let go of a prideful grin, one that showed how proud I was of my witty retort.

Hans, having lost interest in island life, dropped his head back into his hands and started to sob again. There was one option here: change Han's outlook on life.

"Turn on CBS tonight at eight, watch *CastAway*, and report back to me tomorrow. We have training to do," I said. I knew that Hans needed something to look forward to.

"What's on CBS at eight?" Hans asked.

"*CastAway!*" I screeched.

"But there's a *Baywatch* reunion on tonight at eight," Hans said. "My parents will never let me out of that."

"Tell them it's for homework," I told him. "It's not a lie. I'm asking you to do this work at home." Again, pride filled me. I had already begun my training, and the ability to convince people of what they needed to do—and make them feel as if it was their idea—came to me very easily. "Report to my house Sunday morning. First things first. We will train, *CastAway* style, to beat Billy."

Our gym class had ended, and children from all over the grounds became swarms of moving feet and bobbing heads, all running to the one entrance to the school. The large crowd of students became thicker and thicker at the front end of the human bottleneck until one giant body of shoulders shuffled back and forth through the door, chunk by chunk disappearing into the school.

In the sparseness of the moment, with few children blocking my view, I saw Hector. He stood alone across the street in the high school parking lot. He saw me. He didn't wave. Instead, he looked up to the sky and shook his head.

Class, I knew, had to be in session, and I knew that he, like me, had been pushed into the remedial English classroom. He ran his hands through his thick black hair and loped, not back into school, but down the street toward our apartment, disappearing behind the Burger King and reappearing again half a block away before disappearing again.

That night, after Billy had shamed me on the school playground, Hector sat down on the edge of my bed. He leaned in close to my ear and said goodbye. The streetlights shone into our room and landed on the blanket that covered my legs. The strength of Hector's cologne clouded my eyes and made me cough, and I nearly rolled off the bed because he sat right on the edge and didn't think about what that would do to my body.

"Where are you going?" I asked.

"I'm going home," he said.

I was really confused. I mean, I had figured out that he'd been gone nearly every day and night since we moved to Utah nearly four months earlier, but I didn't think he got so stoned that he forgot where he was.

"You are home, Hector," I said. I pulled the covers over my head and thought about how the girls laughed at me on the playground—my mystique had collapsed around me.

"No, Chuy, I'm going home, home. To Dad," he said.

"What?!" I yelled. I couldn't help it.

"Quiet, hermano," he said. "Don't wake Veronica or Mom, and don't tell them where I went for at least two days, okay? They won't even know I'm gone." He patted my leg like my father used to do when he left for the States for work.

I looked at him and knew there was nothing I could say except, "How?"

"I stole Veronica's credit card and booked a last-minute flight," he said. "I'll be there tomorrow, with Dad."

"Does Dad know?" I asked.

He leaned back a bit then stood up, "Of course not, Chuy. He'd never let me come if he did." He walked out my bedroom door holding out two fingers in a peace sign as he left.

Hector was wrong.

Mom and Veronica knew something was different. They knew Hector had gone. A small detail in the house the next morning tipped them off. Maybe it was the absence of his socks on the furniture, or maybe it was the lack of a musty smell outside the apartment door that my mom had gotten used to walking through on her way to work in the morning. Maybe it was maternal intuition buzzing inside them. I don't know. But they knew he was gone.

My mom pulled the covers from over my head in the early morning after Hector left. I begged her to put the blanket back. She pulled on my arms until I sat up in bed.

Veronica stood in the doorway with a cup of coffee, and the smell of fry grease and bleach from my mom's work uniform sat over the room even though I knew she had washed it by hand the night before, scrubbing at the ketchup and mustard and syrup stains over the kitchen sink.

"Where's Hector, Chuy?" she asked. She placed her hand on my leg and looked at me while my eyes did their best to focus on her question and reveal no secrets.

"Where's Hector, Chuy?" Veronica echoed from the doorway.

My nipples felt cold, and, at fourteen-years-old, with two women in the room with me, drilling me with questions, sunlight in my eyes, and the stench of old breakfast suffocating me, I felt uncomfortably exposed. I pulled my blanket up over my cold nipples and what I thought to be my sculpted chest.

"You got nothing to cover up there, boy," Veronica said. She laughed and sipped her coffee.

"Where's Hector, Chuy?" my mom asked again. I was focused on how sculpted my chest had become from cutting grass and hoisting the weed eater in the air for minutes at a time.

"I don't know," I said. "And I do have something to cover up with my blanket."

"Nada," Veronica whispered.

"Mucho," I said.

"Nada, nada, nada," Veronica said.

"Enough," my mom broke in.

I didn't understand how they knew he had left for good. He left in the middle of the night all the time. I had no idea how they figured him out.

"Chuy," my mom said, "We know he's gone."

"How?" I asked. I really wanted to figure out their secret.

"That doesn't matter, Chuy," my mom said. "We just know."

"He made me promise," I said. My older brother, the one I had admired from the day I had met him, or the day I first remembered him, made me promise to keep his secret until he got on the plane to Mexico, but he didn't think I would come under such harsh interrogation so quickly and with full-on insults about my pectoral muscles, or the lack thereof.

"Chuy, tell me now. I need to know," my mom said.

"He made me promise," I said.

My mom pulled her hand from my leg. The soft and gentle approach had failed her, so she stood up next to my bed.

"Tell me now, Chuy," she said. "I don't care if he made you promise. Is he shacking up with some puta? Is he joining a gang? Where, Chuy? Where is he?" Her voice was full of fear and anger, and some of the anger was devoted to me, for not telling her anything.

Veronica walked from the doorway and stood on the other side of my bed.

"Is he safe, Chuy?" she asked. "Where he went, will he be safe?" Veronica talked to me so kindly that I had to answer her. I was in too much shock not to.

"Yes," I said. "He's safe."

My mom leaned in close to me, "Tell us where he went."

But my dear aunt Veronica reached over my bed and placed a hand on my mom's shoulder.

"Let him keep his promise to his older brother," she said to my mom. "It's important."

My mom listened to her.

"When can you tell us where he went?" Veronica asked.

I sat up in bed and let my covers fall to my waist. I felt comfortable again.

"Tomorrow," I said.

"Okay," the women said in unison.

"You promise he's safe?" my mom asked again.

"I promise, Mom," I said.

"I'm late for work. Love you, mijo," she said and walked out of my room.

Veronica turned to follow my mom out the door but turned back around and pointed at my chest, "Nada, nada, nada. You are still a boy."

I wouldn't have to break my promise. After midnight, the phone rang in the apartment. My aunt cursed the air from her bedroom, and my mom ran to the kitchen to pick up the receiver.

Silence hung in the night for a minute or two. As if the apartment had been trapped in a pressure cooker for the day, the thickness of worry that can stifle a household released when my mom gasped and cried into the phone. It was my father on the other end. Hector had made it to Chelem after a very long flight and hitchhiked the twenty or so miles from the Mérida airport.

"He's okay?" she said into the phone. "I agree." After a long five minutes of "hmm," "esta bien," "si, si," and "okay," she started to talk about us here in Utah. Her tears left her, and as he always did when he called each week, he had her laughing by the time she hung up the phone.

Veronica snored in the distance.

Chapter Nineteen

Veronica

Seattle, WA 1924

I'm getting out. I couldn't protect my baby, but I have to protect myself. He can't hurt the baby now, Veronica thought to herself when she reached down and turned off the water. The blood had been washed clean of her, and she had no reason to be sheltered or fed anymore. The baby was gone. So she dressed quickly, praying to get out of the apartment before Jason woke up, and stole every cent from his dresser drawer, which totaled a whopping twenty-three dollars and eighteen cents. She looked out into wet Seattle and, in her heart, knew it would be a very long time before she reached home. That there was a chance she would never make it home at all. She walked toward the front door, but on the way there, she tripped on a stack of Jason's work. The time he would be passed out was disappearing with every breath she took, and her lungs shrank with fear, gasps leaving quicker and quicker from her mouth. She leaned down, the ache in her belly stabbing her like needles, and grabbed Jason's pages, months worth of typing and scribbling to get the words out, all lying cleanly on pieces of paper. She took a small grocery bag from the closet, threw in some extra clothes and the poetry, and ran out the door with the money jingling in her pocket.

A thin layer of mist ran through the streets of downtown Seattle. It wasn't raining, but the air was full of moisture. Flecks of water floated in the air and sparkled when the sun poked out from the overhanging clouds. Water ran down the street, weaving through the creases between bricks, and pooled up on the edges of Veronica's shoes. She stood on the corner of Pike and Third. Rumbling cars pushed to get up the hill, while brakes whistled from those slowing down on the other side of the road. She shivered in the mist. She longed for the warmth of Mérida. The loveseats. The street vendors. Seattle was cold, with nowhere to sit. The honk of a brand-new Ford Touring Car shook her from her daze before it rolled on by, the red wheels spinning up the hill. More honks followed until she was back on the sidewalk.

Directionless, she let her feet fall one in front of the other down Pike. She opened and closed the sweater that she had put on earlier, as if she were walking around the city enjoying the day. The sense of normalcy calmed her and the smell off the Puget Sound woke her little by little. Two blocks down, the noise of the Pike Street Farmer's Market woke her even more.

She walked into the market. Fresh fish moved by her in ice chest after ice chest, giant salmon riding along on the tops of wheeled carts. Men, working since before dawn, had shed their jackets and sweated through white t-shirts. Storeowners, dressed in suits, shouted out orders to the clerks behind the elevated counters and pointed at rock-fish, crab, salmon, squid, halibut, and rows and rows of clams.

Veronica kept walking through the rows of cranberries and apples. She walked by the delivery trucks. The men loaded bucket after bucket of seafood into the backs of the trucks, each truck filling up, dropping the canvas down in the back to enclose the food, and spinning out, their thin tires doing their best to get a grip on the brick roads of the wet city. She felt lost but free. Jason imprisoned her in the apartment. He imprisoned her by not teaching her English. He imprisoned her by not letting her leave, meet people, and learn the language on her own. He imprisoned her with fear.

The market ended, but she let her feet take her down toward the port. The ease of walking downhill led her onto the wooden planks of the port and piers. She walked out to the edge of Pier 40 and stood above the water. The wind from the sound pushed her hair back from her eyes, and the mist fell on her face. Her tears were long gone and replaced by the salty air of the city on the water. She tossed Jason's pages into the water, throwing each into the sea and feeling freer and freer with every page that sank into the waves. He'll never come to get me, Veronica thought to herself: he's too much of a coward. And she was right, Jason never chased after her, like he never came for her in Mérida. She slept on the dock that night. When the sun came up, a fisherman tapped her on the shoulder with the toe of his work boot.

"You'll have to get moving," he said. His tone was civil but strict. "Best get out of here before the police do their morning sweep."

Veronica understood few of his words, but his thumb in the air over his shoulder said enough. She walked away from the port and down the edges of the industrial-lined walls of the Puget Sound until she walked into the train station. The names of cities painted in yellow blocky letters flipped on rotating planks of wood at the entrance, each accompanied by a departure time. She knew the route back to Mexico, so she walked up to the ticket booth and got a ticket to Denver with stops along the way in Portland, Boise, and Salt Lake City. The ticket price to Denver was twenty-two dollars and fifty cents. She bought the cheapest seat and boarded the train. There was no place to sleep. She would have to sit up the entire time, but when the howl of the train shot into the air and Seattle disappeared behind her in the window, and Jason with it, she didn't care. She wore a nice dress that she had bought on her last day in Mérida. It was black with a ribbon around the waist and red and pink stitched flowers around the bottom hem. She looked beautiful when she fell asleep against the window. The Cascades swooshed by her, then the Columbia River.

The sound of train whistles woke her briefly in Portland, but she fell quickly back to sleep and didn't wake again until Boise. The blood loss and the days of vomiting had left her dry inside—she suffered hot flashes and headaches whenever she raised her head from the seat. Her dehydrated state made her body shut down and sleep, doing its best to convert whatever fuel source remained inside her. The train conductor's hand touched her shoulder in Denver, nearly a day and a half after she left Seattle, and shook her gently.

"Miss, we're in Denver. End of the line for this train. Miss. You'll have to get up," he said in a kind voice. As if her legs were weights and disconnected from her body, she lifted them with her arms and stood up. She walked in a daze toward the train station, found a water fountain in the corner of the ticket room, and drank and drank and drank until the skin beneath her fingernails was no longer concave. The water swam through her body and gave her enough energy to walk around the train station and beg the other passengers for enough money to get her a ticket to El Paso, to Ciudad Juarez, and into Mexico.

People's generosity surprised her. They must have seen the desperation beneath her beauty. "Could they have seen the loss of my child?" she thought to herself. "Could they have seen what I have been through? Why are they handing me money when I've never done anything to deserve it?" These thoughts bothered her right up until she was able to plop the money down at the ticket counter and pay for a ride on the rails across the flat plains of Colorado and Kansas, and downward through Texas, a state large enough to be a country itself. She drank as much water as she could and bought a bag of biscuits with the twenty cents left over from her ticket purchase. She gobbled them up, found her seat on the train, and fell asleep again. The exhaustion had overtaken her.

Chapter Twenty

Chuy
Provo, UT 1990

It was a typical October Sunday morning in Provo. The streets were completely empty except for the few people who worked at the few places that were open—gas stations, one or two diners, large chain restaurants, and grocery stores. Most families had already found their way into the rows of seats at the local ward house and committed to the three-hour Mormon church service. Behind the blank walls of the cookie-cutter churches that popped up on every other road in the densely Mormon-populated city, people gave testimonies and cried about Jesus and talked about the evils of the secular world—the alcohol, the caffeine in hot beverages, the sex before marriage, and the "sperm worms".

The sun began to mix warmth with the chill of the fall night and drift out toward the Great Salt Lake. The Rocky Mountains peered down on the playground outside our one-bedroom apartment. The fall colors had arrived. When the sun peeked its head over the eastern mountaintops, the Bigtooth maple trees shone a bright orange. The quaking aspens shimmered a rich yellow, and the scrub oak trees, which are as much a shrub as a tree, stood out among the reds and yellows with their red-brown. The combination of colors resembled a confused painter's palate that, in its confusion, created something more beautiful than could ever be intentionally drawn.

I stood in the middle of the beat-up playground that sat in the middle of our apartment complex. Being a Catholic family from the heart of Catholic Mexico, we had gone to a half-hour Mass the night before. My mom had taken up a second job, calling rich people on the phone and asking them why they had "forgotten" to pay their BMW payment. We went to Mass on Saturday night because she said she reported to el jefe all damned week, and while crossing herself for protection she said didn't need to report to "no el jefe" on Sunday morning. After a long week of waiting tables and calling "rich gringos," the communion wine at the five o'clock Mass would be her first drink, and by the time she fell to her pillow on Saturday night, she would be saturated—not drunk—with the finest Franzia boxed wine we could afford. "It's what they serve in Mass, it's what I serve here," she would say to herself over our traditional Saturday night frozen pizza. She would finish her night off by enjoying reruns of sitcoms with my aunt Veronica and rambling on to me about the sacrifices our father made.

"First, he left Mexico every summer for four years to work the fields and send money home. An educated man, a Mexican tradesman, picking apples for his family. That man had pride," she'd say. Mid-story she would raise her empty, Snoopy-covered McDonald's cup, and I would grab it and fill it with her favorite Franzia flavor, white zinfandel. "All that money so I could apply for, pay for, and get my green card. And in the end, since he had broken the law and been deported back to Mexico, he can never apply to be here without el jefe blanco looking for him." Shortly after el jefe blanco made his appearance in her story, Mom would pass out on the couch with a half-eaten Hostess pie on her belly—blackberry flavor. The jam-like filling would rest halfway inside the pie and halfway outside the pie, like a turtle sticking its head out of its shell. My aunt Veronica would finish a couple more glasses of wine, and yell at me to carry her into bed.

"Poor girl," Aunt Veronica would say before she would turn around and yell at me, "In English! I can tell when your footsteps are in Spanish because they're smoother. Clunk like you try to speak English, like you're clunking, clunking, clunking."

Mom knew how the night would end—knew how she wanted the night to end—so the second she got home from work and Mass, and moments before she dropped the frozen pizza on the oven rack—a sound like a brick falling on aluminum siding—she put on her robe and washed her McDonald's Snoopy cup. She slept in every Sunday morning that followed every Franzia Saturday night, and her late-morning slumber gave me plenty of time to prepare the playground for *Cast-Away* training.

I began by climbing six feet up the flagpole that stood outside the dirt pile of the playground and tying a piece of rope to the pole. I tied on an old tennis ball that our neighbor, Jonas Prickert, used to play fetch with his dog. The ball was so slimy that I had to run it through the grass twenty-five times to dry it off. I took my dad's electric drill from his toolbox and drilled a hole straight through the center of the old ball. It took me twenty minutes to thread the rope through the ball and tie a knot on the end of it to hold it in place, but it worked. No, it wasn't a tetherball, and no, it wasn't a tetherball pole, but the rope and ball did wrap nicely around the flagpole when I smashed them with the end of my hand. The tennis ball, slimy and tiny, made for a more elusive target than the volleyball-sized tetherball, so I knew that if I could master this game, I could beat Billy the next time I stepped onto the court. Beyond that, I had to make the challenge more difficult—a challenge that would prepare me for *CastAway*, a challenge that would make me a winner.

I placed three garbage cans next to my makeshift court, and a small figure walked out from the remaining shadow of the mountains. Like my mom, the silhouette of the figure wore a robe. It fell past its knees, and the bottom edges swayed back and forth in the light breeze that the canyons exhaled that crisp fall morning. As the figure got closer, I saw his face: Hans. He had fulfilled his promise. He had made it to the playground early enough for training. And, apparently, he had forgotten to dress for training. The rays of the sun reflected off the skin of his super-white legs, skin resembling that of a newborn piglet, almost pink in hue. Once he got close enough to wave, he raised his right hand in the air and shook it back and forth. The movement of his upper arm pulled the right flap of his rope up high enough to expose, what I thought to be impossible, the even whiter, pinker skin of his upper thigh.

"Chuy!" he said. "I'm here to train to beat Billy and to be the Knight Rider of reality TV, but I'm not sure how training for *your* show will help." He said *your* as if I owned the show. He stopped, and before I could yell for him not to, he untied the belt on his robe, pulled his arms from its furriness, and threw the robe on the ground, revealing the naked body of a bright-white fourteen-year-old German boy, except for the presence of an American flag Speedo. Hans stood in front of me with a smile on his face so big that David Hasselhoff couldn't wipe it off with a swing of his survival buoy.

"I watched *CastAway*. I did my homework. I am ready to train," Hans said in his thick German accent. "I had to beg my parents to let me watch, so I started it late, but I watched it, and I'm ready to go. Now, where's the alcohol and the hot tub?"

I had no idea what he meant by alcohol and hot tub. I would find out later that Hans turned on the TV after the start of *Island of Seduction*, saw people on an island, and figured it was *my* show. In my mind, at the time, I figured alcohol could mean rubbing alcohol to clean wounds, and his English vocabulary replaced natural hot springs with hot tub, so with little time to waste before my mom or Aunt Veronica woke up and came to get me for the Sunday morning ritual of making a big beans and tortilla breakfast, Hans and I had to get to training.

Hans' eyes fell on me with anticipation, waiting for instructions with a focused glare.

"Hans, go stand by the three garbage cans at the other end of the court," I said to him in Spanish, pointing toward the three cans I had set up for training. Hans, comfortable as a baby in his mother's arms, walked his American-flagged butt across the sandbox and behind the three garbage cans. I took my place in front of my makeshift tether-ball pole and positioned my legs in an athletic stance, feet spread at shoulder width and knees bent—like a shortstop ready for a deadly grounder.

"When I start to swat at the tennis ball, roll one of those garbage cans at me," I yelled to Hans. "We're going to hit the ball while jumping over rolling garbage cans. If we can do this, we can beat Billy and gain immunity."

Hans squinted. His brow wrinkled. And he stuck his hand into the air. He had no reason to raise his hand to ask for permission to speak, but I didn't mind one bit. In my life, I'd always been the youngest, the quiet one, and I'd always had to do what others told me to do, so when the young German boy raised his hand in the morning sunlight beside the flipped garbage cans, I called on him.

"Yes, Hans," I said.

Hans dropped his hand down, placed it on his hip, and extended his thumb and index finger outward to make the shape of a reverse "c." Hans lifted his hand toward his lips like bringing a tiny glass to his mouth.

"Shouldn't we take shots first?" he asked. "And where are the half-dressed women to give us big erections, rub up against us, and try and get us to have sex with them? Will they be coming before or after the rolling of the garbage cans?"

At that moment, I saw something that I never wanted to see again: the thought of the tempting women had already begun to shift Hans' blood flow. Hans did not notice, so I ran toward him, snatched his robe from the ground, and threw it in his direction.

"Hans, put this back on, now!" I said.

"Shots?" he said. "We need shots because without them, the ladies aren't as tempting."

I ran back to the court, wondering what the hell Hans meant by shots and sexy women and temptresses. *CastAway* had women in bikinis, but, for the most part, they weren't temptresses, and for sure, they had no access to alcohol on the island.

With the slimy tennis ball in my hand, I pulled my arm back and threw it as hard as I could around the other side, and an image of the bald spot on Billy's head appeared as a target on the other side of the pole. The ball gave "ffffeeewww, ffffffeeewww" sound as it pushed the thin, dry Utah air out of its path and circled back around to me.

"Start rolling the cans!" I yelled to Hans right before I focused my eyes on the incoming tennis ball. I raised my hand in the air and made contact—like the soft spot of a bat smacking a baseball far into the crowds. The smack stung the soft part of my palm, and the skin between the meaty part of the base of my thumb and the rest of my palm became red instantly, a sensation of pain and pride glowing from my hand.

Hans, with one big push, rolled the first garbage can toward my feet. It came slowly toward me at first but picked up speed and reached my feet as the tennis ball swung back around my way. I jumped, and in mid-air, I swatted the tennis ball—first, the sting on the hand, the sting on the face, second, the swell of pride from hitting the ball mid-jump, the fall head first toward the ground, landing on my face. I had jumped in time but had failed to jump high enough, and the edge of the rolling garbage can caught my feet and upended me. Sand stuck to my face, and my right fist jammed into my chin. The smell of dog shit on the lawn flooded my nostrils, and the world went dark.

I woke to the sound of Hans humming the *Knight Rider* theme song and talking to himself. He had laid his robe out on the grass like a picnic blanket and lay on his back, propped up on his elbows.

He traced his belly button with his finger. His index finger circled his outtie and ran up from there to his chin, where he placed it in his mouth.

"You cannot tempt me, baby doll," he said. "I am committed to my wife on the other island, and I know she is committed to her little German muffin. Don't you dare touch me there, temptress, sexy woman. Please, temptress, please do not touch me there a second time," he said. "I love my wife," he said.

The moment felt like a dream until a loud scream from our balcony apartment sent a lightning-like jolt through my spine to my head.

"Dios mio!" my aunt yelled. "Dios mio!" she yelled again louder.

I'd never heard her speak Spanish before. "Jesús Luis Chavez, what are you doing down there with that gringo pervert?"

She disappeared back into the house and came back out with her rolling pin in hand. Her old body morphed into the ninja I had seen the first day I moved to the United States. She flung her body over the railing and landed on the steps below her.

I jumped up and ran toward her. I hoped I could explain that Hans was a confused German who didn't have cable and, like me, needed to gain acceptance at school. When I got close enough to try and stop her, she focused on a confused Hans. The lack of strength mixed with fear did not raise him to his feet, but rolled him down the hill toward my aunt.

When I got close to her and tried to stop her, she pushed me with the rolling pin, and I fell hard to the ground. She stopped running for a moment, her eyes bouncing back and forth between Hans and me.

She ran toward Hans and gave him three or four smacks across his Speedo-covered ass.

It would take hours of explanation before my aunt accepted that, yes, Hans was kind of a pervert, and, yes, she would let me hang out with him because he was my only friend, but she had one rule: if she ever saw Hans in a bikini again, she would drag him to Father John at St. Isadores Catholic Church and have him baptized, confessed, and whipped.

Hans's parents called later that night. My aunt explained what she had seen. They asked why she stopped whacking him.

Chapter Twenty-One

VERONICA

SOMEWHERE BETWEEN KANSAS CITY, MO, AND EL PASO, TX 1924

VERONICA WOKE TO THE SIGHT OF TWENTY FACES LOOKING DOWN AT her on the train. She placed her hand on the seat next to her leg to prop her body up. When she did, she felt the same warm, thick, moist liquid that she felt in the bathtub in Seattle, but this time a pungent, bloody air came with it. She raised her hand, her arms weak and her fingers tired and her mouth so dry, and saw strings of thick red mucus drape down between her fingers, webs of internal blood.

A man in his late forties split the group in front of her with his arms. His cap said *Conductor* above its tiny bill. His eyes were tiny in his head, like two push pins stuck all the way into their cushion. His face was patched up red in random places—below his left eye, beneath his unremarkable jawline, on one cheek but not the other— and he gasped when he made it through the crowd.

The conductor took her thin, frail arm and lifted her off the seat in her compartment. He led her through one passenger car and the through another. Passengers gasped when they passed.

When the conductor stopped, Veronica sat on top of the cold, white toilet in the caboose lavatory. With all the movement she had left in her, she pulled a towel from above the sink, wet it down, and cleaned herself—first her feet, then her legs, and beneath the remaining clean, new dress she had left in America.

The clicking of the bathroom lock startled her. On the other side of it, the conductor stood with warm towels and a bucket. He handed them both to her. "I don't have any more clothes for you, but I think this will help. When you are done, I have found an empty cabin for you to sleep in until we get to El Paso. That's all I can do."

This time, he did not yank her up. He held her hand and let her to the very back of the train. He laid her down on a bench seat in a cabin that looked like it no longer seated passengers. The seat kicked up dust when she lay on it, and tears ran across the fabric, but it was comfortable enough for her to sleep on in her thin, dirty, blood-stained dress.

Chapter Twenty-Two

CHUY

PROVO, UT 1990

BILLY STOOD AND LAUGHED ON ONE SIDE OF THE TETHERBALL COURT. On the other side, Hans lay on the ground in the middle of the yellow lines. Blood trickled from Hans's nose and onto the ground, leaving dark stains on the blacktop. Billy rubbed a hand over the hairless side of his head. He had intentionally aimed the tetherball at Hans's face and hit it with so much force that it broke my friend's nose.

Hans had played a decent game. He had actually returned Billy's serve and slugged the ball back hard toward the champion. When Hans made contact with the ball, Billy had already turned to his groupies and started to smile, so by the time Billy figured out that Hans was still in the game, the ball had wrapped around the pole twice. Billy's face showed it all. He squinted, scrunched up his nose, curled his lip, and raised his hand in the air like Hans had somehow given him a cheap shot. I'd seen this face before on *CastAway*, when all the players sit down at tribal council and one player thinks he is the safest of the group, and is blindsided when he is forced to leave the tribe. He looks around at his fellow tribespeople and his arms and face look like Billy's did that day, like Hans had somehow blindsided him. All Hans did was play the game.

When the ball came zinging back around toward Billy, Hans moved down the court to cut off Billy's best shot, and Billy raised and threw his arm back as far as he possibly could. Instead of aiming to hit the ball above Hans's head to clear it for a complete wrap-around,

Billy slammed the ball down hard toward Hans's head. It slammed Hans in the face and a flying string of blood carried the crackle of a broken nose out across the yellow lines of the court. Billy laughed and so did the girls behind him.

"Get your sausage eater off the court," Billy yelled to me.

I walked over to Hans. He had rolled up in a ball and cupped the blood that gushed from his nose like there was some chance he could keep it and put it back in. I grabbed his right arm with one hand and lifted his torso with my left until we cleared the court, he gained control of his feet, and we were able to walk to the bench together. Hans cursed in German, die scheiße and das srschloch and bumsen rolling from his tongue. I used my white shirt to wipe the blood from his chin and wore it like war paint when I turned back toward the tetherball court. Hans's blood on my shirt kind of gave me the willies, like I was wearing Hans's insides on my outsides, and the image of Hans's banana-shaped Speedo popped into my mind momentarily before I brushed off the chills and walked back to Billy.

Billy had his following huddled courtside. The girls touched his head. He flexed his fourteen-year-old muscles. They giggled some more. No one besides me seemed to notice or care that Hans sat on the bench with a broken nose. The football boys kept tackling and getting yelled at by the gym coach monitor to not tackle. Cliques of girls moved across the playground, rolled up together like pinballs bouncing around the yard and whispering into the centers of their circles. Even the teachers who stood by the entrance to the school didn't notice the blood dripping from the new student near the tetherball court.

I stood to take my place on the court. Memories of *CastAway* training moved my feet across the blacktop.

"Chuy," Hans yelled to me.

I turned back toward him. One hand cupped the blood from his nose. He had raised the other one in the air.

"Don't fall for the body shots. They'll tempt you every time," Hans said. He cupped his raised hand around an imaginary shot glass and poured some imaginary liquor down his belly and slurped, *Island of Seduction* style. Even though he had practiced the wrong game, he was right. Billy always swung high but delivered low, faking his opponent out and spinning the ball low past his body and upward toward the sky.

I repeated *CastAway*'s motto in my head, "Live another day." With Hans's advice and my practice jumping over rolling garbage cans while hitting a tennis ball mid-swing, I knew I could take out half-bald Billy.

The game went by quickly. Billy had no chance. I countered every hit with a stronger hit. I swung back harder than he expected. His girls gasped behind him. Their half-bald hero couldn't get the ball past me. He delivered low, and I stayed on my feet, swung, and delivered an undercut to the ball. It flew past him. It flew so fast it blew his remaining hair back. The girls gasped. Billy lost. Hans screamed out. Blood splattered on the ground in front of him, but he didn't care. Sweat dripped down Billy's bald side, and my shirt stuck to my body. For a moment, it didn't matter if I was in Mexico or Rose Park or Provo—I was victorious, and in victory, I walked over to shake Billy's hand. I, Jesús Luis Chavez, would not be a bragger or pompous. My dad taught me better than that.

On *CastAway*, when the winner of a challenge threw his hands in the air or gave his opponent a finger across the throat, my father would look down at me, sitting at his feet below our futon, and tell me that pride gets you nothing in this world.

"...But humility gets you everything," he'd say. My father may have been thousands of miles away, but I, Chuy Luis Chavez, would shake my opponent's hand and turn to receive my prize with dignity. I walked past the yellow line that divided sides to shake Billy's hand. He glared at me with eyes that told me to stay away. I reached out my hand to shake his, but he did not respond, so I gave him a quick wave, told him, "Buen juego," and walked back to check on my perverted friend.

Billy's yell broke my confident stride, "Speak English!"

I turned to Billy. He had raised his arms in the air and acted like he was swimming.

"Why don't you swim back across the border to your daddy and take that Nazi friend of yours with you?"

"I'm actually Jewish," Hans said behind muffled lips.

Ten minutes earlier, no one knew our names or that we went to their school, but at that moment, every kid on the playground stopped, looked, and listened as Billy renamed us—the wetback and the Nazi.

Chapter Twenty-Three

VERONICA

EL PASO, TX, 1924

VERONICA STOOD IN FRONT OF THE NEWLY ERECTED UNITED STATES Immigration Services building. Less than three months ago, when she entered the country, the building was a little booth with one man standing inside to hand out entry passes. He had given her a pass that noted she intended to stay in the United States and become a citizen—the only necessary paperwork she needed at the time, established by the Immigration Act of 1921. The act prohibited all Chinese and Japanese immigrants from entering the United States and set a 3 percent quota on Europeans. Agricultural lobbyists, however, made sure Mexicans could enter freely. That changed when the Immigration Act of 1924 put a quota on Mexicans, too, and required that when entering the country they were to be termed "quota" or "non-quota." The ones with the stamp marked "quota" meant they were to work the land. The ones marked "non-quota" meant they were to grow up to work the land one day or they were to birth more children to work the land one day.

The booth had grown into a long, narrow building, and the line to come into the United States snaked its way out of the back of the building and into Mexico. It wound through the tall, drying trees of the border and through the matted-down grasslands of the Republic.

Bright white stenciled letters spelling out "U.S.I.S." covered the rooftop, and a fence and sidewalk lined the US border, starting at the entrance on the US side and traveling east and west for as far as Veronica could see. She had no idea about the Immigration Act of 1924, no idea that the restrictions to enter and leave had become much more stringent and monitored for Mexicans. All she knew was that she wanted to go home. She walked along the fence toward the entrance. She had to weave through all the people walking out of the U.S.I.S to get there. Women in long headscarves passed her, and families huddled beneath the shade of the tree and overhang to stay out of the brutal Texas sun. She walked past the fifty-foot-tall flagpole, and the *wap, wap, wap* of the American flag flapping in the wind thudded in her ears.

She was tired. She could barely believe she had made it and didn't want to think of what she still had to do to make it home alive. But she saw Mexico across the fence and was ready to go home.

The line to leave the United States had one man in it. He wore a nice suit and a hat, and a chain ran from his waist to his right pocket. No one waited on him because the newly appointed US. border patrolmen assisted all the people trying to get into the country, not out of it. The man tugged on the chain and pulled out a gold watch to check the time. Flustered, he threw it back into his pocket and huffed.

Veronica walked up behind him and leaned against the wall as if she were done with it all. She dropped to the floor, closed her eyes, and fell asleep on the U.S.I.S. floor. Veronica moved in and out of consciousness. Her eyes were covered in the chalky remnants of dried sweat, and her hair was matted into big clumps. She had no baggage, no purse, and no one else with her. She slept and woke and slept and woke for another hour, until the line of people trying to get into the United States dwindled to nearly nothing.

She woke when the immigration officers finally attended to the man in the outgoing line. He took one hundred dollars from his coat pocket and placed it in the palm of the officer.

"She fell asleep in the wrong line," the man said. "Look at her. She has to have been traveling through the Mexican desert for days. She must have gotten in the wrong line. She has no one." He pulled another hundred dollars from his pocket and slid it into Veronica's sweater. Veronica felt the man slide the money into her pockets. She reached out for his wrist.

"To get you home," he said to her. "This will get you where you need to go."

She opened her mouth, and the stench of dehydration, gummy lips, and a sandpaper tongue came out. She wanted to say that she wanted to go south, but her body had failed her. She muttered thank you before she passed out again.

"Put her in a nice car, in a nice sleeper? Will you take care of her for me?"

The officer looked down at the newly arrived fortune in his hand and told the man that he would take care of it.

"But what train should I put her on?" the officer asked.

"Any that are going north and out of this heat," the man said. "Now I have business across the border, so I must be going. Promise me you'll take care of her tonight." He reached out his hand to shake on the deal. The officer did the same, and their agreement was settled. The officer didn't even look at the man's papers as he stamped them and pushed open the flimsy outgoing gate. He walked into Ciudad Juarez and disappeared into the night.

The officer walked behind his desk, honoring his word to process her that night. He pulled out an immigration form and stamped it with the word "quota." She had no husband with her. She didn't look pregnant, so, no matter what, she could work. In the 1920s, Mexican immigrants made up nearly 75 percent of railroad workers that spanned the western and central United States. The US government expected the men to go home after the building season ended in October. 525,000 miles of railroad line were laid or soon to be laid in 1924, and companies chartered trains to El Paso to pick up new Mexican workers that crossed over the border at Cuidad Juarez. The Immigration Act of 1917 pushed officials to open the railways to make the influx of an underpaid and under-protected workforce possible—maximum pay of fifteen cents per day was mandated.

The officer reached down and scooped Veronica up. She hung limply on his shoulder. She'd become thinner than thin on her journey, and her weight barely made him grunt when he carried her out the U.S.I.S. doors and across the dirt road to the railroad lot. Mexican men and women hopped into boxcars that sat on the tracks. The boxcars had the names of cities on them, marked in white chalk across the tops of the cars: Denver, Chicago, Kansas City, Sacramento, San Antonio, Portland, Omaha. The railroad had already made connections all the way from the east coast to the west coast—the Golden Spike at Promenade in Ogden, Utah was hammered into the earth in 1869. But the rails were still growing, still needed maintenance, and still needed Mexicans to keep them running. Railroad companies recruited right at the border, promising better lives than what Mexico had to offer.

The officer walked past every car and looked inside. Until he got to the last one, there was no seat to lay Veronica down, the cars nearly overflowing with arms and legs and heads. The last car had a sliver of space at the edge of a seat in the back. In a state of blurriness, she could hear others around her. She felt broken. Salt Lake City was scratched into the swinging door of the boxcar. The officer placed Veronica on the edge of it. Her arm slipped down and over the edge, and she nearly rolled onto the tracks, but four hands grabbed her and held her on the flat surface.

Behind her, rows and rows of immigrants sat. Children cried and laughed. Fathers' eyes hung down in worry, and mothers wrapped their arms around their babies or breastfed them to comfort them. Two men held her in the small space left for her to lay. The officer began to close the doors. When he got close to shutting them, he stopped, reached into Veronica's pocket, and pulled out the hundred-dollar bill the nice man had given her. At the end of the day, he would go home two hundred dollars richer than when he had arrived. He would find a prostitute at a speakeasy, and he would die of some horrible sexually transmitted disease, alone in his bed with rotting testicles and major internal wounds—at least, that is what Veronica would tell her grand-nephew nearly sixty-five years later.

Days and miles of track passed. Veronica swayed in and out of consciousness. Her boxcar companions dipped rags into the buckets of water provided to them for their journey. The railroads were in the cheap labor game, so they gave the passengers enough food and water for their journey to fulfill their needs and keep them strong and ready to work when they got to their new homes. Women took turns holding Veronica and squeezing water from the damp rags into her mouth. She would wake for a moment and then fall back asleep. It took three days to travel from El Paso to Denver and from Denver to Salt Lake City. The boxcars stopped so the passengers could go to the bathroom and get more food and water, but beyond that, the railroad companies swung the boxcars along the tracks and transferred them like they were full of goods. Veronica woke up when the train rattled past Price, Utah, a mining town that spit black smoke into the air and was lined with tiny shanties and rickety taverns. She saw the Provo Canyon open its mouth wide and swallow up the train around her. The sharp Rocky Mountains glowed purple in the light of dusk, and the train pulled itself up over the summit. Like a ball slows over a hill and picks up speed after it crests, the train rumbled from the summit and into Orem Valley, past Utah Lake. It passed by the burning lights of Salt Lake City. The smell of salt and brine shrimp and sulfur flowed into the boxcar. It sat in the air and stuck to the seats. The train headed west, away from the lights of the city, along the edge of the Great Salt Lake, and into the western desert.

Chapter Twenty-Four

CHUY

PROVO, UTAH, 1992

MY MOM LEANED OVER THE ISLAND THAT SEPARATED THE KITCHEN FROM the living room and dining room, her feet spread out on the floor, one foot on the brown shag carpet of the living room and one foot on the hard, dingy, green and yellow carpet of the kitchen. Each of the carpets, I had found through months of serious research, having been repeatedly thrown to the floor by Hector before he left for Mexico, had their own distinct and gross smell. My mom had wrapped the long phone cord around her body, like it was hugging her, held the off-yellow receiver against her ear, and laughed and smiled and cried a little.

"Yes, yes, Chuy is fine," she said. "He's standing right here, waiting very impatiently to talk to you, but I'm not getting off the phone until I'm ready. How's Hector?"

She had already asked how Hector was, like fifty times. Did she really need to know about Hector again?

I thought about going to the end of the phone cord and pulling really hard. My mom would spin out of its long and tight squeeze and I could finally talk to my father.

"Veronica is Veronica," she said. "She's cranky and sweet and helpful all at the same time."

I worried about my mother's sanity. Had she been working too hard? Did she put the words "Veronica" and "sweet" in the same sentence? All Veronica did was make my life hard.

—

CAST AWAY

Two days earlier, I followed my mom into the confessional booth before Mass.

My mom had nothing to confess. She was Catholic to the holy bone and went to confession every Saturday before Mass. She made me go, too.

In the confessional, Father Anthony spoke before I could. "Is that you, Jesús?"

"Si," I said.

"Do you have anything new this week, Jesús? Or is this going to be the same confession as every other time your mother brought you in here?"

"No, I have nothing new," I said.

"Okay, Jesús, please say twenty-five Hail Marys and ten Our Fathers for thinking about all the women on TV and all the Mormon ladies with inappropriate thoughts. And, please, Jesús, masturbation is a sin in the Lord's eyes, and he sees you every time you masturbate, okay, Jesús? I care about your soul," he said. "And your mom wants you to mow our lawns. I think it will give you something productive to do with your hands. She does too. Do you think your friend Hans would like to wash the windows? Your mom told me about him, too."

"No," I said. "He's not Catholic."

"Do you think he would like to be Catholic, Jesús?" Father Anthony asked.

"No, he's actually Jewish," I said. "If he had to give that up, I don't think he'd want to be anything. It's his best hobby."

"Jesús, how do you know so much about this? Do you have homosexual thoughts about Hans?" Father Anthony's voice turned from terse to concerned.

"No, Father, why would you ask that?" I asked.

"Your Aunt Veronica came in to see me last week," he said.

"But she's not Catholic. She says the church is for old men who are control freaks and burras," I said. "Sorry, Father."

Father Anthony sighed.

"She came to the confessional to confess your sins on your behalf.

And she confessed the sins of your homosexual thoughts. And she slammed the confessional door and left an empty Coors can and Snickers wrapper behind her. I believe she said, in Spanish, 'That was a good day's entertainment.'"

"No, Father, I don't have those thoughts. I have the regular ones about *CastAway*'s contestants and about Mrs. Johnson who walks her dog every day in her tight stretch pants. You can't see anything because her outfit covers her whole body, but she doesn't take off her garments when she wears her exercise clothes, so you can see her garments underneath, and for some reason, Anthony..."

"Father Anthony, Chuy," he said from the other side of the confessional booth.

"Right. For some reason, this gives me a lot of impure thoughts. But they're not really bad thoughts, I don't think; I imagine her walking the dog in her garments. Not naked or anything. Understand, Father Anthony?"

"Jesús. You bear the Lord's name. You are in the Lord's house. Do you understand why you shouldn't be telling me these things here?" Father Anthony said. "Do you think it would be a good idea for you to visit me once a week and talk about these things?"

No, I did not think it would be a good idea. He asked the questions. I answered them. I couldn't believe how this had come back around on me. I decided right then that I would never tell the truth in the confessional booth again.

"I was joking, Father. I've actually stopped having all impure thoughts," I said.

"Jesús, lying is a sin too," he said.

"I understand, and I'm not lying. I like saying the Hail Mary fifty times and the Our Father one hundred times, and I knew you would assign those to me for penance, so I told you what you wanted to hear," I said.

"Well, that would have been a lie, Jesús, so you did lie to me today," he said.

"Yes, but so I could say a lot of prayers. I've learned my lesson.

Next time, I'll ask for the penance of a lot of prayers instead of taking the long route to get them," I said.

Father Anthony began to speak.

A knock came on the confessional door. I did not expect to hear my Aunt Veronica's voice. I suspect Father Anthony didn't either because he gasped in either exasperation or fear when he realized she had returned to his confessional. His shadow shifted behind the nearly opaque screen that separated us and sat at the edges of the deep mahogany confessional.

"Wrap it up, Anthony, I need the boy," my Aunt Veronica said from outside the confessional door. "Give him a blessing, do your yadyadyadya stuff, and release him. I have groceries in the car that I need for him to carry inside the apartment before I bring him back for Mass."

"Okay, Veronica," Father Anthony said. His voice cracked a little and faded off. "In nomine Patris et Filii et Spiritus Sancti. Go in the name of the Lord, Chuy."

When we got home, she made me carry all the groceries into the house and refused to take me back for Mass. When my mom got home, I got grounded for not returning. Instead of listening to my story about Aunt Veronica, she said, "You could have walked back. No excuse."

Beneath her breath, sitting next to me on the couch, Veronica whispered, "You should thank me."

On the phone, my mom laughed and when the conversation naturally began to slow down, instead of filling the time with updates and jokes, she began to cry through "I love you" and "I miss you," both repeated five or six times before she unraveled her body from the long cord and handed the phone to me.

I held my father's letters to me in my hand. I had sent him one a week since he'd been gone, running through *CastAway* scenarios and updating him on my training.

I told him about how Hans had been training by eating maggots we found. And repeated, over and over, what the host of the show always said, "A million dollars can change your luck and your life." His letters always disappointed me. They told me that he loved and missed me. He thanked me for my updates, but they never said anything about my plan to bring him home, except that his heart was full because I had made a friend and I was doing well in los Estados Unidos, making my way here.

"Papa," I said into the receiver.

"Chuy, mijo, como estas?" he always started this way. I loved him for it. No one ever asked how I was doing. Mom gave me love. Veronica gave me trouble. Dad always asked how I was. Not in a way that most people ask on the street or when a waiter asks, but he drew out the question, holding it in his mouth before letting out, truly asking, "How are you, my boy?"

"Bien, Papa, pero," I would say. "But I would be better if you were here. With Mom and me. If I could win the show, I could pay people to get you here. With a million dollars, we make our own luck, si?"

A long silence hung over the phone.

"I love you, my boy, but we shouldn't talk about this on the phone, okay?" he said. "You never know who's listening."

I looked around the room. Mom and Veronica had settled on the couch. It was Saturday night after Mass, so Mom had tapped her Franzia box of wine and relaxed.

"It's me and Mom and Veronica," I said.

My father exhaled on the other side of the line, his breath leaving his mouth way across the Caribbean.

"Chuy, mijo, I love you," he said. "I want you to be one of those students who gets to travel the world, to see other people, to talk to a man in Spain or France or Japan, okay? Are you doing good in school?"

"Yes, now I am. Hans and Aunt Veronica help me with my English, and the math and science, they're the same as the math and science in Mexico," I said.

My father chuckled on the other side of the line.

"Are you mowing lawns?" he asked.

"Yep, five a week. I'm making enough money that Mom might be able to quit her second job," I said.

"Good boy," my father said. "Maybe soon enough your mom can go back to school too, eh, mijo? Wouldn't that be good, mijo? If your mom can go back to school, to the university, she can get a better job, and she can buy a house, and become a citizen, and you, too. If you're a citizen, I can visit all the time. Do you like that plan?"

"I like my *CastAway* plan better," I said. "When I turn eighteen, I can apply for the show. Actually, the rules say that I can apply when I'm seventeen as long as I am eighteen by the time the show airs on TV, so I could apply in less than three years. I need more training anyway. I think I can get the physical stuff down. I'm pretty fast and the lawn mowing helps my strength, but I really have to learn to be sneaky and mean and backstabbing. I have a hard time with being mean."

My father laughed again.

"Yes, Chuy, you are a kind boy. I love you, son. I have to go. The card is running out of minutes," he said. "And don't talk to anyone about buying my way back here. They have spies. They'll send you and your mom back in a second if they suspect anything. I've seen it all, Chuy. I love you. Good night."

He hung up the phone.

Chapter Twenty-Five

VERONICA

THE SALT FLATS, UT 1924

THE BOXCAR FINALLY SLOWED AND STOPPED IN THE MIDDLE OF THE
night at one of the temporary boxcar towns that popped up along the
railroads across the United States—a town that, like all the rest, would
disappear.

When the smell of burning coal left the air and the engine cooled,
the smell of food took its place. All the passengers poked their heads
out the windows and looked around. Candles and lamps burned in two
parallel rows for hundreds of feet. Behind the candles, in the pitch-
black night of the west desert of northern Utah, white eyes peered
through the little light. The voices of railroad men broke through the
silence of the night, and as one voice got closer and closer to the box
car with Salt Lake City written on it, the passengers started to gather
their bags and packs and children. Every other car had been unloaded
along the way, as passengers disembarked in San Antonio and Denver
and Wichita and Dallas. One woman took Veronica's arm and pulled
her along with her other children and behind her husband. The railroad
man's voice stopped in front of their car and opened the door.

"Home," he said. "Casa." The first family climbed down out of
the car, and the rest followed. Within minutes, the car was empty and
a mass of people stood in the dark and looked down the row of lights
and eyes.

"Follow me," the railroad man said. He held a lantern up in front
of him. His eyes grew out of the top of a beard. He held a piece of paper
in his hand and walked by the first light in the row. Veronica looked up

to see a Mexican man holding a lantern at the top of a few wood plank steps. Behind him, she saw the shadows of a woman and her children in a small doorway. Beyond that, she could see nothing until the group passed another light. Behind it, a man stood in front of a small doorway with no shadows behind him. The group kept walking past fifteen or twenty more lights and the people that stood behind them on top of a few wooden steps in front of tiny doorways to darkness.

The night became even darker when the group walked past the last light in the row. The railroad man shouted out, "Gonzales!" A family from the back of the pack made their way through the crowd and stood in front of the railroad man. The man shuffled to his left, ascended three wooden steps, and opened up a tiny door that looked like all the rest. He waved the Gonzales family up the stairs. They lifted their bags, climbed the steps, and walked through the doorway and into darkness as if they were consumed by the night. The railroad man followed them in for a moment.

The door shut, the railroad man came back down, and Veronica followed him as he walked another twenty feet and repeated the ceremony for a single man in the group, the night swallowing him up like the Gonzales family. When all the families except for the family who had adopted her by grabbing her arm were led up steps into the tiny doorways, the railroad man yelled out, "Chavez," and the family, along with Veronica, followed him up their stairs and through the little doorway. The man followed them in briefly, as he had done with the rest, and the light from the lantern swung around one long room with no other rooms attached to it. At both ends of the long room lay two beds with a blanket strewn across them. Right in front of her was a toilet and next to it a wood-burning stove. The railroad man swung the light around enough for the family and Veronica to get their bearings and then he was gone.

For the first time since she had been dropped into the boxcar in El Paso, Veronica spoke. "Chavez?" she said into the darkness.

"We are Chavezes," a calm voice said. "You spoke of Chavezes in your sleep, so we laid claim to you as one of our own." The hand that had a hold of her arm pulled her into the full body of a woman and held her tightly. "We told the railroad men that you were our oldest daughter. They didn't protest." The full-bodied woman hugged Veronica, walked her over to one of the beds, lay her down, and pulled another girl up onto the bed. "My husband Juan can sleep alone tonight. It's been a long trip." The man shuffled at the other end of the room. The woman nuzzled her body in between the two girls, pulled them in close, and held them until they all fell asleep and the morning sun shone through the windows of the room early the next day. Veronica woke to find the man pulling up his pants and walking out the little door on the side of the room. The woman stood above the bed and smiled down at Veronica and a very young girl next to her, maybe eight- or nine-years-old. The sun revealed a few wrinkles of a heavyset but beautiful Mexican woman.

"What is your name?" she asked.

"Veronica Chavez," Veronica said.

"So I was right. You are one of us," the woman said, her dialect a little different from the mix of Maya and Mexican that Veronica had grown up with in the Yucatán.

"Si," Veronica said.

"Well, you're stuck with us for a while, at least," the woman said.

"Where are we?" Veronica asked. She sat up from the bed and looked out a one-foot by one-foot window.

"We're in the desert by a great lake made of salt. We're at our new home," she said.

Veronica rubbed her eyes, stood with a wobble, and walked toward the tiny door. There wasn't much more to see inside that hadn't been seen the night before in the small light of the railroad man's lantern: two beds, a stove, and a toilet. She poked her head through the open door. On her left, miles and miles of the flattest earth she had ever seen stretched out forever: the salt flats. On her right, water, nearly as flat and calm as the salt flats, stretched out forever too. At the edges of the salt and the water were brown mountains that rose and fell on the horizon. She walked down the stairs and turned around to see that she had spent the night in a boxcar, a freight car turned into a home. Windows were cut out, two on each side of the door, a metal chimney stuck out from the top, and wooden steps dropped down from the entrance. She walked around the edge of the railroad car and looked toward the city. Railroad tracks shot straight toward it like the shaft of an arrow, and at the end of the shaft sat the Rocky Mountains and a city beneath them. She wanted to be there, not in the middle of the desert, not in the center of dust and sand swirling round her. And in a moment, she realized she was far, far away from her home in Mérida, Yucatán. The flatness of the earth, the dryness of the ground, and the presence of desert fauna were the same. The salt flats mimicked the giant shelf upon which Mérida sat, and the presence of salt in each breath reminded her of home, even as the feeling of being dropped into nowhere overcame her. First, her spine felt weak, and then her hips and her knees, and she fell to the ground—the last thing she felt was the hollowness of her womb, and the mourning for a child that left her too soon.

She awoke in the railcar to the sound of laughter and talking outside. Men and women came to meet the newcomers and bring piles of tortillas and beans and newly stitched quilts. She walked out the door to find hundreds of Mexicans talking in Oaxaca accents and Morelia accents and Baja accents and Ciudad accents. The Chavezes sat in the middle of the group and scooped up pinto beans with tortillas and slathered a layer of butter on top that melted into the beans. Veronica slid between the people and sat beside her adoptive mother, who couldn't have been more than ten years her senior but carried herself like an established and strong matriarch. The woman introduced everyone to Veronica and handed the young woman a pan full of beans and tortillas. Veronica ate them up quickly, her first real meal in weeks, letting the bean juice fall between her fingers and run along her forearms until it dripped from the tips of her bent elbows onto the sand.

It was Sunday and nobody worked. The camp of hundreds of people that filed out of about twenty boxcars sat around and talked and ate until the sun fell over the Oquirrh Mountains that night. She dreamed of her own child, and it hurt in areas of her body she never knew could hurt. Darkness overcame the boxcar camp, and the people turned off their lamps, turned to the west, and shushed the children. On the horizon, a castle lit up the night at the end of a pier of a thousand posts. It was not an ordinary dock but one that held up grand hallways that reached from the shoreline of the Great Salt Lake to the castle-like building known as Saltair. The building's dome-shaped roof was surrounded by arabesque towers capped with more dome-shaped tops. It glowed in the distance and looked as if it floated on air. Veronica's eyes spread wide when she looked out toward the dance hall that, at the time, boasted the "largest dance floor in the world." Cars sped by the boxcar town. The brightness of their headlights was matched by the indistinguishable sound of laughter that spilled out into the quiet night of the salt flats. Car after car sped by until the sound of music and loud conversation bubbled up from the top of the dome and rushed across the salt flats, flowed with the wind past the boxcar town, and headed east toward the city. The 1920s were in full swing along the coast of the Great Salt Lake. Speakeasies popped up along the water. Railroad men and miners walked through the speakeasy doors and drank into the night.

Saltair, owned by the Mormon Church and the L.A. and Salt Lake City Railroads, provided a safe haven for young Mormons to venture off into the night to dance, drink caffeinated beverages, and take part in the flapper era. Their parents could rest easy at home, knowing exactly where they were. They knew there was no alcohol. And they knew every other young Mormon at Saltair was eyeing them.

Veronica tilted her head back into the night and closed her eyes. The coolness of the Utah summer night fell over her face and neck, and she listened to the horns, trumpets, and bass that seemed to breathe life into desert lungs. She dreamed of dancing with other people her age. Her feet twisted in the sand beneath her. For the first time since coming to the United States and losing her baby, she didn't hunger for Mérida but instead hungered for Saltair, for fun. The type of fun she had with her sisters and parents growing up when they traveled to the beach near Chelem and swam all day long in the surf. Her father would sit down with the sunset and play his guitar into the night, and the children danced and laughed and spun until the stars above them became blurry and light and free. She felt like a child again.

The people around her seemed to dream the same dream. Even the children quieted down to listen to the music and the laughter. As if a warden had come along and told them to pack it up and get to bed, the boxcar community stood up together and walked into the dark to their homes on wheels. Veronica collapsed onto her bed. Her stomach was full. She did her best to stay awake until the music stopped, the rise and fall of it giving her a feeling she hadn't felt in more than a year. But she couldn't hang on, and fell asleep in the glow of the evening and Saltair.

The next morning was noisy. The sounds of an ever-growing railroad and lively chain gangs clanked before sunrise. Lamplight bounced outside her window amongst the light of the fading morning stars and the greenish tint of a sun that hadn't quite crested the mountains to the east. Mr. Chavez had already gotten up and moved slowly around the cab of the boxcar. Mrs. Chavez stood by the doors of the wood-burning stove and stoked the growing flames in its belly. Men talked outside the boxcar. Whistles blew. Train cars slammed into each other, and the smoke and steam from the engine mixed with the morning salt air that blew in from the west.

"Get up, Miss Veronica," Mrs. Chavez said. "It's time to work." Veronica and the young Chavez girl rolled around in their bed until they were able to roll themselves out of it. Mrs. Chavez told her to clean up in the public water trough and to walk the rows of the boxcars to ask for small excesses of corn for tortillas. She told her that they would need to make some money outside of Mr. Chavez's work with the railroad to keep food on their plates. Rumor had it that checks sometimes arrived after the train of goods rolled through their boxcar town or when Mr. Chavez might be away. She was informed that this was the nature of the business for railroad families. As a Chavez woman who recently turned nineteen, Veronica would be expected to carry a big part of that load. Mrs. Chavez's tone was not cold, but resembled that of a mother lecturing her daughter. At that time, Veronica wanted nothing more than a mother and father to tell her what to do. It made her feel less like a mother who lost her child and more like a lost child herself.

"Yes, Señora," Veronica said. She jumped out of bed and headed out into the rows of stock cars. She had begged her way from Seattle to El Paso; she would beg her way to a couple of buckets of maize, she thought to herself. When she jumped down from the steps, she noticed something: she had energy again. The last two nights of rest, food, and the warm arms of someone who cared about her had begun to restore her strength. When she stood over the trough of clean water, the morning sun reflecting in the water with her, she saw the color had returned to her cheeks and the pink had returned to her lips. She dipped her head in the water and wetted her hair, rung it out with her hands, and let it dry on her back. She felt alive again, even though the smell of salt and burning coal nearly made her vomit.

The boxcar town was alive, too. Many of the cars at the far end of the line were filled with single men and were being pushed along the rail toward an engine that sat at a railroad junction. Mexican men picked up the stairs and any goods that lay outside the car, threw them inside, and helped push it to clank into place behind the engine and other cars. Within minutes, an engine pulled away ten or twelve cars that were part of the town the night before. The men, once their car was connected and the train began to roll, ran alongside and jumped in the doorway. Most sat in the doorway, hung their feet out, and waved goodbye. "Reno" was chalked on their boxcars. Some would return in a couple of months after their work was done. Others would be shipped to California, Oregon, or Washington to work on the railways there. For the most part, the families stayed hunkered down in the boxcar towns. The men of the household would be taken away for three or four weeks, but the railroad did a good job returning them to their wives and kids after their work had been done. Sometimes the railroad would put families on the railways, loading all their stuff into a car near the junction and sending them to other cities in the West, but this was much rarer than the transportation of the much more nimble work-force of single men. Family men offered these boxcar towns stability, and the railroad knew it. Plus, there was a lot of work needed to keep the town standing. Veronica looked at Mr. Chavez when he walked down the stairs. She followed him with her eyes when he reported to the daily train that would take him a few miles away to repair the railway. Chances are, he would be sent to Ogden to work at or near Ogden Union Station, one of the largest junctions in the United States and very close to the Golden Spike at Promontory Point. The Golden Spike was the last spike to be driven into the railroad that connected the East to the West and made the railroad transcontinental. There was always work to be done at Union Station in Ogden: car repair, loading and unloading, railway repair, and any other kind of maintenance that came along with heavy use.

Veronica walked up to the first car and rapped on the door. A skinny woman opened it up and looked out at the young woman from the Yucatán.

"Que?" was all she said. The warmth of the people sitting beneath the stars and Saltair lit up with music and dancing had gone.

Veronica was as polite as she could be when she asked for any corn that could be spared for tortillas.

"No." The woman slammed the door.

Veronica stood, a little shocked before she moved to the next car down the line where she got the same cold response from the next woman. Woman after woman gave her nothing. Cold hands and faces shut the door in front of her.

One woman looked on Veronica with pity and invited Veronica into her boxcar and handed her few cups of flour. Veronica looked at her, puzzled.

With as much respect as she could muster, she asked the woman, "What is this for?'"

"For tortillas," the woman said.

"Tortillas?" Veronica asked. Veronica had never even seen a flour tortilla. The history of maize ran deeper than Catholicism or devotion to Mayan gods in her culture. No one in the Yucatán made tortillas with flour. She wouldn't know how to do it even if she wanted to, and she didn't. Tortillas were made with corn or they weren't tortillas. It was like saying an apple is an orange. Sure, they're both fruit, but they're not the same fruit.

"Si," the woman said. "From Chihuahua, my type of tortilla." The woman held a pile of fresh flour tortillas in her hands. They were warm and soft and fell over the edges of her palm. Veronica took one off the top, spread a little bit of butter on the tortilla, and ate it. It was smooth and soft, and the butter ran down her throat and coated her taste buds. It didn't have the same rich taste as the corn tortillas she grew up eating, but it was filling, warm, and comforting.

"These pendejas," the woman said. "Them and their corn tortilla prejudice. I grew up on flour tortillas, and the railroad men love them."

The woman mixed the flour and baking powder and salt. She cut lard into the mix and turned the ingredients with her hand until a clump of dough sat on her table. The windows and blankets and toilet all had wisps of flour on them, in their cracks, and on their threads. She sat Veronica down and talked to her about the railroad men. She told her to stay away from them. She took her hand and said that they could not be trusted, even the nicest of them. She told her to sell them tortillas and beans, but to never look them in the eye or smile at them. She warned of young women who were taken away from their families in a rail cart and never seen again. Her daughter was one of them. But they did see her again, beaten and raped on the side of a railroad track on line to Reno. She did not cry when she talked about her daughter. She picked up the dough after it had risen and congealed, kneaded it, chopped it up with her hands, smoothed it out with a roller, and threw it in the frying pan. It fried up white with chocolate colored spots across the top.

A whistle blew outside. It was still cold. The heat from the sun had yet to heat up the desert. At such a high altitude, with no moisture in the ground or humidity in the air, the heat from summer days didn't stick around. It drifted away at night and took its time coming back in the morning, even in the summer months. The two of them walked out together. On the other side of the tracks, men piled out of a railcar and walked toward tables of food that had been set up for them. All the women who had turned Veronica away stood behind the tables and handed food to the railmen in exchange for a small bit of change taken from the men's pockets. When the railroad supply cars came along later in the week, the women would use the money to buy more supplies until their husbands received their minimal checks from the railroad. They barely made it by, but they made it by.

Mrs. Cordova, the woman who had taken Veronica into her car, placed her flour tortillas down on a table next to her railcar. When the railroad men saw her, many of them rushed toward her table and stood in line, leaving the six or seven other tables that served corn tortillas. The other women turned their heads and scowled at the woman and Veronica. Men stood two by two. They threw money onto the table and picked up five or six tortillas and bowls full of pinto beans. Within seconds, the beans were scooped up and eaten and the men were gone, along with all the tortillas on the woman's table. A second train car full of men pulled in and emptied. The woman cleaned up her table. She was done for the day. Her table was clean, and she scooped the pile of change into her flour bag. Some men walked to her table to see if she had any food left. She, following her own rules, kept her eyes down and shook her head, "No." They walked away with disappointed smiles, knowing they had missed her food.

"These gabachos love flour tortillas," she said to Veronica. "I think it's because they're white. The corn is too dark for their white blood." She let out a little giggle.

The men from the trains came and went all day. With luck, some of the other women sold all of their corn tortillas and pinto beans, but they had to stand outside all day long to do it. By the time their tables were empty—and some weren't—salty lines of sweat that looked like dried-up rivers beds ran down their faces, and they were exhausted. By that time, Veronica had carried the flour back to the Chavez car, sat down with Señora Chavez, made a batch of tortillas, and sold them quickly to the third or fourth car of railroad men who stopped by the railcar town.

From Tuesday until Friday, Veronica repeated what she had done on Monday. She walked to the woman's door at the end of the row, helped her make tortillas, sold them to the men, took the excess flour to the Chavez car, and repeated everything until the night came. Señor Chavez rolled back into the haggard town every night around seven and collapsed on the bed. He was beat. Señora Chavez fed him. Most nights that week he fell asleep before she could finish eating. Railroad work was hard work. And no matter what any man did before he became an employee of the L.A. Railroad Company or Union Pacific, it couldn't have prepared him for the backbreaking days along the line.

For the most part, Veronica had no problem sticking to the rules laid out before her on her first days on the tortilla line. Most of the railroad men were stinky, heavily bearded, and crude. As beautiful as she was, she heard every kind of catcall.

"Chocolate heaven, come on over!"

"Sweet, soft baby, I'm your man!"

"I would love to ride your railway of love, baby!"

The catcalls were rarely creative and typically vulgar, but they didn't bother her much. Mexican men in Mérida were the kings of cat calls, much more creative than these hairy, white, stinky men whose fingernails were caked in black tar and whose teeth were caked in a different kind of tar. Even if they wanted to turn her head, when they did, momentarily, she saw nothing that tempted her. "Gross gabachos," she whispered to herself.

When Sunday rolled around again, she saw a different town. The smell of food sat like a mosquito net over the town—white smoke covered the cars and no outsiders jumped out of railway cars and called Veronica a Mexican princess. Saltair glowed in the near distance when the sun dropped over the Oquirrh Mountain range. The music came back, accompanied by crests of laughter, and the townies, despite the rivalry between women during the week, sat around a fire and drank beer that had been shipped in on the Saturday afternoon supply car.

They danced to Mexican ballads that ranged from the style of northern states to the style of the Yucatán. Veronica sat with the Chavezes and smiled and drank beer and missed her family and unborn child, but felt like she had joined another family, one on the salt flats of Utah in the middle of nowhere.

PART THREE

Chapter Twenty-Six

Chuy

Provo, UT 1992

Hans and I were best friends. Hans helped me with my English (one reason my aunt let me hang out with "the pervert") and we both had become somewhat skilled in German and Spanish, respectively. At sixteen-years-old, having successfully navigated Provo, our Mormon classmates, and our otherness, we walked into the homeroom of our junior year with all the confidence that is awarded to the middle of the pack. We weren't cool, but we weren't picked on. We weren't the smartest kids in the class, but we weren't the dumbest. We did everything we could to land the same schedule, and for the most part, besides sixth period, we did. During sixth period, I threw on my running shorts and joined the cross country team for daily practice. I'd found out that I was fast while being chased by bullies in the eighth grade, leaving them far behind me as I sprinted across the park and kicked up dust from the dry baseball infield. Hans joined the debate team and spent sixth period with one hand in the pocket of a sports jacket he had bought at Deseret Industries as his mouth ran on and on. He felt the jacket made him a better debater. His mouth was a natural runner.

On the first day of our junior year, we found seats at the back of the classroom, near the heater. Hans and I exchanged notes in German and Spanish about *CastAway* episodes and upcoming strategic practice. The teacher, a lecturer by nature, stood facing the whiteboard and talked aloud as if he and the board were having a long conversation about the intricacies of a geometrical proof.

Mid-lecture, everything changed. The door of the classroom swung open and an athletic girl with sun-bleached hair walked through. She had long, tan legs stretching from the edges of mid-thigh cut jean shorts that showed her full knee. I didn't have to look at Hans. I knew he'd be lost in his own imagination. As she walked toward the empty seat in front of Hans and me, the thick left strap of her tank top fell from her shoulder and down her arm. Briefly, before she slid it back up onto her shoulder, I glimpsed the curve of her of underarm beneath her left arm. I nearly screamed in ecstasy, but then I looked at Hans.

He sat forward in his chair and leaned over the flat surface of his desk. His hands and arms were tucked beneath it. He looked like he was drowning a small animal in his lap, pushing downward again and again. His eyelids clenched together and his lips pursed downward. He looked like he was in deep pain. He did not breathe until I slapped him on the back. His breath shot from his lungs and his mouth and scattered the blonde hair that lay on the new girl's neck, revealing a tattoo of a surfboard above her shoulder blades. The surfboard had zig-zags of reds and blues and greens and her name, Angela, was scrawled beneath it in cursive. Angela probably felt the power and heat of Hans's exhale on her neck and turned around to look at us both. I'd expected her to get angry, or to ignore us like the rest of the girls in our school did, but she didn't. She smiled and winked at us and turned back around, pulling her blonde hair farther off her shoulders and down across her chest to reveal another tattoo right below her hairline: two tiny surfboards with the letter A beneath one and the letter E beneath the other.

Our principal, covered from head to toe in clothing, stuck her head in the door and said, "Ms. Angela, come with me." She dropped her chin toward Angela and said aloud, "Now. So we can remedy your clothing situation."

Angela stood up and followed the principal out of the classroom, but Hans had no immunity to the girl who had briefly sat in front of him. For the last three years, we had been surrounded by strict Mormon girls and Brigham Young University co-eds in the Mormon

Mecca, and were reminded of honor codes and modesty and sobriety everywhere we looked. For the last three years, if Hans saw skin above the knee, he had to retreat to the bathroom to calm himself in whatever way he felt necessary at the time. Angela, with 30 percent of her body covered with clothing, and with her dark, tan skin, tattoos, and obvious lack of care for what others thought of her, was too much for Hans. Again, his breath left him in a hurry, but this time, his head dropped to his desk, and he sighed.

"Bathroom!" I whispered. With my thumb, I pointed toward the door.

"I can't," he said. He placed his thumb on the desk and swooped it upward.

Hans, my friend, was stuck. If he stayed there, the smell of the new girl would probably put him into some kind of shock. If he got up, the entire class would see how excited he was about the transfer student, so I did what I thought was best to save him: I stuck my finger down my throat, ran to the garbage can, and vomited my eggs and toast into it. Sickened and intrigued by my running and vomiting, the entire class lost sight of Hans as he fled to the bathroom.

The teacher asked how I felt. Besides the lingering taste in my mouth and the soreness in my chest from vomiting, I felt fine. Most of the male students in the classroom, unable to deny their lust for all things gross, hovered around me and the garbage can and examined my breakfast.

A strong air of vanilla softened the stench around me. A hand touched my forearm. It was soft and tan. It was Angela's. She placed it right below my hand, gently moved it up my arm to my elbow, and squeezed it like examining the ripeness of an avocado. Gentle but strong enough to make sure I felt it.

"That was nice what you did for your friend," she whispered into my ear. I could feel her breath and smell her lip gloss. "I see you're not like the rest of these future missionaries."

She had returned wearing a long denim frock that covered her from head to toe. It didn't matter. I knew what was beneath it, so everything inside me trembled and shook. The scent of vanilla and skin came over me. I'd never been touched like that before. I'd never felt the breath of a beautiful woman on my neck before. My nerves got the best of me; I threw up again. Covering her up did me no good; my imagination did all the work. It was even worse.

At cross country practice after school, my empty stomach and I ran along the trail on the mountainside above Provo. For an hour or more each day, I thought about nothing but putting one foot in front of the other and making sure I didn't catch a toe beneath an exposed root and eat shit. The winding trails of northern Utah were my team's training routes. The aspens and maple and sage brush lined the single-person veins of flattened dirt that stretched out beneath the sharp, rocky slants of rock that began at the tree line and reached 8,000 feet into the air, 12,000 feet above sea level at their peaks.

The team captain ran ahead of me. Every time I tried to catch him, he sped up and left dirt in my teeth. I popped out from a cluster of trees and saw my high school in the Provo Valley beneath me.

Angela's lower thigh boinged in my brain, too. The curve her underarm. The smell of vanilla hit me. My foot came down on the rounded curve of a slick rock, and I flew forward and slammed my face into the ground.

Runners came up behind me, picked me up, and asked if I was okay. I was. I'd fallen before while letting thoughts of bikini-clad girls on *CastAway* pop into my brain mid-run. It was as if their beauty saved me from pain, or at least the initial pain from eating shit on the trail above the city. The rest of the run was pain-free. I had somehow put the thought of Angela's skin out of my mind long enough to follow the trail down the mountain, onto the Provo streets, and into the parking lot at school.

But there she stood. For the sake of self-preservation, and because I had no more food to throw up, I turned and walked in the exact opposite direction from where she stood. I found myself heading toward the Mormon church that sat across the street from the school, a place where all my classmates went for church, a parade of Mormons crossing the street in long pants, long shirts, and halos on Sundays. I had no idea what I was going to do when I got to the church. My clothes were in the locker room in the gym directly behind Angela. My backpack was there, too. But I kept walking until I walked through the front doors of the seminary and was greeted by seminary teachers.

They scanned me up and down and reached out their arms.

"Hello, brother," they said in near unison. "You're new to seminary. Have you heard about the church and is that why you have come today?"

"Yes, I have," I said. I glanced back over my shoulder to see if she followed. My short, short running shorts nearly exposed me.

"Where did you hear about the church?" the taller one asked. They made eye contact with each other and smiled.

"I live in Provo," I said, answering their question about the church. My tone was not sarcastic, it was informational. My mind was on the left lower thigh of girl outside the seminary building. I knew she was there. I knew she smelled like vanilla. Somehow, I knew she would wait for me to come out of the seminary building, and I was scared shitless of her.

"Of course, of course," one teacher said. "Would you like to come in and talk more about it and learn the teachings of Joseph Smith?" They both walked toward me and placed a hand on each of my sweaty elbows. They smiled at me.

"No, thank you," I said. Aunt Veronica would beat me with her roller if she knew I even stepped into this place. "I'm here to avoid the new girl. She scares me a little."

The taller teacher kept talking about Joseph Smith, the new New Testament, and the virtues of the one true church. The other teacher put his hand on my shoulder. Like a switch had been turned off on his vocal cords, his voice turned from preachy to sincere.

"I understand," he said. "She's beautiful. I can see that. Follow me, and I can get you out of this."

The room, covered in white paint and pictures of a very white Jesus, made me doubt my decision to flee into the church in the first place. Paintings of Joseph Smith in the forest with Jesus and Moroni; Joseph Smith translating the Golden Plates; Joseph Smith with the Urim and the Thummim, covered the walls. It seemed a little pompous to me, but I channeled my father's respect for someone else's dedication and thought about Angela's beautiful face.

"What is your name?" one man asked.

"Chuy," I told them. Every time the door opened and closed behind me, I got a glimpse of Angela, and every time I saw her, she was a bit closer to the door.

"Jesús!" the man said. "The name of our brother-lord. We're happy to have you, Jesús. Our lesson today is about the importance of chastity. Join us! We have an extra seat."

The door swung open again, and there she was, right outside the door, ready to enter. I felt the juices in my stomach swirl and more sweat leak from my elbows onto the man's hands.

"Yes," I said. I followed the two of them through the double doors of the conference room.

The taller teacher stood in front of a table at the front of the room. He placed his hands on a wooden, portable pulpit that sat on the table, pulled out a few pieces of paper from beneath it, and began to talk.

"Outside these walls are temptations that we can't even imagine. TV shows tempt us with sex and violence. Advertisements for clothing show half-naked women and men dancing and writhing together in hot showers." He did not take on the persona of a preacher, but one of a friend. His voice was calm, understanding, and even forgiving of the nasty world outside the seminary doors.

"I mean, I get it," he said. "Sex sells. I'm not dumb. You're not dumb." He lifted his hand from the pulpit and pointed to a young man in the first row. "And I am a man too. A young man. With hormones." The group of high school students leaned backward in surprise like a giant hand gave them one big push when he said the word sex out loud and in church. Mumbles circled through the room.

"We all know that our bodies are designed to procreate. We all know that our hormones are part of a natural instinct to keep us alive. While some teachers will not talk to you about this, I will." He found my eyes with his, stared right into them, and did not blink once.

"Temptation is coming toward you right now, and even if it is the most beautiful thing you have ever seen, you have to be strong and not let it control your instinctive bodily response to its beauty. Not here at least. Not in this building," he said. Most of the other students listened to him and took the last few things he said as metaphors, but I knew he was talking about my teenage, hormonal burst when Angela walked in and sat down next to me. My wet legs stuck to the vinyl chair and sweat fell onto the floor around me.

"Hi, again," she said to me. Her voice broke into the middle of the teacher's talk about the necessity of chastity and sexual purity.

"Hi," I whispered.

"Are you feeling better?" she asked. "It looks like you've stopped throwing up. How's your friend Hans feeling?" I had expected her voice to be sultry, a mix of Michelle Pfeiffer and the devil, but it wasn't. Instead, it was soft with a little bit of depth to it. "Why did you come in here?" she asked. She tilted her head to the side, smiled a smile that barely upturned her lips, and raised one eyebrow. She seemed truly inquisitive. No, she seemed truly concerned. "You don't belong in here, do you?" she asked. Her voice got higher at the end of her question, as if she would feel abandoned and alone if I did belong in the seminary room after all.

"No, not really," I said. "The guy talking seems pretty nice though."

"Yeah, I'm sure he is," she said. "But do you want to go for a walk with *me* instead of listening to him?"

"Not really. Thank you," I said. I had no control of my stupid mouth, but at least I knew these words would save me from doing something tonto.

"Okay, maybe later," she said.

This beautiful girl, this girl with skin that was an extension of the sun, this girl with the color of the ocean in her eyes, this girl who had no business talking to me.

I sat in my running shorts in the middle of a crowd of students and waited until the teacher stopped talking and dismissed the class. Angela tapped me on the leg and said goodbye.

"I'll see you in class tomorrow, Chuy," she said. Before she left, the taller teacher approached her. He shook her hand. She shook his back. She nodded, and she walked back out the front door, this time with her head dropped a little, with a slight reverence that I hadn't seen in her yet that day.

Our apartment complex roared with the sounds of music and laughter and conversation that night when I walked into the parking lot. Fall in northern Utah had arrived. The maple trees on the sides of the Wasatch Mountains splashed red and yellow and pink in the path of the sun that dropped over the lake. The summer's heat had left, and the autumn breezes, cool and clean, flowed out of the canyons like the rivers that cut the great rock walls leading into the valley. The smell of Asian and Indian and Mexican food met in the air outside the open doors of the apartments, and smoke from ovens and frying pans crawled along the ceilings, over the tops of the exterior door jambs, up along the edge of the rusting overhang, and upward into the heavens. Nowhere else in the city smelled like this complex, like this diverse mix of rich aromas.

I walked past the burnt, grassy area that had never grown back to its original half-green and half-gray after it was burned down by the ash of a cigarette, and headed into our apartment through the open front door. Like in every other apartment, a steady stream of smoke rose from the kitchen and crawled above me to escape into the evening. The landlord had promised years ago that he would install fans above the stoves, but never got around to it. It seemed that few people stuck around long enough to complain a second or third time. From my count, we had lived there the longest, nearly three years, except for Mrs. Yamamoto, who lived directly below. I'd never met her, but

I knew that she was nearing one-hundred-years-old, and she had lived in Seattle when she first arrived in the States. She was put into a camp, what is now the Puyallup Fairgrounds, during World War II, because they thought she was from Japan even though she was actually from Okinawa. Despite this, both her sons served in the Vietnam War. She now lived alone, except for my Aunt Veronica's daily visits to her door with Mexican pastries.

But apart from Mrs. Yamamoto, everyone else came for a bit and then left. Which kind of pissed me off.

I knew my Aunt Veronica could have money. I knew she owned her house in Rose Park and could make a really good bundle on it if she were to sell. She bought it in the late 1940s, when the streets were laid out in the shape of a rose and filled up with railroad workers and the second batch of immigrants from Mexico and China. I knew she could have made a lot of money off that house, since the city was now filled with white-collar workers that couldn't afford homes in the Avenues or by the university and felt like progressive, white explorers for buying homes in the middle of the most diverse neighborhoods in the city.

It was Wednesday night. *CastAway Island* would be on in less than an hour, and Veronica stood over the stove and fried chicharrones in a small, black, crusty frying pan. I loved everything she cooked except for her chicharrones. She fried them so long that they shriveled up into tiny nuggets of teeth-breaking pork skin. One bite could take out a tooth. One bite could ring in your ears for days. She told me that she liked them that way and that if I wanted any I had better start to like them that way, too. I think she cooked them that way so she didn't have to share.

I threw my running bag toward the couch, but before it hit the cushion, Aunt Veronica yelled at me from the kitchen, "Do not drop your bag on the couch. Take your stinky bag and walk it to your bedroom and let it hang out in there with the rest of your filthy, stinky clothes." She continued to fry her teeth-breakers. "Shower, too," she yelled. "I can't sit by you when you stink like a baboon's ass. Go shower and come help me finish dinner." She chuckled under her breath.

Veronica and I cooked before *CastAway Island*, keeping with tradition with my father before he had been ripped from our home. Her hands had become so frail that I had to do all of the kneading for the flour tortillas.

"Your Grandma Rosa loved four tortillas. I taught her how to make them," she said.

"I know. That's how my father knows. That's how I know," I said.

She turned to me. "My hands are getting too old to knead the dough."

"I will help you," I said.

An hour later, we sat together on the sofa—Mom had gone to work and Hector had been gone long enough that we had established our own routine—and watched the opening flashes of jungles and challenges and, my favorite part, women in bikinis bending over and struggling to pull something out of the sand.

She crunched on her chicharrones. I did my best to not get excited. The world felt right.

"You're not a joto are you?" Aunt Veronica asked. The question came out of her mouth in the same, mellow manner, like she was asking me what I wanted for dinner. "You and Hans together all the time, never with girls. You a joto? He's European, and they are more open about that stuff, but *we* don't tell people we're jotos. So do his parents know something about you two that I don't know?"

The question, the tone, the implication, did not surprise me or bother me. Last week, out of nowhere, she asked if I knew the difference between men who liked girls and men who liked men. I kind of expected this question was next in her line of interrogation.

"No, Tia, I'm not gay," I said.

"You're never around girls. You're a handsome boy. You have a strong mix of asshole conquistador blood mixed with the fierce face of your Mayas. You a joto?"

The commercial after the opening and before the first of the episode rolled in front of us.

"I talked to a girl today after school. So beautiful," I said.

"Did you ask her over here for dinner?" she asked.

"No," I said. "She asked me to go on a walk with her, but I said no."

"She's beautiful?" she asked.

"So beautiful," I said.

"And you said no?" she asked.

"Yes," I said.

"Yep, you're a..." the episode began, and she stopped mid-sentence.

During commercials, as was our tradition, we talked about the game and who would be kicked off and who was evil.

The credits rolled after the expelled player spoke, and my Aunt Veronica finished her sentence, "...joto. But I'd love you no matter what, Chuy. You can love whoever you want. Just don't bullshit me."

Chapter Twenty-Seven

VERONICA

THE SALT FLATS, UT 1924

VERONICA WORKED THE TORTILLA LINE FOR SIX MONTHS. SALTAIR boomed every Sunday night. Man after man after man tried his best to get her attention. When the men realized that catcalls didn't work, they changed tactics.

"What's your name, chica?" the white men asked.

"You're Veronica, right? You're beautiful." Some held up the line to talk to the twenty-year-old girl who, in the last year and a half, had run away with a poet, carried his child, lost that child—a child she thought about every day—and escaped its abusive father. She had ridden in the backs of railcars to get to El Paso, dehydrated and nearly dead, and found her way to the railcar town in the desert. The men could try their best, but Veronica had gone from a silly girl to a strong young woman in less than a year. Her resolve had grown strong. Her will could handle any slurs from men who became angry when she rejected them.

"Fine, slut," one man said after his advances fell on deaf ears.

"I wouldn't touch you anyway. You'd probably give me some kind of disease," another man said.

Under her breath, Veronica would whisper, "I hope your dick falls off from some prostitute," or "I doubt I could even feel you if you tried." The innocent girl who chased women and men in the streets of Mérida was flushed out with the blood that flowed from her womb a little less than a year earlier. After a while, she looked forward to the catcalls and eventually angry words from the men. She loved the power her silence gave her. These men got angrier and angrier every time they tried to talk to her and she ignored them. She crushed their dreams. She put them in their place. She realized that men had no control over her—not because of her sexuality, but because of her will-power. She was stronger than them, had more resolve, and couldn't be swayed by their sweet words like she'd been swayed in the past. And she reveled in their anger. She swam in it. It made her smile to know that no pretty white man could get to her again. She would never fall for another white man with blue or green or light brown eyes or hair. She may have been, at one time, naive, but she was never stupid.

One morning, however, she did lift her eyes to a man that stood on the other side of the tortilla table. She had gotten very good at pulling tortillas out from beneath the towel, scooping beans into a bowl, and handing both to the men. They didn't touch their hands, look up, or need to aim. She made their hands come to her, and the men adjusted. That morning, she saw a set of dark brown hands—not the dark hands of a really tan gabacho, but the darkness that comes from generations living beneath the Yucatán sun. The hands reached for her tortillas.

"Dios bo'otik," a voice said, and Veronica's head popped up. He didn't say "thank you" or "thanks" or even "gracias" but "Dios bo'otik." She had not heard Dios bo'otik since leaving Mérida more than a year ago. It was said in the streets of Mérida from the vendors that lined the Cathedral at the city center. Instead of "gracias," many Mayans said, "God pays." It was one of the few common phrases from the merging of the Spanish and Mayan that hung on in Mérida. It separated those of Spanish descent or Spanish and Mexican descent from those Mayan families that were, mostly, made up of Mayans.

Her head shot up for the first time on the tortilla line. Señora Cordova slapped her on the leg, not understanding why Veronica looked up at this man. They'd seen hundreds of thousands of Mexicans, men from all over Mexico, and Veronica never faltered in her resolve.

She responded, "Hach Mixba'al"—"you're welcome," in Mayan.

"Veronica," Señora Cordova barked. "Keep your head down. These men. You know these men."

With her head down, she said, "Taak tu lakin." "Until later."

"Taak tu lakin," he said and moved toward the railcar.

Señora Cordova slapped Veronica on the back of the arm. "You know these men. A traveling railroad man is a traveling railroad man. It doesn't matter if he is Mayan." Señora Cordova was no fool. She figured out what happened immediately.

The young man came the next day and the next, and the exchange was exactly the same.

"Dios bo'otik."

"Hach Mixba'al."

"Taak tu lakin."

"Taak tu lakin."

Each day she caught a tiny glimpse of his face before he turned and headed to the railcar. He had the same Mayan features as all the Mayan men she wouldn't respond to in Mérida. Her eyes were set on the American men in the tweed suits back then. Any Mayan man that asked her out had no chance. His eyes were nearly black from edge to edge, with a hint of brown in the irises to separate them from his pupils, and his hands were small. He cupped the tortilla, and the edges of flour dangled from the front and back of his palms.

"Dios bo'otik."

"Hach Mixba'al."

"Taak tu lakin."

"Taak tu lakin."

When the young Mayan left on the third day, Señora Cordova whacked the back of Veronica's calves with her rolling pin.

"No more of this," Señora Cordova said. "No more of this foolishness."

Veronica leaned back and massaged the growing welt on the back of her calf.

"I don't understand the problem," Veronica said.

She handed a man a tortilla and scooped up beans to put into his bowl.

"Hello, beautiful," the man said to her. Frustrated with Señora

Cordova's comment and whack to the back of the legs, Veronica dumped the hot beans on the man's hands instead of in his bowl. He yelled at her, threw the beans on the ground, and reached over the table to grab her, but Señora Cordova whacked him with a giant wooden serving spoon and filled his bowl with beans and waved the man away.

"I'm saying you're welcome and see you later," Veronica said in one of those yelling whispers that mothers invented and perfected over centuries.

"That's enough to get you into trouble," Señora Cordova said. "If he's riding the rails with those gabachos, his soul is gone. It's hard enough for the married men who came with wives and children to stay good men. Many run off to bigger cities. Many come home with diseases from prostitutes. And many never come home. It's too easy to live on the rails, drink at night, whore around, and not worry about their families. It's too tempting." Señora Cordova waved her spoon around in the air. "Look around, over the last six months, how many husbands do you see come back and stay back? Your Mr. Chavez is an exception. He is a good man but look around. They're gone. Sometimes they still bring their money back. Sometimes, like Mr. Chavez, they push to work closely to their family so they can come home nearly every night, but sometimes the rail takes them, the booze gets in them, and the call of the next whorehouse down the line is too tempting to pass up. If it doesn't get their bodies, which it usually does, it will get their souls, dampen them, spit on them, run them with rivers of silt."

Veronica looked around the camp and saw women doing laundry in the water tub, serving tortillas and beans on the line, and sweeping the steps to their railcars. She tried to think of how often she saw their men. She saw them, usually, on Sundays, when the beer flowed and the sky lit up with laughter and music. On Sunday nights, the women of the town were kind and happy. She scanned her memory of those nights. Her world had become so small. She saw the Chavezes and Señora Cordova. Saltair glowed in the distance, but beyond her little circle of family, she couldn't place the faces of too many men. She never cared to look, but now, she saw that Mrs. Cordova was right. There was no real consistency of men, outside a few men like Señor Chavez, around the campfire. They were blurs in the night. They all looked the same—tired and wrinkled and drunk—but she couldn't, with any certainty, say that she saw the same men standing around with their families. Monday mornings and the crabbiness of the women when she asked for supplies made a lot more sense now. Veronica had been trapped happily in her bubble of family for so long that she never saw the pain the railroad had brought other families. She had two women who loved her, talked to her, looked after her, and mentored her. She had Mr. Chavez who came home nearly every night and sat and talked with the family like her father did. She was happily unaware, and this realization pissed her off. It was the same type of naivete that got her there in the first place, the same type of loving blindly that impregnated her and beat her, and stole her from the rock walls that lined the streets of her hometown.

"You're right, Señora," Veronica said. She continued to hand men their tortillas and dump beans into their bowls.

The next day when the young Mayan man said "Dios bo'otik," Veronica said nothing. She kept her head down and gave him his food. He repeated himself two more times before giving up and walking away.

Winter had come and with it 1925. The skies dropped snow over the tracks. Life became blurry and cold and slow. Railroad men came less and less. The working season began to die with the turning of the trees. Orange and brown and red leaves fell on the mountainside of the Wasatch Range, and Veronica missed the young man who spoke her language every morning. Chances were that he had moved on to Reno or Sacramento or down to San Diego with the railroad. Winter came, and it was tough. Señor Chavez used most of his money to buy wood from the railroad company to heat the wood-burning stove for cooking and keeping the railroad car warm enough for the family of four. Veronica kept close to Señora Cordova. She stayed there most nights and listened to the middle-aged woman's stories about her dead husband and dead daughter.

But they all made it through the winter well enough. The four-foot snow drifts that built up along the sides of the railroad town began to melt. The railways did a good enough job to keep their tired workers fed and warm, even handing out extra supplies at no cost during the toughest months of the year. Utah is a desert, but at 4,400 feet above sea level, it gets its fair share of snow and ice and blizzard winds. The winter of 1924 to 1925 wasn't easy, and it was definitely cold. Brine shrimp lived on the water throughout December and January, turning the Great Salt Lake pink, like looking at a giant wedding cake that smelled like a pig's ass. The entire lake became frothy and rich and covered in brine shrimp eggs. The smell was almost unbearable, but Veronica had felt worse, seen worse, lived worse than the pink-infested waters of the Great Salt Lake.

All of a sudden, at the point in time when it seemed like the winter would never end and life would never be warm again, spring came. The local fishermen skimmed the brine shrimp off the waters, the snow began to melt, and warmth came back into the encampment. Veronica waited for the railroad men to come back. They were money. They were entertainment. They were life. The cold winter months were claustrophobic at best, and she yearned for the work of the tortilla line.

In her heart, Veronica wished for her Mayan worker to come back, but he didn't. March became April. Saltair lit up again. Mormons and non-Mormons flocked to the tiny city on the pier. They danced on the dock supported by 2,000 posts and the night came back to the great lake.

The railcar town sat around on an early April Sunday night and the palace boomed in the early spring air.

The cars full of hungry men came back too. Most of them stumbled through the bartering process. Most of them still said please and thank you and gracias. They were new to the railroad, recently picked up from El Paso or the poor houses of St. Louis, Kansas City, Wichita, or Denver. Veronica felt comfortable and part of the Chavez family, but lonely at the same time. She held on to the love Mrs. Cordova gave her too, but with both the Chavezes and Mrs. Cordova, they, unintentionally, held back a bit from her. Mrs. Cordova, having lost her husband and daughter to the railroad, had hardened to a point where she protected herself by pulling back if Veronica got too close to her soul with questions about family, or love, or friendship. The Chavezes gave her a bed and food and a table to sell tortillas, but they too held back the deepest ends of love. Mrs. Chavez never wanted her daughter to feel as if Veronica intruded on their relationship, and Mr. Chavez was too tired to give most the time. It was a father's attention and a child that she ached for the most.

Chapter Twenty-Eight

CHUY
PROVO, UT, 1992

THE PRINCIPAL, A BLOCK OF A WOMAN COVERED IN CORDUROY, POPPED her head into class to check on Angela. Her eyes scanned the girl who sat in front of me.

"Where are your clothes, young lady?" she asked Angela.

"I have clothes on," Angela said. "Unlike you, I don't need a tent to cover my big fat ass." She said this loud enough for me to hear it, but not loud enough for it to make it through the chatting voices in the classroom and into the principal's ears.

"Let's go get another dress for you to put over your clothes. Let's go, missy," she said in front of the whole class.

Two girls, covered head to toe in long dresses and long sleeves, whispered to each in the corner of the room, "That slut should go home," and "I bet she had to leave California because she slept with everyone in her school and needed to come here to find more people to have sex with," and "Look at her, she doesn't care to cover up what our Heavenly Father gave her?" Their voices were quiet, but the entire class could hear them, even the principal, but she did nothing to stop their chatting or from being so cruel.

Before the principal left the room, I swear I saw her smile and wink at the two girls in the corner of the room, like she was giving her approval for the nasty things they said about the new girl.

Angela shifted in her seat uncomfortably. Her head dropped down a bit. She didn't respond to the old, blocky woman or the girls that called her names on the other side of the room.

I know I shouldn't have done it right then, but an uncontrollable urge raised my hand and placed it on her shoulder.

"Don't listen to them," I said. "They're mean."

Angela turned to me and grabbed my hand. She gave a slight smile that said, "They don't bother me, Chuy." Her eyes met mine. They were light blue and beautiful, and they softened. I gazed at her for what seemed like a week but must have been two or three seconds. And she looked back at me in a way that no girl in that town had ever looked at me before. She squeezed my hand again, this time with her fingers and palm, and she released my hand and slowly removed her fingers from it, rubbing them over my skin.

"Thank you, Chuy," she said.

Some students laughed at the whole exchange. Some whispered, and others sat quietly in the uncomfortable moment, but the two girls in the corner of the room continued their hazing. "What do you get when cross a Mexican and a slut?" one girl asked the other.

"I don't know," the other girl said.

"A mutt—you know, a Mexican and a slut combined—a mutt," she laughed.

"Yeah, a mutt."

I couldn't believe the teacher let this go on this long. He stood there in front of the class and listened to the girls call us names and insult us. Out of nowhere, he walked over to me and Angela, rapped his knuckles on my desk, and asked both of us to stand up and go to the principal's office.

"No public display of affection will be tolerated in my classroom," he said. "Go to the principal's office and explain to her that you two can't keep your hands off each other."

"Let's go," I said to her.

"Do you know where her office is?" Angela asked me.

"Yeah, follow me," I said. Angela took my hand. She slid her fingers between my fingers and gripped them tightly as we walked down the hallway. I couldn't believe it. I felt warmth that crawled from my hands to my chest and made the hair on the back of my neck stand up tall. Chills shot through my spine.

"Those girls are mean," I said.

"They're like Cinderella's ugly stepsisters, but less attractive," she said. She did something I loved. She laughed so loudly at her own joke that she snorted. This beautiful, perfect girl snorted in the hallway. "They look more like her stepsisters' butts than their faces." She should have stopped after the first joke because it was funny. The second one was not funny at all. She totally messed up the first one with the second, but she didn't care. She laughed and snorted and laughed and snorted again. She tried to insult the girls again by talking about how their hair looked like hyena hair.

Hans, coming out of the bathroom, saw Angela and me walking together. I saw his eyes nearly pop out of his head. Subtly, he lifted his hand to his side and gave me the cheesiest thumbs-up I had ever seen, accompanied by the cheesiest grin I had ever seen. I hoped Angela didn't see him, but she did.

"Your friend thinks you're pretty cool," she said. "Does he love David Hasselhoff?" She laughed again, as if she were the first one to ever make that joke about Germans. But she was right. Hans was right. I felt cooler at that moment in my life than I ever had before, so I slowed my pace. I didn't want to get to the office because I would have to let go of her hand. She smelled like vanilla. My arms were warm. My ears burned. And I didn't want any of it to end. So I slowed way down, methodically holding my feet back from walking until I stopped.

She stopped with me and turned and looked at me.

"Geez, I'll hold your hand again," she said. She had obviously figured out my plan. She laughed again at her comment, and we walked into the principal's office together.

"We cannot allow this to happen. We have standards. If you want to be loose with your morals and ban yourself from the beautiful kingdoms, you'll have to do it on your own time," she went on and on and on. All I thought about was the next time Angela might let me hold her hand and Hans's face when we passed him in the hallway.

I looked at Angela, who stared blankly at the principal. All the smiles and crying from laughter had gone away and a straight face had replaced them.

"Chuy, I'm disappointed in you. You're a nice young man," she said. She pointed her finger at my eye and wiggled it around as if she were trying to drill her words into my skull with it.

"Now, both of you get up!" she said. "Come look out the window with me." We walked around her desk. She stayed seated in her chair, covering up every square inch of leather beneath her. She pointed out toward the other students, two of them being the girls who called Angela a slut ten minutes earlier. "You see those young people there. Those are children of the Lord. See how they dress. See how they cover up their skin in the presence of the Lord. I know you two can be children of the Lord. Angela, I know your family. They are good, practicing Mormons. Chuy, I've met your parents. They're good people. Can we not remedy this?"

The two girls who had taunted Angela and made her cry earlier walked past the window and smiled in on us.

"See them," the principal said. "See how, even when you are in trouble, they are good-spirited and smile your way. The Lord is their short shorts," she said. Angela's lips quivered. "The teachings of Joseph Smith give them what your sex gives you."

Angela pushed air out between pursed lips like she was in Lamaze class. *Stop woman, please stop.* I thought to myself. I knew Angela couldn't handle it.

"The one true church gets them high."

Angela's lips rose, and she did her best to keep it together.

"Jesus is their crack cocaine." That was it, the last straw, the stupid straw that broke the stupid camel's back. Angela buckled over, nearly falling to the ground, and laughed, unintentionally and with no malice, in the principal's face, spit flying from her mouth and landing on the corduroy tent.

"Oh my gosh, Chuy! Can you see it? Those stuck-up girls snorting Jesus and smoking the church to get high!" She laughed so hard that the tears came back and then the snorts. She rolled her eyes to the back of her head as if she were imagining the girls chopping up Jesus and snorting him up their noses or putting him on a spoon and injecting him into their arms.

"My parents are Mormon," she yelled. "But thank god they're not Utah Mormons." Snorting and laughing, her voice filled the room. "Utah Mormons are different from everyone else. Oh my gosh, Chuy, why isn't this funny to you? Maybe you need a shot of Saint Jameson! Augh, Saint Jameson! I kill myself."

I wasn't laughing, although I loved the sound of her laughter and the sight of her smile, because the principal was writing down everything Angela was saying. The principal picked up the phone and asked for her assistant to get Angela's parents on the phone. Angela still laughed.

"Chuy, you can go back to class," the principal said, and shooed me with her hand as if I were an annoying fly buzzing in her space.

"I'm fine," I said. "I'm happy to stay."

"Chuy, I was trying to be polite. Leave, now," she said.

I walked out of the room and past the assistant. Her eyes scanned the electronic directory of parents on her computer. She dialed a number on her phone. The call to Angela's parents was imminent.

I didn't go back to class but decided to hang out outside the principal's office and wait for Angela to come out. You never know. She might need someone to hold her hand or maybe her upper arm or maybe…my mind drifted up above her arm to that slight smile on her face. I sat down on the wooden bench outside the office. I put my ear against the wall to see if I could hear anything, but the thick white walls trapped the sound behind them. A door opened and footsteps sounded my way. I expected tears. I expected a sullen girl who had gotten reamed by her parents and the principal. Instead, what was said was, "Jesus is their crack cocaine! Is the Quorum of the Twelve their gangstas?"

"Get out of here, now!" the principal yelled, and slammed the door behind Angela.

Angela rounded the corner and saw me sitting on the wooden bench.

"Did you hear that Chuy?" Angela said. "Was I the only one listening to that bullshit? I mean, I grew up Mormon, but come on!"

"What happened?" I asked her.

"Aw, nothing. I couldn't stop laughing, which got my mom laughing. I told her that the principal said the Lord is their short shorts, and my mom asked if their Lord needed Nair for their short shorts or if he didn't mind if he had a beard up there. I laughed so hard that I peed a little. So, Mrs. Corduroy hung up the phone and kicked me out."

I was sad she wasn't sad. I wanted to hold her hand again, to feel her soft fingers between mine, and to get that buzz that flew through my body, but she wasn't sad, so I stood up and said, "Beard!" and tried to laugh.

"Oh, my jumping bean," she said. She held out her hand anyway, and we walked back to class. Hans still stood in the doorway of the restroom with a face frozen in amazement at the world.

For weeks, all Angela and I needed to be happy was to be with each other, away from the world, so at night we drove her car to the edge of Utah Lake, parked at the edge of a closed marina, hopped the gate, walked to the end of the pier, and sat down to dangle our feet in the water. We never had a lot of time.

We didn't waste any time throwing off our shoes, dropping our feet into the water, and slamming our hips against each other in that intoxicating cloud of hormones that swirled around us. Those nights were a blur of ecstasy and slobber. Neither one of us took notice of style or grace in our making-out technique, and I used every ounce of self-control to hold my feet in the water and talk for a minute before I moved close to her and we started smacking lips. A touch on the leg or the shoulder turned me toward her, and all she needed was my turn and the full-on make-out would begin. Legs flew out of the water and hands grabbed any exposed flesh. We rolled around on the dock like a rolling pin spreading out a tortilla. Our lips became raw. Hours would pass. Only when the sun would sink behind the Rocky Mountains, the warmth of summer would leak into the sky, and the cool, arid air would ski across the water, would we stop making out. She would drive me to the apartment and drop me off.

Aunt Veronica would wait for me in the kitchen. She always stood next to the oven in a nightgown that dropped straight down off her shoulders. She wore her nightgown like a judge and her face like a decided jury, ready to hand out a sentence.

"Ella es Mormón?" Veronica would ask even though she knew the answer.

"Si," I would say for the fortieth time.

"Your face is red like a baboon's ass," she'd say. "You look like that Mormon girl tried to suck your lungs out through your mouth. You look like you might have to buy new jeans because the front is almost rubbed through."

"I know, Aunt Veronica, you don't like her."

"I don't like her? I don't know her. When you going to bring her around to meet your aunt and your mom?"

"Why, so you can hit her with your rolling pin when she says something wrong?" I asked.

"Has all your blood gone down there, Chuy? When do you talk to me like that, Mr. Sexy-Sexy?"

"I promise to bring her by the house soon," I'd say, but never meant it. I never planned to bring her by the house, never planned to show her how we lived in a cramped apartment that smelled like frijoles and chicharrones, never planned to subject her to my Aunt Veronica's torturous questions.

Instead, I imagined running away with her after high school to some exotic place like Reno, Nevada. I saw her driving up to the apartment and calling for me with some exotic bird sound. Angela would do it too because she had always loved to squawk at anyone on the street who wore brightly colored outfits.

"Look at the peacock," she'd say. She would make a noise that sounded like a drunk chicken and quack until the peacock person disappeared.

I'd run to her car, grabbing my lawnmower and Weed Eater and shoving them into her hatchback. We would disappear into the western desert and come back for birthdays and holidays and long weekends and when my Aunt Veronica cooked a feast of panuchos and chili verde and fresh salsa with frijoles.

In my mind, the western desert opened up for us. We rolled down the windows, let in the dry air of the summer, and drove until the lights of Reno came into view. In Reno, we rented a little apartment by a greasy-spoon diner. She got a job as a waitress, using her outgoing and funny personality to charm the visiting gamblers and local college students out of tips. She laughed and patted them on the back and told them thanks for supporting her cute little beaner of a man at home. Yes, she called me a beaner, and no, I didn't take offense to it. I started my own landscaping company and hired hard-working illegals like my dad, so they could someday bring their families to America. We got married in a roadside chapel by a Catholic priest so my mom wouldn't pray the rosary over our heads before she killed us in our sleep. Soon enough, children ran around our apartment and spoke English and Spanish and traded baseball cards and Catholic saint cards. And, once we got settled, I made my fortune on *Cast-Away* as the first winner not born in the States. After my fame grew, we moved out of the apartment into a bigger apartment by the nicest casino and ate chocolate-covered hard candies every night before bed. There was no stopping our love. It lasted until the day we fell asleep in each other's arms and passed away while Season 1,178 of *CastAway* held jury.

—

One night in the real world, where Aunt Veronica sat behind me at the window of the apartment as the Mormons walk by, Angela picked me up with tear marks on her cheeks. It was obvious that she tried to wipe them off, but the tears, though salt water, left silhouettes on her skin. Her cheekbones were rubbed red and webs of tears stretched across her eyelashes. When she opened the car door to let me in, she yelled, "Oh, my cute beaner wiener!" and laughed, but her laughter lacked the guttural depth that usually echoed from her mouth, which was my clue that her laugh was a ruse.

I lifted my hand to her face and plucked at the tear webs in her lashes, but she turned away, thrust the stick into first gear, and sped off, avoiding my eyes and staring straight forward at the road ahead.

"What's wrong?" I asked.

"Nothing, Curious George," she said. She gave me another half-assed laugh.

"Really, what's wrong?" I asked again.

"Nothing, now shut your trap," she said. This time she really laughed at herself and turned to me with a real smile, exposing her tiny teeth. "I'm good now that I'm with you." I expected her to call me a cute pet name like "my Latin cupcake," but she didn't. Instead, she held onto "you" for an extra syllable. It was the most honest, non-humorous, in-the-moment thing she had ever said to me. She lit up inside, her impossible-to-hide smile rising in her mouth and cheeks. We were together in her car, heading out to the marina at Utah Lake to dip our feet into the water and, eventually, make-out until it hurt to kiss anymore. We would end the night holding each other beneath the bright stars that popped out from behind the jagged peaks of the Rockies and dropped down behind the rolling tops of the Oquirrh Mountains.

We pulled up to the locked gate outside the marina and ignored the sign that told us to not enter after dusk, but before we made it to the end of the pier, wood cracking beneath our feet when we walked, Angela began to lose the battle against her tears. She used her hands like wipers to skim them off her face and trick me into thinking there was nothing really wrong, but by the time we sat down at the end of the dock, she had begun to snort the mucus that comes with a real, genuine cry.

At that moment, on the pier, her tears starting to flow down her face and puddle up in her lap, I did what any teenage boy would do. I tried to make out with her. Kissing her with love seemed like the best way to take her mind off any sadness she felt that evening, so I leaned over to her, put my right hand on her thigh and my left hand on the small of her back, opened my mouth, and did my best to ram my tongue down her throat like usual.

That was the first time in my life that a woman (besides my Aunt Veronica) slapped me. And she slapped me hard. The sting ran from the skin on my cheek and rattled my brain around in my skull.

"Wake up, Jesús," she said. It was the second time she'd used my real name since the first time we met, when she asked if she needed to keep the door open behind me for all the angels and saints, the twelve disciples, and my mother Mary.

She slapped me again.

"Why'd you do that?" I said.

"Because it felt so good the first time," she said. From beneath her crying, she giggled a bit. "I slapped Jesus." Her lips turned upward for a brief moment.

The lake water rose and fell on the pier posts and the night fully appeared above us. Provo and Orem glowed behind us, a glowing dome of light hovering above them and slowly fading into the western desert and giving way to the light of the stars and the drifting white of the Milky Way. I didn't know what to say. The one woman I had ever been around while she cried was my mother, and she hid away in her room to keep her tears from Hector and me. I knew that she cried because she missed my dad and no words from me could stop her from missing him. His walking through the door was the one thing that could stop her tears, so like I did with my mother, I ignored Angela's sobs because I figured I could do nothing to stop them.

"Wake up, Chuy," she said again. This time she did not smile.

"I'm awake," I said, "but I have no idea what to do." Making out, my idea for a solution, had failed miserably.

"How about wrapping your arms around me and holding me and asking me what's wrong?" she said. To help me out a little, she scooted over on the pier and leaned in toward my chest. That's when I tried to make-out with her again. She slapped me two more times and stood up.

In my defense, she had never gotten close to me like that unless she wanted to make-out. My body became very confused.

Angela stood on the edge of the pier and cried. With her ten feet away, I felt my humanity come back to me and the hormones dissipate a little.

"What's wrong?" I asked.

"Chuy, come here," she said, "and keep that mouth snake of yours to yourself."

I walked over to her with my arms open and wrapped them around her. She trembled despite the 80 degree weather that night. Her trembling further calmed my hormones, and the world seem to slow down.

From her pocket, she pulled out a photo of two children, one boy, and one girl, both with long blonde hair and Angela's nose. The children smiled into the camera with bright eyes, hugging each other, and happiness seemed to color the photo with mellow oranges and warm reds. They sat in front of a fireplace and two Christmas stockings with the names "Elliot" and "Anna" on them hung behind the kids on a mantle.

As if I had confirmed the authenticity of her sadness by realizing that the children could be no one else's but hers, Angela cried harder than I had ever seen my mother cry in her bedroom. Her chest rose and fell like the lake waters while she looked at the two beautiful children in the picture. She knew from her previous experience with my ignorance that I had no idea what to do, so she lifted her shirt, took my hand, and placed it under the waistline of her jeans. My hand had never been there before. For a moment, I thought about how Hans would be so proud of how far I had gotten, but before I could make any kind of move, Angela gave me a look to calm down and rubbed my fingers back and forth on the skin beneath her clothes. Her skin had soft ridges, and when she squeezed my fingers around her flesh, I could feel the striations in it.

"I love my stretch marks," she said. "They are the one thing reminding me that I really did carry two children inside of me." She left my hand on her skin and raised the photo to the light of the moon. "They're nearly two now, and I think about them every day, Jesús." She said my full name again. I guessed it would be used when she was pissed or when she was sad, basically the same way most use the name Jesus.

She told me about her pregnancy and her abusive boyfriend. Her story pulled me into her somehow. Like I was with her when they took her boyfriend to jail for petty theft, like I sat in her room when she rubbed her belly in the mirror and cried, like when she said goodbye to her children when she decided to give them up for adoption, like I held her hand when she had to have an emergency C-section, when the doctor cut her open, and when the nurses took the babies away, popping her head out from behind the sheet to hear them cry and see the operation room door shut behind them.

"I love and hate these photos," she said. "Their new mom is so sweet and agreed to send me anything I wanted, but the photos rip me apart. Probably how it feels to be kicked in the nuts." She laughed, and we shifted our feet together, continuing to hold each other until we reached the end of the dock. We sat down, the water lapped up against the wooden posts, and we didn't talk for a long while.

She broke the silence with, "I would have never named him Elliot. That's for sure. What a dorky name. She better send me photos of his black eyes and ripped underwear." She laughed again and we made-out, but instead of a whirlwind of hands and lips and spit, we kissed with soft lips, and I ran my fingers back and forth over her beautiful memories beneath the waistband of her pants.

Chapter Twenty-Nine

VERONICA

THE SALT FLATS, UT 1925

"DIOS BO'OTIK."

Someone said at the end of the tortilla line.

"Hach Mixba'al," Veronica said back immediately. She looked up to find a Mayan man in front of her, but it was not the same Mayan man she wished would come.

"You must be the beauty of the salt flats that every man from Reno to Wichita talks about," the man said. He took the chance to speak to her when her head snapped up to respond to him.

"No," she said. "That's not me." She dropped her head down immediately. This was not her friend who spoke to her.

"I think it is you," he said.

"Move on," Señora Cordova said. "There's a line behind you." She waved her hand in front of him as if shooing a fly.

"Taak tu lakin," he said to Veronica.

"Taak tu lakin," she said instinctively.

"When will I see you again," he asked.

"Later," she said.

"Okay. Later," he said. He repeated, *later, later, later* until his voice followed him into the train car.

The next morning, a trainload of men and families were dumped into the railcar town. Four or five of the railcar spots and cars had been empty for a while. The men who had lived there were specialists at one task or another, and when they were needed no more, they hooked their homes up to the end of a train that chugged away with them in tow.

The same man who showed her and the Chavezes to their home that dark night nearly a year before showed all the newcomers to theirs. Veronica didn't pay close attention to the newcomers and continued to roll tortillas in the comfort of Señora Cordova's trailer. Spring in Utah had been kind in 1925. Winter ended early, and February and March were pleasant, with breezes that floated into the valley from the mouths of the Wasatch canyons in the east. The mountains sprouted green and pink in the distance, and the men who came through for tortillas and beans were somewhat pleasant and respectful. She did, however, wish her sweet Mayan friend would come back to talk with her in her native language and say goodbye with that gentle appreciation in his voice.

The women left the cars with a stack of tortillas in their hands. They placed them next to a big bowl of steaming pinto beans and got ready for the rush. The women down the line scowled at the beautiful girl who served the most popular tortillas. While serving a young, Chinese worker, she felt a tap on her shoulder.

"Dios bo'otik," a man said.

She turned to see the man from yesterday morning standing on the wrong side of the tortilla line, in the center of the camp where the locals lived, where it was clearly off limits to transient workers.

"Dios bo'otik," he said again. "I live here now." Beneath him lay a duffel bag of clothes and a lunch pail.

Veronica turned back to the tortilla table and ignored him.

"Taak tu lakin," he said.

"Taak tu lakin," she said with respect.

"When will I see you again?" he asked.

"Later," she said.

His foreman yelled for him to throw his gear into his car and get on the next train for work in Ogden.

"Good, later, I can't wait," he said. "And you *are* the famous beauty of the salt flats. There's no doubt about that."

His voice bothered her in a way she couldn't describe. She hated the way he complimented her. His compliments reeked of sex and anger and loneliness.

The day went as the rest of the days went, and by the time the tortillas were gone, Veronica was tired. Her legs ached, and her shoulders dropped. The warm air left with the sun, and the blanket of stars covered the camp. The men who got on the railcars that morning didn't come back—it was common for them to stay in small tents near the Ogden depot overnight. Deep, long tunnels ran beneath 25th Street in Ogden. On the surface, it was business as usual, but beneath the blacktop and concrete, the tunnels stretched out for miles where railroad men bought liquor and women. Casinos were carved out of the ground and lined the caverns. Nothing good happened in those casinos. Railmen fought miners and drunks killed prostitutes. The Chinese built the tunnels to avoid taxes, but the catacombs quickly turned into the most dangerous mile of hollowed-out earth in the country, rumored to even scare off thugs like Al Capone.

"I wouldn't go there if they paid me," he once said.

In the early morning, men lay three layers deep beneath the crust of the earth, and above, no one would know the difference.

When the railroad men came back from their time in Ogden, they were beaten to hell. They reeked of puke and urine. And they fell into their railcars as if they'd jumped from a high dive. This group, including the Mayan man, came home Saturday night, climbed into their bunks, and slept until midday on Sunday. The camp went about its business that Sunday afternoon, cooking, laughing, drinking bootleg liquor, and waiting for Saltair to open up and compete with the stars. Veronica slept in late and woke to the singing of Mrs. Chavez and her daughter. Mr. Chavez drank coffee on the steps of the railcar and basked in the sun. A local priest came from the Cathedral of Madeleine in Salt Lake City and celebrated mass between the railway cars. Many of the men who spent the last couple nights in the arms of prostitutes and the throes of liquor lined up to give their confessions before the priest left, as if their ten Hail Marys and ten Our Fathers could cleanse them from their railroad lives.

The young Mayan man stepped out from the railcar that doubled as a box of penitence. He pulled his hair back from his face, and Veronica took her first long look at him. He was taller than other Mayan men. He was handsome. His thick, black hair complimented his sharp nose and long chin. Beneath his shirt, veins and muscles cut into his dark skin. Veronica made the mistake of staring for one second too long, and he caught her eyes. He smiled, and she saw it was a nice, straight smile, both charming and shy. He raised his hand and acted as if he was tipping an imaginary hat on his head. He walked back to his car and shut the door, presumably to sleep off the sin and alcohol and women.

For three spring Sundays in a row, the Mayan found her at the campfire, sat down next to her, and smiled at her until she waved at him to leave her alone. But he didn't. He talked at her in a mix of Spanish and Mayan. He'd get a little drunk and some of the things he said made her laugh even though she didn't let the laughter leave her lips. She wouldn't give the man that satisfaction. He lacked the sweet charm of the Mayan who first approached her in the tortilla line. He lacked that cautious intent that left his voice hollow with insecurity. This Mayan had been on the railroad too long, saw too many prosti-tutes, drank too many bottles of whiskey, and woke up too many times half-clothed on the side of the railroad tracks, but some of the little things he said made her laugh. Mainly, he made fun of the old Mexican women around town.

"They hate you, don't they?" he'd say. "Because they are fat cows and you are a goddess. Where I come from los vacas always have the longest, skinniest utters, and they hate anything that comes into their pasture that is beautiful and hasn't been sucked dry of life." What he said wasn't necessarily funny, but the truth behind it made Veronica smile inside. Most of the women at the camp would never look at her, let alone talk to her.

"They're jealous of your flour when all they can cook is corn. They know the railroad men like your flour tortillas more than their dry-ass corn tortillas, but they refuse to cook them. Stubborn old vacas," he muttered more with every warm beer that passed over his lips, and he got sweeter too.

"Honestly, I've never seen a girl as beautiful as you. Es la verdad," he'd say. "It's the truth. You are the beauty of the salt flats that men talk about all across the southwestern United States." He'd mumble and raise his hand in the air and scan the horizon with his palm like he was touching all the southwest. "On long trips, I tell them that I talk to you. They call me a liar. I tell them the truth; you never talk back and they believe me," he'd say and laughed. His eyes drifted back and forth like he was talking to all those men. "Yep, they believe me." The first two nights he sat with her, Mr. Chavez sat on the other side of Veronica and listened, making sure the Mayan didn't say anything inappropriate. He, too, thought the Mayan's commentary about the old women of the camp and the legend of the beauty of the salt flats was a bit vulgar, but harmless and amusing, so he let the Mayan talk and drink beer and pass out on the wooden chair near the fire. On those two Monday mornings, he rolled out of the chair, grabbed his gear, and stumbled, tired and groggy, onto the railcar that would take him to Ogden for work around Union Station.

One Sunday in mid-April, the Mayan placed his chair down next to Veronica as the sun drop behind the Oquirrhs, and he listened to the music rise from Saltair. He didn't talk about the old women, and he didn't drink any beer. He sat and listened and remained quiet until midnight rolled around and the camp began to close down. Veronica brushed the sprinkles of ash that rose off the fire and landed softly on her dress and, for the first time, mainly because the Mayan hadn't passed out, she said, "Good night."

The Mayan rose from his chair. He, too, brushed the ashes off his jacket, and like a young man at a fancy ball, he bowed, lifted his right hand, and said, "Veronica, would you like to accompany me to Saltair next Sunday? I got tickets to the ballroom and didn't drink beer tonight so I could buy you anything you would like to eat when we go. It would be my honor to escort the beauty of the salt flats to the concert."

Veronica, on one of those rare occasions in the entirety of her life, was shocked and speechless. This time, she was not ignoring him but couldn't honestly come up with anything to say.

The Mayan bowed lower.

"Get up, you idiot," Mr. Chavez said from behind him. "You look like a goddamned clown bent over like that."

Veronica, however, thought it was nice, the sincerity of it all, the way he didn't drink that night after a long week of working to buy her hot dogs.

"I don't have a dress," Veronica said. "Only these rags. They are stained with lard and butter and beans."

"I will take you in them," the Mayan said. He pushed his hair away from his forehead and wiped puddles of sweat that had built up in his wrinkles into his dark, black mat of hair. The sizzling sound of a fire being put out by a bucket of water crackled in the air behind her. Carload after carload of revelers flew by the camp. Music played loudly from their radios and girls yelled into the night as the salt air blew their hair back. Veronica heard them every Sunday night and wanted to be them, to let the world and her worries, her memories of her lost child, and her regret for leaving Mérida blow past her in the wind and fly away with nothing but sagebrush and sand to listen to them.

A hand fell on her shoulder and squeezed.

"I can make you something," Mrs. Cordova said. "I have no idea why you would ever want to go out there and dance and act like a crazy person who hangs out of a car or the window of a trolley in the middle of the night, but I can make you something. Probably not a dress. They wear pants. Those little girls. They wear pants that flap around when they dance like they are wearing curtains on their legs, hija."

"Thank you," Veronica said. "Thank you."

"Do you trust this tonto on his knees? I don't," Mrs. Cordova said.

"I do," Veronica said. "I trust him."

Mrs. Cordova nodded with hesitation but walked away, not fighting the young woman who had dispelled hundreds of men over the last year, the young woman who never said yes.

The Mayan remained on his knees. Mr. Chavez kicked him again and told him to get up because he looked like an idiot. But he did not.

He stayed there until Veronica finally said, "Yes, I will go with you." He stood up from his knees, pulled a beer out from his back pocket, and chugged it down in one lift of the bottle to his throat.

"In celebration," he said when the empty bottle dropped to the ground. "I will see you next Sunday, beauty of the salt flats." He walked away.

Chapter Thirty

CHUY

THE GREAT SALT LAKE, UT 1992

HANS DROVE THE CAR TOO FAST FOR MY AUNT VERONICA'S COMFORT. We headed north toward Saltair, a concert venue that had been rebuilt in the 1990s after a fire burned it to the ground decades earlier. Everyone knew the story of how Saltair burned down in the 1920s. The radio stations always billed it as a great place "to see concerts, and ghosts, too," referring to the history printed on the back of every concert flyer. We covered the fifty-nine miles from Provo to Saltair to see our favorite band play.

I sat in the backseat alone and thought about Angela, the girl I planned to grow old with and have babies with and sit on wicker chairs with at eighty-years-old. She'd taken over my mind and my soul. I rarely saw Hans. And he was not happy about it, either.

Though Hans and I had been able to avoid bullying for the most part, our old nemesis, Billy, went on hot streaks of hazing us when he got a chance. Along with four or five of his friends, he would chase Hans through the hallway and slap paper swastikas on his back even as Hans yelled that his family was Jewish. They started calling him a Jew-Nazi after that, to which Hans would yell that that didn't make any sense, so they ended up shoving him to the ground and moving on.

They liked four-on-one more than four-on-two. I was always with Angela at school, and we found our way to the corners of rooms or the school grounds to talk and kiss and look at each other. When the bullies did see us together, if it was Angela and me, they yelled, "Look, it's the mutt, going off to make mutt babies." Angela would give them the finger and tell them, heartily, to "Fuck right off!" And I loved that about her. When the three of us were together, they'd call us the Nazi and the mutts. Angela would, in turn, forcefully tell them to "Fuck right off!"

They never got violent unless they caught us alone, and they had been catching Hans alone a lot since Angela and I had started dating. The tradition of them yelling that we'd make mutt babies seemed to be fine with Angela for a while, but I could sense that it started to bug her after the first forty times. She started retreating from the bullies, pulling me down other hallways when they approached. I think their shaming had finally gotten to her, but I wasn't completely sure because she wouldn't talk about it. And we stopped kissing at school.

"I don't think we need to bring extra abuse on ourselves, my skinny chili cheese fry," she would say. I wanted to tell her chili cheese fries were Tex-Mex and really had nothing to do with Mexican food, but I didn't care enough to do so.

"Okay," I said.

"Okay," she said. "Tonight we can kiss when you come over."

"Do you want to come to my apartment instead?" I asked.

"No, let's go to the lake," she said. "It's all easier that way."

"What's easier that way?" I asked, because I could easily be near her anywhere on the planet. To me, being with her was easy all around. I loved her.

"It's easier to not involve family and stuff," she'd say.

"Okay," I said. "The lake it is."

At school, Angela had found some friends, too. I didn't mind so much. They were really nice to her, and they were nice to me, too. Many times, when Angela and I sat with them at lunch, they asked me question after question about Mexico and how it was to live in a two-bedroom apartment by the interstate. One day, I talked to them about the true difference between corn tortillas and flour tortillas, and how, since living with my eighty-six-year-old aunt, I had been converted to the flour tortilla side. Angela, unlike herself, stayed pretty quiet while I talked about how flour tortillas don't break as easily and how they absorb the bean juice much better than corn tortillas. I had to make sure and tell them, however, that corn tortillas were much more traditional in the Yucatán. And that got me talking about my proud Mayan heritage and how we held off the Spaniards and Revolutionaries and the dictatorship longer than any other civilization and society in the Mexican states. We were small but we were strong, I told them.

A day before the concert, I told Veronica that Hans, Angela, and I had planned to take off early from school the next day to see a concert at Saltair.

Veronica, standing in her bathrobe on the porch of the apartment complex and bitching about the smell of fake food to Mrs. Yamamoto, turned to me and said, "You cannot go unless I go with you, Chuy. Okay? We'll leave at four and come home right after the concert." She turned and continued to bitch to her friend about how all white people know how to do is mass produce shredded beef and fake cheese in giant fryers.

"Okay," I said. I'd learned to not fight with her. I'd learned that I would never win, and that my mom would kill me if I told my aunt no.

When I told Hans, he shook his head and said that he could drive. When I told Angela, she told me that something had come up and that she couldn't go. With my aunt, I figured she wanted us to stop by her Rose Park house for something. With Angela, I figured she didn't want to go because my Aunt Veronica was going. And I couldn't ditch Hans anymore. The poor guy.

We drove along the edge of Salt Lake City on I-15 for about forty minutes before Hans took I-80 west toward the Great Salt Lake, Saltair, the western desert, and Nevada. I'd expected Aunt Veronica to tell us to swing off the interstate and stop at her home, but she didn't. She stared out the window as the car moved along the road toward the flat, salty, stinky earth surrounding the lake.

Cars lined the shoulder of I-80, engines idling and slowly inching forward, car after car, to enter the parking lot next to the newly painted concert venue that rose up out of the marshy fields at the edge of the lake. It was a lone structure with no others around for miles. Its architecture mimicked that of European castles and mosques but poorly blended, covered in stucco, and painted beige. It was really nothing to see, a large concrete building in the middle of a flat, dry desert and half a mile from a receded ancient lake.

We slowly inched forward with each car that pulled into the parking lot a mile ahead of us.

Veronica had been quiet for most of the ride, until she yelled at Hans to slow down or to turn off his "pendejo music."

With about a quarter mile left before we turned into the lot next to the eyesore of the concert venue, Veronica opened her car door and stepped out into the early evening.

"I'm gonna walk from here," she said. The eighty-six-year-old woman, dressed in green pants and a flowered shirt, shut the car door behind her before I could say anything to her. She walked over the mound of rocky dirt that separated the road and the salt flats and walked out into dried up salt beds. She placed her hands on her head and looked northwest toward the glowing red and orange sunset and into the nothingness.

"She's so strange," Hans said.

"I know," I said.

"Why'd she come with us?" Hans asked.

"I have no idea. Did you want to tell her no?" I asked. She stood in the middle of absolutely nothing.

"Hell no," Hans said.

"I guess it doesn't matter," I said.

Hans moved the car ahead ten feet.

Veronica, after about three minutes, turned directly west toward Saltair and began to walk, nearly keeping pace with the line of cars. I kept an eye on her the whole time, but, in my mind, I knew I didn't have to. She needed no one.

We pulled into the parking lot and found a spot for the car. We walked toward the edge of the concrete and waited for Veronica to make her way to us. She did, her feet in her super cushioned black shoes moving across the salt beds.

When she reached us, I could see that she had been crying. My Aunt Veronica cried. I really didn't think she was anatomically capable of crying.

A softness had taken her, one that I had never really seen in the two years I lived with her. She placed her hands on my shoulders, breathed in a heavy and salty breath, and let her eyes meet mine for a few seconds before she said, "This place used to be so beautiful. It was grandioso. It was wooden with great spires and arches and open-aired rooms for dancing and music. Every inch was painted by hand. Every foot had been carved. The wood was smooth, and it stretched out with its promenade and boardwalk and wooden bridge for half a mile into the water."

"Are you okay?" I asked.

Her softness hardened again, and in a way, I felt so much better— secure in the world—when it did.

"Shut your face," she said. "Now it's ugly concrete built for kids like you to get hard-ons."

I said okay, asked Hans to give her the keys to the car, pointed her toward our spot, and walked toward the metal detectors at the edge of the big, ugly, concrete building. My aunt whispered to herself when she thought we were too far to hear her, "Sweet, sweet boy."

When we got to the entrance, I turned to hopefully find her asleep in the front seat of the car. Instead, I caught a glimpse of her bright green pants as she rounded the far north side of the venue, headed out toward the lake's edge, and sat on the salt-filled sand, placing her hands behind her in the earth, staring at the setting sun again.

Chapter Thirty-One

VERONICA

SALTAIR, UT 1925

BEFORE DAWN, VERONICA DRAGGED THE MAYAN'S DEAD, STIFFENING body across the sand of the Great Salt Lake toward Saltair. The light sun of mid-April scattered across the thick and salty water like the bouncing of candlelight on darkness. Blood dripped from his lips and belly, and the wooden fragment of the dock she used to cut him remained stuck in his torso below his left ribcage. The rising and falling waters of the lakeshore reached out and erased the trail of blood left on the sand, like the hand of God had come to cover her tracks and clean up any evidence of what she had done. Workmen would be there any minute to clean up after the dancing the night before and continue to ready the pavilion for the long summer season to come. She saw the train's smokestack crawl toward her. The smoke rose into the air and became bigger and more opaque the closer it came to her.

She pulled his body. Her calves became tight and tired with every yank, but the smokestack chugged toward her in the distance. The train began to blink as the sun reflected off its shiny engine.

She had never gotten to see Saltair close up until the night before when the Mayan took her there. She was finally there: the light of the moon faded into the sky behind the glowing, Moorish-style structure that sat at the end of a quarter-mile pier in the middle of the great lake. Domed caps, like those that adorned the La Mezquita de Cordoba in Spain, perched above the water like rainbows of welcome. The crowd swarmed around Veronica. They walked along the wooden-planked dock toward the great dance hall and the Coney Island of the West. A giant roller coaster screamed above their heads, a Ferris wheel spun on the edge of time, concession stands stood by, and people decked out with flapper hats and dapper ties walked toward the sounds of R. Owen Sweeten's Jazziferous Band like they were sailors caught in the trance of the Titan's sirens. The *toot, toot, toot* of the brass ensemble was more captivating and invigorating than Veronica had imagined it to be when she sat amongst the immigrant rail workers in her camp a couple miles away. The music made her feet move. Her heels splayed outward and back together in time for her toes to do the same. Back and forth they danced beneath her. Once they made it onto the main deck, the stripes of the ceiling and the stripes on the domes that covered the gigantic structure mesmerized her. She felt more alive than she had since walking hand and hand in the Mérida sunlight with her poet lover.

Even as the night approached, swimmers hung on buoys in the middle of the lake, but it didn't take much to stay afloat; the salt content of the lake made every swimmer a buoy of their own. A tiny finger placed on the shoulder of another swimmer who had a finger on the buoy could keep a person afloat. That was part of the charm of the lake. You really didn't have to expend any energy even while swimming; the water itself held you up, and you could relax beneath the sun and into the night beneath the stars and not grow tired. When she and the Mayan made it into the great hall—the dance hall that battled Coney Island for the biggest in the world—it took her breath away. Thousands of people danced to the music of the Jazziferous Band. The monstrous oval floor was surrounded by a wooden track used for a circling bicyclist that pedaled around and around the dancers on the floor inside the track. Arched trusses swung upward toward the circular center of the ceiling. The smell of salt and perfume floated in the air like the swimmers floated outside on the lake. Veronica and the Mayan danced for three hours until the train caller came in and announced the departure of the last train home.

She and the Mayan ran out of the dome with all the other dancers. Her face hurt from smiling and her calves ached from the long night of dancing in borrowed heels. They ran along the pier toward the trolleys and trains, hand in hand. She thought about how, at first, this young Mayan put her off in so many ways—his smile angered her, his use of their shared language made her fume, and his corny jokes at the camp-fire over the last month made her weary of his intentions—but at that moment, when the trains pulled up to load passengers, she adored him and how he had convinced her to go out with him, and how nicely he had treated her the entire night, bounding off the dance floor to get her Coca-Cola and water and popcorn.

Right before the train closed its final doors, the Mayan yanked her away from it.

"What are you doing? We have to get on that train or we'll have to walk back to camp!" Veronica yelled. "It's miles away!"

"I have something even more spectacular to show you," he said. He pulled her arm again. The second pull did not feel like the flirty type of pull a man gives a woman when he wants to whisper some-thing sweet into her ear or steal a kiss. It was a hard yank that sent pain through her shoulder and into her neck.

"Ouch!" she yelled. "What are you talking about?"

"Basta," he said. "Venga conmigo!" He had yanked her off the pier and down into the sand beneath the dock while the final revelers boarded the train and disappeared into the night. He pulled her dress up above her waist and dug his fingers into the skin beneath the tops of her undergarments. He did not care that when he pulled downward, chunks of her flesh filled his fingernails like the dirt from a day work-ing on the railroad. She slapped at him, dug into his face, and tried her best to fill her own fingernails with his flesh and blood. He held her down with one hand and pulled his pants down with the other. His daily work hauling and hammering and picking made him too strong for her. He'd held down the hot steel rail as another man hammered spikes into the earth. He handled Veronica much easier. But the sand beneath them made it hard for him to gain any leverage and move himself into her. He picked her up and threw her against a post that held the pier in the air. Above her, the giant wheels of the train began to turn. The engine snorted and screamed into the night air, drowning any attempt she had to launch her own scream into the night and the ears of anyone who could help her.

He tried to use the post to ground her, but she wiggled beneath him. He slapped her, but she still struggled beneath him. The train wheels caught the track above her, and the shift and pull on the dock splintered the post that the Mayan pushed her against. She found a long, thin piece of wood that had been shed by the motion of the train, and she plunged it so far into the Mayan's gut that his back arched up like a stretching cat and his strength left him immediately. To make sure he could not come after her again, Veronica found the piece of wood with her hands, pulled her knees and feet to her chest, and kicked the wood into him even farther. She sat in shock as blood leaked from him and the air from his lungs left him in short choppy breaths until it was all gone. She pulled him by the arm to the lake that crept up beneath the pier and pushed his body in, hoping he would disappear.

The first time she tried, he didn't sink. She figured that once his clothes and body were wet enough, he would sink and she could leave, but the damn salt content of the water did not fit into her frantic plan. The Mayan's body floated in front of her. When the sun began to rise, she knew that the workmen would be on their way. The workmen who kept Saltair running throughout the season were the same men who bought her flour tortillas and beans every morning.

She had to get rid of him, so she wrapped her arms beneath his armpits, lifted his torso, and dragged him three or four feet at a time. She tugged him, yank by yank, up and around the spiral ramp to the main pier that led to dance floor and the concession stands, and the Hippodrome.

The wooden planks beneath her splintered into his belly and arms, and his blood stained the pathway. Her trail had become visible like children using breadcrumbs to lead each other into the forest. The Hippodrome, the center for roller skating and movies, stood in front of her with the lake at its back. Wooden planks spun around the domed ceiling, and the Mayan's blood seeped through his clothes onto the entrance. She stood in a wooden world and knew that when the workers found the trail of blood, they would find the Mayan, and when they found the Mayan, they would find his home, and when they found his home, they would find out that he left the night before with the beauty of the salt flats. And she would be taken away from the Chavezes and Mrs. Cordova to god knows where—prison would be a paradise compared to where she imagined American men would take a beautiful young girl with no family to miss her.

Veronica dragged him. She dragged him until she reached the top of the steps that led down beneath the Hippodrome and into the Ali Baba Cave, a wooden cave made for long, romantic walks (that could be chaperoned by church officials, of course). She couldn't toss him into the lake because he would float back up. She couldn't bury him in the sand because she didn't have enough time, and even if she did, the water would dig him up in a couple of days' time. Her best option was to drag him to the farthest point in the tunnel and hope that by the time the workers found him, she would be able to jump a train to California and disappear into the crops with all the other immigrants. She sat down on the last plank in the tunnel, and a wooden sliver sliced into her calf. It burned beneath her skin like someone had pulled a poker from the fire and pressed it against her skin, and she saw the Mayan's cigarette lighter drop from his pocket and where it opened on the planks. A wind fanned the flame.

The next morning, *The Salt Lake Tribune* ran an article that reported on the great fire at Saltair that broke out in the Ali Baba Cave beneath the Hippodrome. "A wall of flame about four feet wide and running the length of the cave," described L.S. Peterson, a firefighter, to the *Tribune* the morning after the fire. He said that he tried to beat it out, but "I hadn't been gone over two minutes and in that time [the fire] had started up again and spread before the wind." The hot winds from the south rose to the wooden fortress, searching for hot embers beneath the flames, and blew on them until the fire consumed the Hippodrome, the giant dance floor, the concession stands, the roller coaster, and thousands of wooden posts that held above the water. The smoke and ash blew up into the sky and blocked out the sun for hours. The domes burned and fell. Firefighters came from all over the Salt Lake Valley and Sugarhouse and Farmington and, according to the *Tribune*, "Tongues of the flame and smoke leaped fifty to one hundred feet and shot out and licked up the timbers and beams of the great structure as though they were cardboard," driving the firefighters away until the great Saltair was nothing more than ash and burnt wood.

Veronica ran to the mountain across the tracks from Saltair, climbed the desolate face of it, sat on a rock that pushed out of the dirt, and Saltair burned into the night. Sounds of sirens wailed, punctuated with loud pops of wood burning and collapsing. Smoke rose into the air and stained the black of night with dark grey. The red-orange flames danced along the water's edge and consumed the bloody path she created by dragging the Mayan across the dock. The flame burned the blood-stained wood and the undocumented Mayan who had no dental records or family to identify him. The flames died down, and Veronica laid her head down on the surface of the rock and fell asleep.

PART FOUR

Chapter Thirty-Two

CHUY

PROVO, UT 1992

EVERYTHING WAS PACKED. THE ROOM AROUND ME HAD BEEN SWEPT into a bunch of suitcases and placed beside the door. My mom and I were to leave for Mexico at midnight. We had found the cheapest flight—the red eye that took us directly to Mérida from Salt Lake City. For the return trip, we bought tickets that left at three in the morning, something I was not looking forward to. We had to fly through Dallas for customs, but I didn't worry about that before we left. I was excited to see my dad and Hector for the first time in two whole years.

I was imagining ways to bring my dad—and Hector, too, if he wanted—back to the United States.

The day before we left, we walked through Deseret Industries in search of used luggage for our trip. My mom picked out a bunch of handbags, large ones, to hold the massive and mysterious contents of her purse, and I picked out the biggest suitcases I could find, hoping my dad would agree to be stuffed into one and thrown beneath the plane to come home with me. He and my mom talked so much on the phone that I thought he might take one look at her and jump in the suitcase, say, "Hasta pronto," and let me zip him up in there.

"You don't need a suitcase that big, Chuy," my mom told me after I had climbed over rows of suitcases and somehow maneuvered a travel trunk with stickers all over it from beneath ten or twenty other soft, zip-up suitcases. The trunk looked like one I'd seen in cartoons forever, with wooden sides, metal framing around the edges, and stickers from all the places the traveler had been. For a moment, I had forgotten about folding my father up into a cube and began to think about all the places that trunk could take me. We had spent a full year saving for a short trip to Mexico and were currently at the thrift store buying luggage, though we had barely enough money to eat and pay the rent. Even with that, we had to borrow a bunch from Aunt Veronica to make it by, even though my mom worked two jobs and rarely came home. I wasn't quite sure why this whole United States thing was even worth it, why my dad disappeared for four years to pay for us to get here, or why my mom spent those four years making the three of us "legal."

"I really like it," I said. And I did. One of the stickers on the top showed an illustrated picture of the Mayan ruins. Uxmal sat in the center of the sticker. I grew up less than one hundred miles from the pyramid that once hosted human sacrifices. The blood of old Mayans streamed down the massive, steep stairs of the tall structure, but I had never gotten the chance to visit it. It cost too much money to see. Only tourists got to see the ancient Mayan ruins that rose from the ground all around us in the Yucatán. And the ruins that weren't blocked off, gated, and too expensive for locals to visit, were covered in graffiti, and tags from local gang rivals. But the sticker made me so proud that the man or woman who owned that trunk had put Uxmal right on top and in the center. Maybe Yucatán had become his favorite place in the world. Maybe he was Mexican, like me, and did everything he could to get back home.

On the side of the trunk, another sticker spoke to me. It read FARGO in a faded, red, bubbly font, and that was it. Images of the most beautiful country sprouted in my brain. With a name meaning GO FAR, it had to be one of the most coveted destinations in the entire world. I could see the advertisement for it: "You must Go Far to get to Fargo, but it will be worth your while—or your while worth, because once you get there, you'll never want to go home, or home go." In the woods of Fargo, there must be streams and lakes and fruit. There wouldn't be any season except for autumn, and the temperature would be 70 degrees all year long. It wouldn't snow, burying people in the winter, as it did in Provo, and it wouldn't get too hot, like the humid, burning summers of Yucatán. Fargo would stay perfectly cool and breezy. The men would be able to wear shorts and tank tops all year long, in case they wanted to jump in the lakes and streams, and the women would wear comfortable sundresses that let the breeze flow around them. I had to go to Fargo one day because I, too, wanted to Go Far.

"It's expensive," my mom said.

I had saved up some money from mowing lawns. I handed most of it over to my mom every week for groceries and to send a little back to Hector and my dad, even though my dad protested every time we did. He had his old job back and was doing fine, he'd tell us, and my mom always let me keep a little for me, for clothes and music, like Roxette and Poison.

"I have some money. I'll get it, Mom. I'm gonna go far," I said.

She gave me the strange look she always gave me when I spoke.

"Okay, mijo," she said. "It's up to you. Do you even have enough stuff to put in there for the trip?"

"No, but I'm hoping to bring about 130 pounds of stuff back with me," I said.

Again, the same look of confusion as to what the hell I was talking about ran across her face, but she shrugged and moved on, snatching up a small carry-on bag for her clothes and makeup.

Back at the apartment, our luggage sat next to the door. My big trunk and my mother's bags.

At about seven in the evening, Hans knocked on our apartment door.

"You ready?" he asked.

"Where you going?" my mom asked from behind me.

"Where's this Angela?" Veronica asked.

Hans looked around me, knowing that if Veronica asked a question, he had to answer. "She's waiting in the car."

"Why won't she come to meet us?" my mom said. Veronica echoed her from the couch.

"Not sure," said Hans.

"I'm ready. I'll be back in two hours so we can go," I said.

Hans and I walked out to the car. Angela sat in the back, pointing for me to sit in the front seat with Hans.

I climbed in and turned to her in the back, reaching for her hand. She held it and smiled.

"What's this party?" I asked.

"Oh, I got invited by some friends," she said. "And since you're leaving tonight, I thought it would be a good way to see them and see you too."

She wore jeans and a T-shirt that read "CTR" on the front. I'd never seen it before, but I missed a lot of things. Hans, however, did not miss it.

"Choose The Right?" he asked.

Angela slapped him on the shoulder to shut him up. I'd seen that kind of slap before. Veronica slapped me like that on a daily basis.

"Let's go," she said. "Chuy has to get back in less than two hours."

When we walked up to the house, one that sat on the east bench of Provo, adjacent to the BYU campus, I felt like I had entered another world—maybe one like Fargo. I mowed lawns three or four times a week, but I had never set foot on such a perfectly manicured lawn, covered in perfectly manicured trees and bushes and flowers. A path led to the door, brick after red brick, with clean white mortar in between, and every third brick was etched with a short scripture verse. On the windows that flanked the beautifully carved wooden door, CTR had been frosted on the glass.

I turned to ask Angela about it, to ask if this was some kind of fireside, a Mormon conversion party, or something like that, but she had already opened the door and walked into a room full of students from our high school, the same I'd barely spoken to in the nearly two years since I first walked through the doors of Provo High School.

Most of the kids greeted Angela with hugs. Girls who sat in the seats in class that everyone understood were saved for anyone but me, smiled at me and Hans. A fire had been lit in the fireplace at the center of the room.

A very tall boy walked out from the kitchen with a glass of water, shook our hands, and sat in a center seat of a circle that had been set up in the living room. A young girl, the host of the party, passed around small candies and cups of punch. Angela reached for my hand and gave me a light kiss on the cheek. She sat me down next to her in the circle.

Hans stood frozen in the doorway. When a girl approached him, his eyes as wide as his open mouth, he began to creep back toward the door. Someone had shut it since we entered, so he backed into it but kept his feet moving, as though he could still pass through it.

"Please stay," a girl said to him.

He looked at me. Angela held my hand tight.

The girl led him by the hand to a chair on the opposite side of the circle from me.

Everyone else filled the remaining ten or eleven seats around us.

"Shall we begin?" the tall boy in the center seat said.

Everyone bowed their heads.

Hans turned and looked at me. He grinned the grin he grins when he is about to lose it.

"Heavenly Father, thank you for this gathering of young souls who live to serve you. We are gathered here today with our guests. We are so fortunate to have them join us to share in the word of our Lord and listen to the words of our prophet Joseph Smith."

Hans kept his eyes on me. Then he shifted them to Angela.

"I want to begin today with a tale of the Nephites and the Lamanites," the boy said. "I want to read a passage from the Doctrine of the Covenants. It shows how Lamanites are descendants of the Jews who killed Jesus, and how, with open eyes, they should all find their Savior."

Hans stood up, his face red. He had told everyone for years that he couldn't be a Nazi because he was a Jew, all to protect himself from ridicule.

"This is from Doctrine of Covenants 27, 'Which is my word to the Gentile, that soon it may go to the Jew, of whom the Lamanites are a remnant, that they may believe the gospel, and look not for a Messiah to come who has already come.'"

The boy sat back down.

I had no idea who these Lamanites were, but I had the feeling I would find out soon enough. Hans would not. He left the circle, shouting that he'd be in the car. The door slammed behind him.

"That's too bad," the boy said. "But Chuy is still with us, so we can talk about how the Lamanites will all come to see the light of the Lord." He continued. "Lamanites were evil and power hungry. When they aimed to kill Nephi, the chosen one of the Lord, God cursed them with dark skin."

Everyone in the room looked at me.

Angela held my hand tightly and smiled.

I was ready to exit, but I remained and tried to stay calm to show Angela that I cared enough for her to see the evening through.

"The Lamanites fought as the true opposition to Jesus Christ for centuries. Here, in the Americas, they killed the Nephites, remaining to rule Central America and South America as hunters and gatherers until Joseph Smith brought the lost scriptures home. It is our job, our mission, to bring Lamanites back into the fold, and that is why Chuy is with us today," he said.

And that's when I stood up.

I had no idea what that dude was talking about, but I knew my family was the dark people in the story, and I was not joining the church.

I walked toward the door, opened it, and stepped outside. Angela followed me. She reached out for my hand.

"I love you," she said.

"I love you, too. Let's go. I have a plane to catch to see my dad," I said.

She gave me a light kiss on the forehead and said she was going to stay and that she wished me a wonderful time in Mexico. She walked back into the house before I could protest.

Hans waited for a very dazed version of me to get in the car.

He dropped me off at my apartment. For some odd reason, he gave me a hug before he drove off.

I couldn't sleep on the plane, and neither could my mom, so we got to talk for the first time in a very long time. It seemed like we hadn't gotten to spend any time together since we got to Utah. Mom worked so much. Every day. Most of the time, she came home briefly between jobs to change clothes and head out again. She didn't jump on board with the "stuffing Dad in my trunk" idea, and she didn't like the idea that I didn't buy a trunk for Hector, too, even though she said the idea was "que improbe." She thought that if I was to plan a heist, I should think of my brother, too. I agreed with her and asked if it might be possible to buy another trunk in Mexico for Hector. She nodded her head at her stupid boy.

She asked about Angela, but I couldn't bring myself to talk about that night with her. She told me she loved me before I left, and I held on to those words and the kiss on my cheek as tightly as I could. I knew that if I told her Angela decided to stay behind that night, my fear that something had changed would become too real. I had to hang on to her saying that she loved me and believe that was the absolute truth. Because I loved her so much.

When we landed in Mérida, my mom sprinted ahead of me up the jet bridge. My father stood outside the gate with his arms open wide and his hands clasping at the air, as if practicing to squeeze us both. By the time I got to the top of the jet bridge, my mother had already thrown her arms around him, but unclasped one arm from around her back and waved for me to join them. He squeezed so tight that I could barely breathe. But I could smell the hot metal of his work over the flames, a smell that never left him. I would have given up breathing for that smell.

I missed my dad so much, but I didn't know how much until I got to see him again. It was weird; I missed him more when I was around him than when we were apart. It ached inside of me.

We walked toward the baggage claim with his arms around us. He didn't even attempt to take them away. Hector had somehow snagged my trunk and Mom's bags before we even got there.

He had grown tall and so much bigger than I expected. His biceps looked like they were trying to escape the skin of his upper arms, and his neck had grown thick like a man's, large at the base. I barely knew that muscular man who held my trunk like it was made of feathers. He smiled. A big smile. He had grown up. And I could see it in him that he was happy.

But when I approached him for a hug, my dickhead older brother threw his fist into my shoulder, and I could swear something broke.

"Chuy, you're too skinny, hermano," he said.

He turned to my mom, picked her up in his arms, squeezed her tight, and said, "I'm sorry, Mom. I'm sorry I left. I'm sorry I was difficult. But, I'm glad I'm here with Dad in Mexico. It's my home. I love you, Mamacita."

My mom cried in Hector's arms like I hadn't seen her cry, ever.

We all knew that Hector had begun to work with my dad. We all knew that he was doing well at home, but to see him so strong and happy and mature made it all real, almost real enough to take away the deadening pain in my shoulder.

We drove home in our old Nissan Sentra, the four of us packed into it like we'd always been in a life before this one. The streets of Mérida were full of people. Thirty minutes after we left the city, my father pulled our car onto the dirt-covered driveway leading to our two-bedroom home, blocks away from the giant beach houses that had sprouted up on the edge of the Gulf of Mexico since I was a child. Our cinder block and cement home had been painted yellow, and new windows had been placed in the front of the house. It was modest, clean, and tidy. I had missed it.

Hector unloaded our bags. He carried Mom's stuff into the house, through the living room, and into her bedroom, a room she hadn't seen in two years. He unzipped her bag and laid it on the bed for her. This new Hector kind of made me wonder if he was up to something, but

I didn't want to awaken the sullen, dickhead of a brother that I had known for most of my life.

My father and I carried my trunk into the house. We set it down in my room.

He sat on my bed with me. Hector had moved out and was renting an apartment in Mérida, close to the city center. According to my dad, he planned to begin school at Instituto Tecnologico de Mérida in the fall to "grow the business."

"Is that your trunk, mijo?" my father asked.

"Si, te gusta?" I replied.

"Si," he said.

I knew that my opportunity had come, so I took it. I pulled all of my clothes out of the trunk and threw them on the bed next to my father.

"Watch this," I said.

I dropped my body into the trunk and folded myself up. I fit perfectly inside.

"Want to try it?" I asked my dad, who sat there and shook his head.

"I'm not getting in your trunk, Chuy. You can't ship me back to Provo, mijo," he said, "but I love that you still hope we can all be together in the United States. It's not possible. The second I step back into our apartment in Utah, they would snag me again and send me here."

"But that's not fair," I said.

"It's fair enough, because I know they could have found a way to send you and your mom and Hector home, too, if they wanted to. They have laws, but they don't follow them. And, for the most part, I didn't either, but you and your mom and Hector did, and that's all I care about. Let's talk about other things, Chuy."

Every single time he told me this, patiently, on the phone, or through letters, it broke my heart. I would rather try to drug my father, put him in a trunk, and ship him to Utah than accept what he told me.

"I'm gonna win a million dollars on *CastAway Island*. You can do anything with a million dollars," I said.

My dad leaned off the bed and pulled me out of the trunk. He placed his hands on my shoulders. He kissed my forehead like he had always done.

"That's a fantasy now, Chuy," he said. "I love you. Let's go eat some dinner."

We all got into the car. We drove to the east side of Chelem and pulled into a local restaurant. As if Provo had come to us, it was full of white people in flowered shirts and beige shorts.

Hector caught me looking at them all.

"More and more every year," he said. "All the houses in town are being bought, torn down, and replaced with gigantic houses with beach views. Mostly Canadians but some Americans, too."

My father called for his friend, Jorge, who owned the restaurant.

"Give us the lobsters and the freshest fish plate you have. Oh— and the fresh octopus and squid," he said.

We'd never ordered that stuff before. Hell, we'd never ordered anything other than the cochinita pobil at Jorge's.

"Hector's paying," he said.

I thought Hector would fight him, but, instead, he smiled and told us that he had wanted to do this since he was little, something I never knew about. But, unlike the movies, torturers rarely reveal their inner thoughts to the tortured.

We ate lobster soaked in butter.

This was exactly what I wanted forever, but I wanted it in Utah with Angela. And, to be honest, I wanted it with Veronica, too.

"Chuy has a girlfriend who is scared to meet me and Veronica," my mom said.

"She gordo, Chuy?" Hector asked.

"She's actually very pretty," my mom said.

I took slight offense to her use of the word "actually," but I accepted it as too close to the truth to deny.

"She won't meet you?" my father asked.

I shifted in my seat and coughed, spitting pieces of food on Hector. His eyes widened, and I could see that the new Hector wanted to turn back into the old Hector and beat the shit out of me, but, instead, he calmly wiped the lobster off his shirt.

"She wants to. I promise. It hasn't been the right time. I swear, Mom, when we get back, you'll meet her the next day. I promise," I said.

"Okay," my mom said. Her eyes saddened.

My father placed his hand on hers on the flowery, plastic tablecloth. She didn't want to go home. For her, for all of us, Chelem was home.

We had three great days of laughter, three great days of food, and three great days of forgetting that our family had been divided in two and separated by thousands of miles, a string of mountains, and the Gulf of Mexico. In those three days, we had more money in Mexico than we'd ever had, with my mother's US wages in her pockets, Hector's extra income, and my lawn mowing contributions, all piled on top of the money Dad had always made. We bought clothes in Mérida and went to see movies in the capital city. But with each peso spent, I knew what the money meant—it meant Mom and I had to go home soon. Mom wanted to stay. I was torn. I couldn't decide if I wanted to stay or if I wanted us all to be in Utah. Angela, the love of my life was the determining factor, however. With her in my life, I knew that I wanted my entire family to be together in Utah.

With the dollar stretching long and far in the Yucatán, we stayed in a hotel by the airport the night before our flight home and woke at two in the morning to catch our plane. Hector had said his goodbyes the night before, after joining my mother and father to sip beers after dinner, groggily lifting his hand to wave before we shut the hotel room door.

My parents and I took the shuttle to the airport. Mom and Dad held hands. I was excited to go home, see Angela and Hans, and tell them both about my weekend with my family. I kind of missed Veronica, too, the crazy old woman who haunted my life with a rolling pin. On the shuttle, with the darkness of morning all around us, I thought about how much Veronica had done for us. A smile unexpectedly curled my lips. She'd become real family.

My dad came with us to our gate.

They called our seats.

Mom cried.

Dad shielded his eyes from her when she turned to walk down the jet bridge.

I hugged him. My tears fell on his shirt.

"You would fit in my trunk," I said.

"I know you don't understand now, Chuy. But you will someday," he said.

With his small, strong hands, he turned my shoulders to the bridge and pushed me toward home.

Mom slept on the flight to Dallas.

I did some homework that was due later that morning.

Two hours later, we stood in the customs line at the Dallas airport. Mom's hand shook. She held her Green Card and every paper with an official stamp that she had ever received, her trembling fingers passing between the documents and her chest where they made the sign of the cross over and over again.

I couldn't understand why she was so nervous. On the card, right next to our photos, it read "United States of America, Permanent Resident." That meant they would let us through, but I guessed that her superstitions had gotten a hold of her.

The line went pretty quickly. I stepped up to the customs officer before my mom. I handed my Green Card to the bald man with crooked teeth behind the glass, answered his questions, and got a wave to head back into the United States.

"Well, that was easy," I turned to tell my mom. But when I turned around, I didn't see her next to me.

Instead, I saw four customs officers surround her at the window of another customs box. She shook her head. She held up her card and all her paperwork.

A female officer walked behind her and grabbed her arms behind her elbows. A second officer slapped handcuffs on her wrists.

"Mom!" I yelled.

I ran back toward her. An officer tackled me right before I crossed the red line that separated me from customs and my mother.

On the ground, as I wiggled beneath the officer on top of me, my mom caught my eyes. I saw her whisper from across the giant, cold room, "I love you, mijo. Don't give them a reason. I love you. Go home."

The officer pulled me up from the ground. He took me into a plain white room. He asked me more questions. I told him the truth and asked why they took my mother. He walked out of the room before answering me.

When he returned he said emotionless, "She was guilty of knowingly housing an illegal alien or helping smuggle an illegal alien to the United States within, before, or after five years of her arrival into the United States of America."

The room got colder.

"It looks like you will miss your flight if you don't get moving," the man said.

He escorted me through the Dallas airport.

He walked with me down the jet bridge and placed me in my seat and told me that if I tried to leave the plane, I would also be deported. He said he guessed that since my mom was caught that I would probably be next, but, sometimes, once you're back in the States, they never get around to you. If you keep your nose clean.

He slapped my shoulder and placed his hand on the gun at his waist, then turned and walked down the aisle.

Chapter Thirty-Three

VERONICA

SALT LAKE CITY, UT 1925

VERONICA CLIMBED DOWN FROM THE ROCK ON THE EDGE OF THE Oquirrh Mountains. Saltair lay in ashes below her on the beaches of the Great Salt Lake. Firemen from all over the Wasatch Range helped pick up the pieces of the dance hall after a long night of battling the flames with their hoses. She would find out later that no one other than the Mayan died in the fire that night, and that gave her solace.

Veronica thought about walking across the train tracks, crossing the sandy, dry desert, and finding the Chavezes.

"It's time for me to no longer be the beauty of the Salt Flats. It's time for me to find my way home," she whispered into the air.

She hopped aboard one of the freight trains that led into the city, the edge of the Great Salt Lake receded behind her, and hopped off at the railroad station a few blocks from downtown. The bright Mormon temple, where Moroni shone golden in the sunlight, sent a blinding light across the entire valley. She had nothing to change into and no money to buy food, so she walked toward the city in search of a place to sleep in the April sunlight.

Veronica walked up toward Pioneer Park and fell asleep on the lawn next to lovers who had come there to picnic. The two couldn't have been any older than her, but their faces carried a purity and innocence that had long left Veronica. Their giggles and flirty playfulness lulled her to sleep beneath a tall maple, and before she knew it, the world had become cold with the incoming night. To get warm, she rolled beneath a shrub and pulled the edges of it over her like a blanket. She lay awake until the morning sun popped up over the Utah Savings and Trust Building east of the park. The sounds of the city made her feel alive. Trolleys tinkered by. Cars puttered in all directions. Children came out with their parents to play in the park. And the winds from the canyon released their last breath of early morning air. She walked up and down Main Street and State Street until the hunger in her belly begged for her attention. She knew she had to do what she did to get to El Paso, and she had no shame when she sat on a park bench in the center of town and asked an old man, in broken English, if he could spare a few cents for her to eat. He scoffed at her and walked away. She cursed him and moved on to another man hanging around outside a pastry shop. He treated her the same way. She talked to nearly thirty people before anyone gave her a cent.

After being rejected by a family heading to Temple Square to listen to a concert in the Tabernacle, a woman and her husband approached Veronica from behind.

"Do you need food?" the woman asked Veronica. Her husband stood back. Veronica smelled of soot and perspiration and dirt. Her clothes were grey and dropped ashes on the ground when she turned. She had dirt between her teeth. Beyond being a dark woman in the middle of a bleached-white Mormon world, she was a dirty dark woman, alone, with very little English to help her out. The husband did his best to distance himself from the scene.

"I would like to buy you food," the woman said.

Veronica understood well enough. She held out her hands with her palms up to take the woman's money, but the woman gave her nothing.

"No, I would like to buy you food," the woman said. Her husband and Veronica shared the same confused face. The woman took Veronica's hand and walked with her into the nearest restaurant, asked for a table, and walked with the girl through the crowded place. Patrons turned their heads and gasped for clean air when the two women and the man walked by. Some grunted in disgust, and some even asked aloud if they really planned to eat there.

"Mind your own business," the woman said.

The woman wetted two napkins, wiped the soot from Veronica's face and hands, and gave her a roll.

Veronica, trying not to offend anyone, daintily picked apart the roll, even though she wanted to shove the whole thing in her mouth.

"What's your name?" the woman asked.

"Veronica," she answered.

The woman looked the young girl up and down. She looked at her face to see if she was joking or making it up. She put her hand on Veronica's arm and rubbed it back and forth. Ashes fell on the white tablecloth.

"Would you like to come home with us?" the woman asked.

"Are you sure about this?" her husband asked aloud.

"I'd like to take you home with us and clean you up. Would you like that?"

"Why are you being so kind to me?" Veronica asked.

"I've never been good at looking away," the woman said.

"This is true," her husband said. "This is what she does."

Veronica finished her meal, rode the trolley with the couple to the Avenues district, and followed the woman up the stairs to a single apartment that sat at the top of their home. The woman showed her around the place. It was small with slanted ceilings, but it had a toilet, a bed, and an oven.

"It's yours as long as you want it," the woman said. "Now, why don't you take a bath? I'll bring up some clothes." She left Veronica alone.

She sat in the bathtub, and for the first time since she lost her child, she wept.

Veronica slept for twenty-four hours and didn't stir until she felt the back of a hand sweep across her forehead. She jumped up, the face of the Mayan following her in her sleep, and swung her fists through the air, but when she opened her eyes she saw the kind woman who had taken her off the street.

New clothes had been laid on the foot of the bed. Veronica's dark skin was in contrast to the white dress the woman had given her, and it was beautiful. She took a long look at the woman before changing, unashamed, in front of her. The woman had blonde hair, but it was layered in thick, golden hues. Her skin was not the same white that wandered the streets of Salt Lake City, but a beige that had seen the sun, and her eyes had a few wrinkles beneath them. But she was beautiful. A gentle, half smile revealed wisdom, patience, and strength.

"When you're ready, please come downstairs for lunch," the woman said. She stood, left the room, and shut the door. Veronica listened to her footsteps as she walked down the outdoor wooden staircase that led from the rooftop room to the grassy lawn.

Veronica washed her face in the bathroom sink and walked out the door and down the stairs. She imagined herself walking down the stairs with the same regal posture that the woman carried, the smell of the Great Salt Lake coming in from behind her and the breeze lifting her dress a few inches at her ankles. For the second time in two days, she felt free of all the burdens she had been carrying over the last two years.

She rounded the northeast corner of the house and knocked on the front door of the main floor. The door had been left slightly open, so when her knuckles wrapped on it, it opened enough for Veronica to see the couple sitting at the table. An infant boy nursed on the woman's lap. She could see the back of his head and the golden blonde hair that he shared with his mother. The husband scraped up butter with his knife, spread it across some bread, and crammed it in his mouth.

"Please, Veronica, please come eat," the woman said.

Veronica walked over to the table and sat in the extra chair on the other side of the table from the husband. She folded her hands and placed them on the table's edge and waited.

"Please, please eat," the man said. All of his hesitation had disappeared in his home. His face was smiling and warm, but Veronica felt no warmth from him.

She took a piece of bread and some eggs that had been set out for her. She placed the eggs in the center of the bread and folded the corner of the bread to make a tortilla and placed the warm breakfast in her mouth. Her belly filled up quickly. It had shrunk. And even if she wanted to eat more, she couldn't.

"Finished?" the woman asked. She introduced herself as Claire and pointed to her husband and introduced him as Frank. With his mouth full of bread, he waved his hands in the air like he was being arrested. He laughed on the other side of his full mouth, and Veronica let out her first laugh too.

"Honey, will you grab the newspaper?' Claire asked and pointed to the cabinet on the other side of the dining room.

He stood, selected another piece of bread for the long walk, and put it in his mouth. He picked up *The Salt Lake Tribune* and handed it to his wife, who was still nursing their boy. Claire held it out in front of her for a minute, opened it up flat, and dropped it on the table in front of Veronica. Two photos covered the front page: the rising flames of Saltair in one photo and the ruins of the great dance hall in the other.

In perfect Spanish, Claire asked Veronica what she knew about the fire. The woman's smile disappeared and so did her husband's. Veronica remained quiet until Claire told her that the soot and ashes on her dress said more than enough.

"Por favor, Veronica," Claire said. She asked her if she started the fire.

Veronica remained quiet for a minute longer. Her eyes scanned the paper for mention of a young Mayan woman, but her English was not nearly good enough to read the bulk of the article.

Claire reached across the table and put her hand on Veronica's.

"He took me there, and he tried to rape me beneath the docks," Veronica said in Spanish. She did not cry. She did not break down. In her mind, it was done, and whatever Claire and Frank wanted to do they could do. "So I killed him to get away, and I burned it all."

Claire stood up, handed her son to Frank, and walked around the table to Veronica. She leaned down close to her and wrapped her arms around the nearly twenty-year-old woman. The warmth from Claire's body filled Veronica with emotion, and she broke down again, the second time since leaving El Paso. It wasn't anger that broke her, but love.

"I knew it," Claire said, her Spanish clean and smooth and fluent. "I knew it. Do you want to stay with us?" Claire asked her. When Veronica said she couldn't because she could never take and not give something back, Claire explained that they could use the help with their boy, Charles. She explained that she and Frank were new professors at the University of Utah and that both of them were gone at different times during the day and sometimes those times overlapped.

"Maestro?" Veronica asked in shock. Until that point in her life, she had never imagined the possibility of a woman professor. She never imagined a woman doing anything but cleaning fish or making tortillas.

"Si, si," Claire said, brushing off Veronica's bewilderment, and asked again if Claire would like to stay and help with the boy.

"Si, si," Veronica said. Her eyes looked toward the boy in Frank's arms. First a smile and then a sigh.

Claire saw the change in Veronica's face immediately and asked what was wrong.

"Nothing," Veronica said. She stood up, walked to the baby boy, asked for him by waving her arms in front of Frank, and pulled Charles close to her chest. He took to her immediately, pushing his little face into her neck and long, brown, nearly black hair. His fingers grasped at her clothes and wrapped around the hair that fell over them. Veronica whispered into the little boy's ear something quiet and unheard by Claire and Frank.

"He already likes you," Claire said. She wrapped one arm around the young Mayan woman who held her son. "I'll teach you English, and Frank, here, will teach you math and take you downtown to fill out the paperwork so you can stay and work here. If you want, that is?" Claire kept her arm around Veronica.

"Si, si," Veronica said. There was hesitation in her answers, but she said nothing but, "Si, si." She handed Charles back to his mother.

Claire said nothing. She took Charles back to her chair and finished nursing him.

"The hard part," Claire said, "is that everyone is going to think that you're Frank's second wife, living up in our single-living space upstairs. It's not surprising. Three or four families on this street have two wives hanging around, and ten kids screaming out during the day."

Frank choked on another piece of bread that he had tried to swallow whole.

"They can think what they want to think. They can eat shit for all I care," Claire said.

Veronica smiled, stood up from the table, and walked into the kitchen. She scanned the cabinets for flour and lard and a pan, and within minutes she placed a stack of fresh tortillas on the table in front of Frank and Claire.

"Thank you," Veronica said. Her English was frail and shaky and nervous, but she wanted to shed what had kept her on the outskirts of society as quickly as she could.

Frank jammed a whole tortilla in his mouth and smiled as wide and as full as a mouth of tortilla allowed him to smile.

"You're welcome," Claire said. "Now go back up and rest some more."

Veronica stood up and walked out the front door of the main house. Spring had come. Buds popped out on the edges of branches, the sun fell on the face of the Wasatch Mountains, and Veronica waited to let the morning embrace her. She smiled.

For the next year, Veronica woke up, bathed, and read whatever Claire had given her to read. It started with children's books, moved on to fairy tales, and by the end of the year, Claire had Veronica addicted to the classics. She fell in love with anything that transported her to the wilderness—Shelley and Whitman, Thoreau and Muir—with them, she stood on mountaintops and in rivers and along the edges of the frontier. She heard their voices in her head as they walked her through the pines and redwoods and along the edges of cliffs.

She filled her mind with the words of nature and pulled her hair back and walked downstairs to meet Charles and his parents at the door. Claire and Frank headed to the university and returned as soon as they could, rarely leaving Charles with her for more than five hours at a time. While Claire nursed the boy, she taught Veronica English, and Frank, days after her arrival, took her to the courthouse, handed the clerk the slip that was pinned on her shirt in El Paso, and filled out the necessary paperwork to keep her in the United States as a citizen. With immigration laws being so new, Frank talked his way around the clerk's questions, forcing the clerk, out of frustration, to stop talking and sign the papers.

As the seasons changed, the mountains turned brown in the summer, bright red, orange, and yellow in the fall, bright white in the winter, and again, after a day with Charles and a lesson with Claire, Veronica stood outside the front door and saw the spring sun hit the mountains. Veronica stretched to bring the day fully in, and then dropped her shoulders a tiny bit—a small enough motion that most wouldn't have noticed—before she headed upstairs to dive into the woods with John Muir.

On the anniversary of meeting Claire and Frank, Veronica woke, bathed, and read, but when she opened her door above the stairs that led down to the main house, it knocked against a package. She leaned down and gently tore through the wrapping. She found a card, an envelope, and a few folded dresses.

FROM CLAIRE, FRANK, AND CHARLES: You'll find everything you need to go home in this envelope. There is money, tickets for the railroad and ferry, and a US passport. We understand if you go and never come back, but if you do come back, you will always have a home here with us. We love you.

P.S. There are also a few new dresses for the journey. You'll need them in first class.

Veronica ran down the stairs and flung the big door open. Claire, Frank, and Charles waited for her at the table, smiling.

Claire used a hanky to dab at the tears around her eyes, but Veronica did not attempt to hold her tears in. She ran to Claire and threw her arms around her. Claire lifted her left arm, her right arm holding Charles, and pointed to the dress that lay on the chair in the living room.

Chapter Thirty-Four

CHUY

PROVO, UTAH, 1992

AUNT VERONICA WENT TO HER ROOM TO TAKE A NAP. DRIVING TO THE airport tired her out; eighty-seven years had begun to show on her. Navigating traffic and people and airport cops wore her out. She rarely broke into those spry movements she did two years earlier when we first got to Utah. Those flashes of energy and life had become very uncommon.

Most days, she would wake in the morning and stand over the stove cooking for an hour, take a late afternoon nap, spend an hour talking with Ms. Yamamoto, and take another nap in the late afternoon. She even found it difficult to give me grief, so when she picked me up at the airport and found out that my mom didn't make it back, that she had been held up by immigration officers in Dallas, she fell asleep in the car while I drove us home, her head caught between the headrest and the window. It was the first time I'd ever seen her saddened but having no anger attached to her melancholy. At sixteen-years-old, I had begun to love her, so when she walked to her room and crawled onto her bed, I worried she would not crawl out again, and I would be left alone in the United States with no any family at all.

I called Angela's house first, but her mom said she went out walking along the lake with a friend and that she would have her call me when she got home. I felt a little jealousy pop up in my chest, but of course she needed her new friends, especially while I was gone.

Hans had been whooshed away by his parents to visit the Universal Studios *Baywatch* attraction in California. I called him at their hotel, and he said, "Chuy, I'm sorry, my friend. I'll be home in two days, and we can talk about how to get your parents back."

The Speedo kid had grown up since we first met. He was always kind. His tears on the playground two years earlier showed that his heart had very few booby traps to keep away pain, but he had become someone I trusted, and I think Veronica had begun to like him too. "I'm sorry, amigo, I'll be back soon. Maybe we can think of another way to get your parents here that doesn't involve winning a reality TV show." I knew what he meant, but it hurt a little bit, because I saw no other option to bring my whole family back than to get on *CastAway* and win. The other options, the legal ones, seemed even more daunting and unconquerable than the reality show route to me. I had no power, no money, and no way of getting any in los Estados Unidos. But I forgave him immediately because I knew he wanted to help in any way he could.

The apartment had become so quiet. Veronica slept in the bedroom. Mom and Dad and Hector slept in Mexico.

And I felt completely alone.

Later that night, Angela called back. Her voice rattled across the line. The otherwise confident girl who would easily take on a bull if it charged, whispered into the receiver.

"Chuy, want to come over?" she asked.

"Of course," I said. "I really need to talk to you."

"Okay, good," she said. "I'll meet you on the pier."

Veronica's Lincoln Continental, all twenty feet of it, sailed along the Provo streets and out toward Utah Lake. It was Sunday night, and the world had become nearly as quiet as the apartment. Everyone had gotten home from church. They opened their bibles and Books of Mormon and spoke kind words to each other in their living rooms—or their Mormon rooms with a couch, chairs, and a table built specifically for visits from home teachers. Most newer Utah homes had them, and they helped sell houses.

The red and orange of the sun fell over the western mountains of the Wasatch Range, onto the waters of Utah Lake. Housing grew thinner the farther west the road went. And the houses got bigger, too. The road emptied, and the world grew even quieter. My mom would have loved it, the sunset by the lake, but she never saw it. She spent her days cleaning and her nights bussing, and never had a chance to see the beauty of our new country. Hector left too soon, and my father felt that if I could make it in los Estados Unidos, that if I could experience the sunsets in the land of opportunity, then his life had been fulfilled. He had told me this in his letters, in his phone calls, and at our home in Mexico the day before. But I didn't believe him, and I didn't believe it was fair, either. I couldn't enjoy it all if he couldn't get what he deserved for all his hard work.

Angela sat at the end of the pier with her knees against her chest She was as beautiful as the rays of the sun. And I loved her.

My footsteps fell hard on the pier. She turned her head and smiled. She patted the wooden planks next to her.

I sat.

I turned to hug her, and kiss her, and once our lips had grown tired, tell her about my mother. But instead of inviting me in, Angela placed one hand on my chest to keep me from her.

A rush hit me. Not a good rush. Not one of love. And not one of hope that she had to burp—this had happened before. This time, the stiffness of her fingers and the strength of her elbow locked behind them said something different.

I pulled away from her and gave her the space she wanted. Tried to be calm. I wanted to cry and tell her that my whole family was trapped in Mexico without me—well, except for Hector, who had found the life he wanted there—but she began to talk before I could.

"Chuy," she said, "I'm sorry, but I've met someone else. Someone I think might be better for me. Or better for the me I want to be ten years from now, I guess."

If I could have dived into the lake and swam across it until I hit the other side more than a mile away, I would have. My ears burned and my cheeks felt numb. Sweat built up in the most uncommon places: a little speck on my lip, drips on the back of my elbows, and a heavy rush of saliva between my tongue and the roof of my mouth.

"I love who you are today," I said. "Who do you want to be? And how am I not good for you?"

She shifted farther away from me, and, naturally, I shifted back, too, like we were two negative ends of magnets pointed at each other.

Angela pulled her shorts down as far as she could toward her knees to cover her thighs. She tugged on a sweatshirt to blanket her torso.

"Chuy, sometimes I get this burning in my bosom," she said.

I looked as far up in the sky as I could, because I was not going to look at her bosom when she said this.

"Okay," I said, with my head tilted upward.

"Chuy, you can look at me," she said. She pulled my chin downward with her thumb and index finger. "I think the burning comes from Jesus."

Okay, good. She didn't pronounce my name right, but maybe she wanted to speed things up a little bit. We could have a ten year goal of getting married and having kids, and, hey, she could start calling me Jesus, too. I felt like it was time people stopped calling me Chuy anyway. I mean, I had turned sixteen-years-old.

"This other boy," she said, "he points me to Jesus in a way I never knew could be possible. He makes me feel like I have a place in the church. No one has ever done that for me. They all saw me as a person who doesn't fit the mold, a person who got pregnant and, obviously, had sex before marriage. I went along with that, thinking I could never really be part of that world again. But he makes me feel like my journey has brought me to this point, and that Jesus—not you, Chuy—planned this for me. He knew that when I did return to the church and its teachings I could be one of the strongest believers there. If I didn't have sex, have my baby, and date you, I could have never loved Heavenly Father and served Him as passionately and purely as I can now. Understand, Chuy?"

All the burning and numbness came back to me.

"No," I said, but I meant "no" in Spanish and not "no" in English. There's a difference.

"I loved you, my little burrito brain, but now I love him. I love Jesus. I found him this week, while you were gone, through the guidance of Thomas Bingham. I'm sorry," she said.

I stood up. She stood up. I don't know how I did it, but I gathered myself and showed her no emotion. I held in the tears because it was the tears that made the moment sad. I hugged her softly and walked down the pier toward Aunt Veronica's car.

An hour later, my face covered in dried strings of salty tears, I walked into our apartment.

Aunt Veronica sat on the couch. She crocheted a doily and had turned on *CastAway Island*. The recap from the week before rolled as a montage and a teaser for the next episode followed. The handsome host said, "You'll never believe what will happen on tonight's episode of *CastAway*. It will shock you. The blindside of a lifetime."

No, host, I thought. *I experienced the blindside of a lifetime.* My heart didn't feel real anymore, like it had been smeared with butter and was slipping around inside of me.

Veronica did not look at me. Instead, she placed an arm over my shoulders and pulled me into her. She smelled like Clorox and grease. I let myself fall into her and stayed there until someone was voted off the island.

When the show ended, she walked into the kitchen, opened the oven, and pulled out warm sopapillas. She slathered them with jam and butter and brought them to the couch. She placed a plate of them down on the coffee table in front of us and began to talk.

"La chica Mormone?" she asked in Spanish. She never spoke it to me.

"Si," I said.

"Encontro a dios, si?" she asked.

"Si," I said.

"Si," she said.

She pulled a sopapilla apart with her old fingers. She dropped it onto her tongue and spoke with food in her mouth, something I had never seen her do and something that would warrant a smack with the rolling pin if I did it. Somehow, she pulled her legs up beneath her like a teenage girl would do.

"Did you love her, Chuy?" she asked.

"Tia Veronica, I did," I said.

She ate more of her sopapilla.

"Did you have sex with her, Chuy?" she asked.

I had no idea how to answer this. It felt like a trap, but I remembered her telling me that I should thank her for getting me out of the confessional that day. Maybe it wasn't.

But I hesitated.

"Chuy, did you know that I was about your age when I was first assaulted by a man?" she said.

All the burning and spinning and sweating that hit me at the beach hit me again on the couch, but this time, I felt a different kind of sorrow, the kind of sorrow you feel for the ones you love, which I knew could be so much deeper than the sorrow you feel for yourself.

"I didn't know that, Tia," I said. "I'm sorry."

"I lost a child, too," she said. "When I was pregnant I had a dream that I should name him Jesús and call him Chuy."

The spinning was almost too much now, so I stuffed a hot and greasy sopapilla in my mouth, and it worked—it calmed me a little.

"I'm sorry, Tia," I said.

Veronica put her hands on my knees and said, "It's okay, Chuy. I'm not telling you this to make you sad. I'm telling you this so you'll know that life, real life, has come to you this week. Your mom. Your girlfriend. Your heartache. You will never be the same. I think about what men did to me every day of my life, and will never forgive them, Chuy, so I have to ask you something," she said.

She let the moment hang out there, something a practiced and wise person can do.

"Si," I said.

"When you were *with* her, were you gentle with her? Did you listen to her? Were you kind? When you were *with* her did you treat her like a beautiful person?"

"Yes," I said. "I did, Tia."

"Did you ever do anything she didn't want or didn't ask you to do?"

"No, Tia Veronica. She led me through it," I said. "I could have never hurt her."

Veronica stood up. She walked around the back of the couch. She draped her arms around me. She squeezed me tight. She whispered, "There will be another for you, my sweet boy. Don't you worry."

PART FIVE

Chapter Thirty-Five

Chuy

Salt Lake City, UT 1994

IN THE FALL OF MY SENIOR YEAR OF HIGH SCHOOL, I WALKED OFF THE
bus and onto the grass of Sugarhouse Park in Salt Lake City for the
state championship cross country meet.

Hans drove Veronica to all my meets. She and Hans had become
close on those rides. He told me that he told her everything.

He stood at the bus door with a video camera in his hand. He'd
been filming me for weeks. His blonde hair had grown long and scrag-
gly in his best impression of Kurt Cobain, and he wore ripped jeans
and a flannel. He'd become the team manager, too—not to be with his
best friend, but to go to all the meets and see all the girls run in their
short cross country shorts and tank tops. He said the video was for a
school project about immigrant families. He said he filmed himself a
lot, too. Not wanting to know more about that, I told him it was okay
to keep filming.

"Jesús, tell me about your father," he asked, right after I stepped
off the bus.

"My dad's in Mexico," I said. "You know this."

He stuck the camera in my face.

"Yes, but they don't know this," he said. He pointed to the camera
lens with his free hand.

"Why is he in Mexico?" he asked.

"You know this. He got deported right after we got to Provo. They
took him because I got caught swearing in the parking lot of our apart-

ment building," I said. "Please move. I need to go warm up and stretch and run in the state championships."

Hans turned my head so the shadows of the trees didn't cover it.

"Are you running in memory of your father?" he asked. "Are you running for him today?"

"Yes," I said. "I'm running in memory of my father, who is alive, and in Mexico. Come on, Hans."

"Good luck today," he said. "I'll be filming you for all the ladies."

I realized that though I was being sarcastic when I said I ran for my family, looking at it honestly, I did. I ran to prove that I wasn't some poor immigrant from Mexico. I ran because every time I called my dad, he always seemed so proud I was running, always talking about how the Mayans were the first people to run for sport.

"We ran or we died," my father would say. "In the ruins, you can see the runners carved into the walls of the stadiums. You're a Mayan. That means you're a runner, Chuy." He would never let me talk about how I planned to bring him home. He would always shut it down and say, "They know who I am now. They know that I have family there. Keep your nose clean. They'll deport you like they deported me. They'll lock you out like they locked your mom out. Don't give them a reason to send you back, Chuy."

"What if I want to come back? What if I want to be with you and mom?" I would say.

"You would forget all we sacrificed. Would you do that to me? Make me feel like I left my family for years and years for nothing? That's selfish, Chuy," he'd say. I'd drop it and talk about running, and he would tell me about Mayan history.

So, yeah, I was running for my dad.

I had gotten to be pretty fast, too. Veronica also told me that it was old Mayan blood that surged through me, that our ancestors used to run across the great shelf of the Yucatán plains and play games in giant arenas, and that we ran from the Spanish longer than any other indigenous people. I thought it was because I ate a lot of beans and tortillas and that other kids ate crap like hamburgers and stuff.

I was nervous. It was cold. The rolling grass hills of the park were intimidating. Teams filed in from all over the state. Runners with really long white legs, nearly as tall as me, did warm-up sprints and stretches on the grass. The other runners looked so confident when they dashed up the grassy hills and bounced up and down to stretch out their calves and get warm on a morning when the mist still lay heavy on the valley and the dew wetted the grass.

Veronica walked slowly from her car. "Run like the Mayans, Chuy," she said. She walked to the start line, plopped open her lawn chair, sat down, opened a mini bottle of wine, and started sipping from it. An official walked up to her, and I could see him run as fast as he could from her while she spat at his legs.

I smiled in the hope that she wouldn't worry about the nerves in my gut that nearly brought me to my knees, and I headed down to the starting line to huddle up and stay warm. The announcer blurted into a microphone that we had about ten minutes until we needed to be lined up along the large red piece of tape placed on the ground.

Minutes later, I stood at the starting line and waited for the gun to go off. When it did, I shot off the line like no race before. In past races, I held back, saving my energy to run faster on the last 2.5 kilometers than on the first. This strategy had gotten me tenth place at regionals and a qualifying spot in the state championships. But I didn't even think about strategy this time. I ran as fast as I could through the first mile lap—I *was* running for my father—rising and falling on the grassy hills and passing runner after runner until I saw Hans with his camera standing next to the lap marker and the giant numbered screen that showed my race time: 4:55. I had run my first mile in four minutes and fifty-five seconds, a minute faster than the first mile of my regional time. I stayed with the top five runners for the second mile, and, again, my second mile. I was exhausted. The lactic acid pulsed through my legs and made it feel like I was heaving stacked bricks from one step to another. I fell behind, and behind, and behind.

I pushed it up the next hill, and the pain from the lactic acid drained from my legs. I could see the leaders ahead of me and gave it everything I could to chase them down. I saw the finish line, and I had jumped into the top five again. There was no way I would catch the leader, but one kid in front of me was catchable, so I pushed hard and sprinted past him across the line.

Fourth place. My best time ever: 15:27. I fell onto the wet grass. The cool dew felt good against my skin. I'd forgotten to breathe during my sprint to the finish line, so my world went dark. Hans shook me awake and pulled me up from the grass and walked me over to a bench where he made me sit and plied me with water and bananas.

My Aunt Veronica walked toward me with a man in a bright blue jacket following her.

When they got to me, the man stuck out his hand from beneath a BYU insignia.

"Jesús," he said.

"Chuy," I said.

"Would you like to come run for the Cougars on scholarship?"

"Sure," I said. "Why not?"

"What does that mean?" Veronica asked.

"It means we'll pay for him to go to college if he runs for us," the man said.

"What about the rules, mister?!" Veronica yelled.

The man yanked on his shirt collar and opened up the top button of his shirt.

"Well, Chuy, you'd have to sign the honor code," he said. "But a good kid like you, raised in Provo, having gone to Provo High School, shouldn't have a problem with it."

"Okay," I said. I could see my dad's face. I could hear him shout with joy. I could feel his pride in his son. He would be fulfilled.

"What's that mean?" Veronica asked.

The man, again, loosened his collar and unbuttoned another button.

"You won't be able to drink, and you won't be able to have any of what we consider to be intimate relationships, unless you get married of course. There is a strict dress code, and you'll have to make sure and go to church every Sunday with the team."

Veronica walked up behind the man and placed her hand on the small of his back. He leaned into the old woman with streaky silver hair and, thinking that she was supporting him, he put her arm around her.

She promptly threw his arm off.

"No way is he going to follow your rules!" she yelled. She disappeared into the crowd of runners.

"What do you think, Chuy? Is this all open for discussion?" the man asked.

I had to say yes. I had to follow the rules. College for free. A degree from BYU. My dad would be so proud. I could get a degree and make enough money to bring my family back, if I didn't win on *CastAway*.

Veronica showed up again, this time with a man in a red jacket.

"Meet Chuy," she said.

The man in red stuck out his hand.

"Hi, Chuy," he said. "Would you like to run for us?" I traced the U on his shirt with my eyes.

"Will I have to sign stuff and go to church?" I asked.

"No, but you'll have to drop a minute off your time by next fall," he said with a smile.

"Okay," I said. The man in blue walked away toward a group of other runners.

Hans filmed the whole thing.

Chapter Thirty-Six

Veronica

Mérida, Yucatán 1925

VERONICA STOOD ON HER FATHER'S DOORSTEP, TWO YEARS AFTER SHE had left with Jason.

She stood stoically. Nervous. A little angry. She wore a clean, red dress with a simple white sash wrapped around her waist. She raised her hand to knock on the green and white door at the edge of town in Mérida, but the door opened before her knuckles hit the wood. Her youngest sister, five-years-old, stood in front of her. The little girl wore her Sunday best. She looked up at Veronica. Her little face scrunched with confusion. When Veronica left, Rosa had turned three-years-old.

"Veronica, hermana, tu has regresado!"

The little girl's bright smile and untamed happiness brought Veronica to her knees. She pulled Rosa to her and squeezed her so hard the little girl almost cried. Behind her, her mother approached. She gasped at the sight of her twenty-one-year-old daughter who had been gone for so long. She looked at a woman who no longer had the face of the girl who left home. None of the girl who had gone away remained in her daughter. She'd lost a child.

Her other sisters ran to her from behind her mother. They swarmed Veronica and brought her into her home like ants carrying food along the path back to their nest. They sat her down at the kitchen table and stared at her. She had left with a handsome poet to los Estados Unidos; she had lived a life so different from theirs for two full years; and she had returned more womanly and beautiful than when she left, wrapped in a bright red dress with a white sash purchased at an American store. They wanted to hear every word, to hear every story, to listen to her tell them about her luxurious life north of the border, way up in Seattle, Washington, where Jason was from.

Are you married?

Do you have niños?

Do you have servants?

Have you come to bring the whole family, or, at least, your sisters back with you to los Estados Unidos?

The questions came fast, and her mother, yet to hug her, stood in the kitchen and gazed at her daughter, catching her eye every couple of minutes and looking away from her.

Veronica sat quietly, somewhat enjoying the attention from her sisters but not responding to them, nodding and smiling and trying to avoid her mother's eyes.

Rosa, while all the other girls dug into Veronica with questions, dug into Veronica's travel bag, a clean, green bag Claire had lent her. She stopped digging when she found a fancy hairbrush, also borrowed from her generous employers in Utah.

"Is this for me?" Rosa said. She held up the hairbrush. On the handle of the brush, she read an etching, "Salt Lake City, Utah."

Veronica moved from her seat to her knees, took the brush from Rosa, Rosa's eyes beginning to swell, and ran the brush through the little girl's hair. When she left Utah, her host told her that all that was inside the bag, including the bag itself, was Veronica's if she chose to stay with her family, which Veronica had chosen to do the second she said goodbye and thank you to those who had taken care of her over the last year, to the family that had clothed and fed her from the day of the great fire.

"Yes, yes, it's for you," Veronica said.

Rosa smiled so big that her eyes swelled with tears of happiness. She ran the brush through her hair and repeated over and over, "Salt Lake City. Maybe I can move there someday, too."

All of Veronica's other sisters asked if she had brought them gifts, so Veronica let them dig through her bag, telling them that it was all for them and apologizing for not having wrapped everything up. She hadn't intended to give any of it to them, but felt bad for not buying them gifts, and happily let it all go. She was home. And she would have everything she needed here.

She relaxed back into her chair while her sisters rummaged through her bag and fought over her stuff. Left alone at the table, her mother came to her, knelt in front of her, held her hands, and placed her head on Veronica's lap. Tears ran across the backs of Veronica's hands. Veronica put her head down on her mother's and took in the smell of her. She had come home, and at that moment felt all the love and comfort and history of her life before she was pushed into the back of the train when she crossed the border into Texas so long ago. She breathed and breathed and breathed, long deep breaths that brought in the smell of her mother and the sounds of her sisters laughing and tussling.

"Do you have flour, mama?" she said.

"Si," her mother said. "For what?"

"Tortillas," Veronica said.

"Tortillas? We have corn for that."

"I am going to make flour tortillas, okay?" Veronica said.

"I don't understand why, but, okay, Veronica, okay," her mother said.

Rosa joined Veronica in the kitchen. She dug her hands into the dough. She helped with the lard. She looked up at her older sister with so much loss and love and happiness that she had returned. When they finished, Veronica gave Rosa the first tortilla, and the little girl looked up at her and said, with a mouth full of tortilla and butter, "I will always make these tortillas."

The front door shut and her father whistled as he turned the corner into the kitchen and dining room.

—

He didn't say anything to Veronica, not for a very long while.

He yelled at the girls who rummaged through Veronica's bag. He told them to get off the floor and that none of that stuff that they pulled out of "that grandiosa bag" came as a gift from their selfish older sister who left the family and decided to never write them to say hello or tell her mother that she was okay. He asked his wife, calmly and with a gentle voice, to stop adoring the little girl who made her cry every night for the last two years. He helped his wife to her chair at the table and ushered the rest of the girls, even little Rosa who had placed her hairbrush into her blouse, out of the house and into the garden to leave him and his wife alone with Veronica.

He didn't say anything to Veronica, even after he himself had filled a cup with coffee and taken a seat across from her at the kitchen table, the one at the head where he always sat.

Veronica sat quietly in her place like she had been gagged and tied down by the anger of the man who sat at the head of the table. Her mother remained quiet, too.

He slurped his coffee. His giant sigh said everything Veronica needed to know. He had not forgiven her. Not even on her return.

When her father finally spoke, he said, "Mija, have you been happy while your mother cried? Have you eaten the gringo food while Rosa forgot your name? Have you lived the life of a white woman up north, and have you had servants as dark as you clean your home, wash your dishes, and nurse your blanco babies while your mother had no help with your younger sisters? Have you eaten fish while your father baited lines and hauled in nets and spent extra hours gutting and cleaning and hauling while your mother had no help at home? I hope you have." His voice was sarcastic and cruel.

"Esta bien. Ella esta ahora aqui," her mother said. She reached across the table and placed one hand on Veronica's and one on her husband's.

"No, no esta bien," he said, "not until she answers, not until she apologizes, not until she asks your forgiveness. Her family's forgiveness."

He lifted his wife's hand off his and set it down on the table.

He slammed his fist against the wood. It shook the table, the floor, the house.

Veronica wanted to tell him everything. She wanted to tell him, "No, Papa! No, I was not happy! I was hurt. I was alone. No, Papa! I was not happy while you cried and worried, but I have shed enough tears for myself, Papa!" But she didn't.

She looked at her mother. She had slumped over the table and wrapped her face in her hands. Her father, behind his anger and his disappointment, was glad she was home. She could feel it in him. He sounded like he had prepared this speech for two years and had to deliver it, or he would not be a good husband to his wife or father to his daughters.

"Si, Papa. Lo siento. He sido feliz," Veronica said. "I have been happy."

Her mother finally cried again, sobbing heavy and wet tears into her hands. The tears were those of relief and not sadness, deep gasps of moist breaths.

Her father let his guard down, too, listening to the sound of his wife's tears wetting the table.

"Okay," he said. "Okay."

He stood up, walked over to Veronica, and gave her a hug.

He called his daughters into the house. They cooked a feast of fish and pickled onions and rice. The family sat around the table and Veronica made up stories about her travels to San Francisco and Los Angeles and Chicago and Yellowstone Park, eating capers and bagels and chocolate cake while looking out over the ocean, and they smiled and imagined it and ate until they felt full.

At the end of the night, her father told all her sisters to grab their blankets from their rooms and put them on the floor in the hallway so that their tired sister could sleep alone in their bedroom for the night. He escorted her into the room and said, "Good night, Veronica. I'm glad my little girl has come home."

The distance she felt from the little girl she was when she left to become the woman who had killed a man beneath the rickety timbers of Saltair was vast.

Veronica took a pen from the desk all the girls shared to do their homework and scribbled out a letter saying, "I love you. I'm okay. Thank you for all the love. I will write every month, and I will send money. But this is no longer my home."

She folded the letter, placed it on her old pillow, and climbed out the window to avoid her father once again. She walked into the night and headed back to Utah. Before she walked away, she turned to the house with her family sleeping inside and whispered, holding her hands up into the air as if holding her thoughts in them, "I've been hurt, beaten, and left for dead, but I survived. I didn't survive to hurt you by telling you these things, Papa, but I survived to stand here and let you sleep and wake up believing that I am okay. Because I am now."

She raised her hands higher in the air, released the thoughts she held there, and walked away.

Chapter Thirty-Seven

CHUY
PROVO, UT 1994

I GRADUATED HIGH SCHOOL.

Veronica had really begun to show her age. She was my sole blood relative in the United States—my mom was never able to return because the INS accused her of helping my dad to illegally cross the border. My dad and mom tried, for a while, to get her back to me, but, after a few months, the situation seemed impossible to overcome.

Veronica, however, since the night I came back to the States alone and lost Angela, all within the span of twenty-four hours, had become my blood family and my loving family. We had grown closer, spending many nights together watching television or talking with Ms. Yamamoto. I did my best to stay home most evenings—Hans would often join us—and sit with her on the long balcony that connected all the apartments in the complex.

We laughed a lot.

One night, after Veronica had polished off four Coors (and let me have a couple with her), she told me her story and broke my heart in one evening. I couldn't believe everything she went through. She finally told me about how she had burned down Saltair, made her way home, and decided to come back to Utah. She let me hold her hand while she sipped on another two Coors and let me have one more. When she was finally near to falling asleep that night, she walked to her bedroom and lay down on the top of the covers. "I dreamed of you, Chuy," she whispered. "God put you in my life. He took a long damn time to do it. That selfish bastard." She fell asleep.

—

One month later, Hans and I packed up the apartment. We took boxes from behind the local grocery store and filled them with the very few things Veronica and I could take with us. The rest, we threw in the dumpster at the edge of the apartment complex parking lot. Veronica sat in a fold-out deck chair, drank Coors, and bossed us around. She even gave Hans a couple of slaps on the butt. She told him, "I never dreamed I'd know some crazy Jewish German kid, that's for damned sure, but I'm glad ya joined us." She'd begun to drink more during my senior year of high school. It kind of suited her, to be honest. She was a nice drinker. "In this life, all I did was work and sleep. I didn't ever have the chance to drink. Now, I think I'll enjoy myself," she'd say. I agreed with her.

When the apartment was cleared, we packed it up in the back of a Penske truck, along with Hans's stuff from home. We drove the thirty-five miles to Salt Lake City and stopped at Veronica's house in Rose Park first. It didn't take long to unload the few things she had. Inside, the house smelled stale. No one had really been in there for four years, not since they took my dad away and Veronica moved to Provo to help my mom out with me and Hector. It'd been a long four years, but the sounds and smells of the neighborhood were as beautiful as when we left so long ago, almost a quarter of my life for me, but a snippet of Veronica's.

She walked inside and sat in her favorite chair.

Hans and I followed her inside and sat down on the sofa. We didn't want to leave her immediately, but she didn't want us to stay either, because she knew we shouldn't.

"You two assholes need to get going," she said. "I sure as hell don't need you hanging around some eighty-eight-year-old Mayan. Go to school, now."

She waved the back of her hand at us, shooing us away like two eighteen-year-old flies.

I hugged her and said I would see her Sunday for dinner.

"Okay, Chuy. I'll cook," she said. "You're a sweet boy."

She kissed my cheek.

We drove up the east side of Salt Lake city, and I pulled the Penske into the parking lot of the dorm for international students at the University of Utah. The registrar had put us both there because we had yet to become full citizens, although we both had lived in the country long enough to feel like we were. We called and complained multiple times throughout the summer, but they said that if we wanted to be roommates, we would have to wait for them to move us after our first quarter because all the other dorm rooms had been filled—unless we wanted to split up. We chose to stay together.

We checked into the dorm office, picked up our keys, and ran to the second floor.

We walked off the elevator, and I saw the exact opposite of what I saw when I walked into my first classroom in Provo. Filling the hallways of the international dorm, people from all over the world darted back and forth with boxes in their hands. People from Asia. People from Africa. People from the Middle East. People from Central and South America. People from the Pacific Islands. Hans tapped me on the shoulder. He approached a young man who looked to be from South America and asked him, in English, where he was from. When he said Columbia, Hans began speaking to him in perfect Spanish. He introduced Eduardo to me, and the three of us, not caring about unloading our truck, spent the rest of the afternoon and evening in the common area of the dorm, talking to each other and to any student who wanted to join us.

Chapter Thirty-Eight

VERONICA

SALT LAKE CITY, UT 1994

VERONICA SLEPT A LOT THAT WEEK. SHE HAD GROWN SO TIRED, WENT
to bed early, and didn't watch *CastAway* for the first time in a very
long time. She found it hard to get out of bed—not from sadness, but
from a new weakness in her muscles and bones. She sat on the porch
of her Rose Park home as the cars went by and the sun dropped over
the lake.

She lost energy quickly, so she began to cook on Thursday afternoon for the big meal with Chuy and Hans on Sunday, making the
pinto beans first, and splitting the good beans from the pebbles in the
burlap sack. She cooked them all night long to soften them, and mixed
in a little bit of ham hock to make them salty.

On Friday, she cooked the chili verde, taking her time to make
sure every piece of the pork simmered long enough to pull apart with
the slightest tug and that the chiles became rich in their own sauce.

Saturday morning, she woke up early to fry the chicharrones. She
ate half of them while cooking, so she had to fry up another batch.
They crackled in the frying pan, and their smoke wafted from her
kitchen window. That night, she walked to the local store, Jun's Market, owned by a Korean man named Jun, and bought a six-pack of
Coors, found a marathon of M.A.S.H. on television, drank her beer,
and fell asleep on the couch, waking at nine in the evening and moving
to her bedroom.

She got up at four on Sunday morning, knowing that the boys
would probably sleep in until noon, and stumbled in smelly and raw

shortly after, and began to cook flour tortillas the way Mrs. Cordova taught her to so many years ago on the dry-edged salt flats of the Great Salt Lake.

She took her time, her hands not working like they did a few short years ago—the last time she made them in this house—and so much more slowly than they did seventy years ago, when she was still so young. She whisked the flour, salt, and baking powder together in a bowl, her wrist spinning with the handle of the whisk tucked tightly into her grip. She took a bucket of lard from a large cabinet next to her feet, and dug her hands into it, grabbing a large fistful of the gooey fat, and mixed it into the powder until the mix became thick and hard and soft at the same time, an exact feeling that she knew when she touched it. She kneaded it slowly, taking a break to shake out her aching hands, and split the dough into twenty balls.

Her rolling pin hung above her. She took it down and pressed the smooth, round edge of it down against the first ball of dough, rolling it until the dough became flat, and dropped the tortilla in the hot skillet that was sizzling on the burner. While one tortilla cooked, another would be rolled out until all the tortillas lay warm and flat in a ceramic pot that she placed in a warm oven to sit and wait for the boys.

She opened a can of Coors, walked to the front porch during sunrise, and waited for the boys to roll up in Hans's car, getting up and out of her chair to grab another beer and add food to the warm oven. First, the beans, next the chili verde, and finally the chicharrones, all of it warming up for her guests.

The car rolled in early at 10:30. Veronica shot up from her chair and waved. She did her best to not act so tired, to not move so slowly, to not let him know that she knew the end was coming. Chuy was alone. The boy was tired and excited and couldn't stop talking about all the people from all over the world who lived with him in his dorm. He stood next to her and kneaded the dough for extra tortillas. The rest of the food had been simmering for hours, but they needed the tortillas to wrap everything up together, to make the meal whole. He talked and talked, and she listened, leaning against the counter to try to act like she wasn't as tired as she felt in her bones. He even asked her to sit and said he could finish up, but she stood as tall as she could next to him and as she saw her great-grandnephew make the same flour tortillas she had taught her baby sister to make nearly six decades earlier, she smiled.

He talked about the kid from India who had played a horrible joke on the boy from Nigeria who in turn played a horrible joke back on the kid from India. He talked about the beautiful girls from everywhere, telling Veronica that he now understood why women truly were the light of the world. And he talked about how ten or so of his new friends went on a shopping trip early Saturday morning to the international market in Salt Lake City, bought ten different kinds of ingredients from ten different parts of the world, broke into the dorm kitchen that was closed for the weekend, and cooked a feast so big and beautiful that he thought he might eat too much to run cross country that fall for the university. He rubbed his non-existent belly and smiled at Veronica.

Every time she stood up to get the boy more food, she rubbed his shoulders on the way to the stove, and he patted her hands with both of his.

"Where's that horny German?" she asked Chuy.

Chuy rolled his eyes, the ones that had changed from those of a fourteen-year-old boy to those of an eighteen-year-old young man.

"If you can believe it, he met a girl who loves language as much as he does. Since they both know four languages, they are teaching each other the two they don't know. That's all they did yesterday, and he woke up early this morning to meet her at the park to learn Arabic," Chuy said.

"More food?" Veronica asked.

"Por supuesto," Chuy said.

Veronica, for old time's sake, whacked him softly on the elbow and said, "No, en Ingles."

Chuy settled into the couch after they ate. He didn't stop talking.

He couldn't stop, it seemed to Veronica. When he did stop, he fell asleep. Veronica covered him with a blanket and let him snore into the afternoon air.

At 2:30 in the afternoon, Veronica's phone rang.

She picked it up.

It was Hans.

He spit out his words so quickly, mixing German and English and Spanish, that she could barely understand him.

"He's sleeping," she said.

"Get him up!" Hans screamed.

"What is so important to wake a man from sleeping?" she asked.

"It's *CastAway*. They called. They want Chuy on the show. They loved his video," he said.

Veronica looked at the boy on the couch. He looked like his father, like her little sister, like *her* father. He always had.

"What video? Chuy didn't make no video," Veronica said.

"I know. I know. I did," he said. "And they loved it."

Veronica thought about how she felt that morning with her great-grandnephew, the warmth he had given to her and her home, and the dream she had about him so many years before he was born. For a split second, she wanted to tell Hans to eat a pile of cow shit. She had felt so lonely. But she took a longer look at the boy whose whole immediate family had been deported and who had held onto that dream for so long, and she told Hans that she would make sure Chuy was at his dorm in less than twenty minutes.

She hung up the phone and shook Chuy awake.

"Chuy, you need to go now," she said. "*CastAway* called Hans. They want you on the show."

Most boys would tell her to stop making fun of him, to stop teasing him, and that this wasn't a funny joke, but Chuy did none of that. The boy with so much light and hope and determination rose from the couch, sprinted out the front door, and jumped in the car.

Veronica waved to him from the front porch and caught his eye.

He slammed the car into park, jumped back out, ran up to the porch, and kissed Veronica on the forehead.

"Thank you for lunch, Tia Veronica," he said.

"Por supuesto," she said.

He drove away.

She walked back into the house, rummaged through her junk drawer, took out a pen and paper and wrote Chuy a very short letter. She sealed it up and placed it on the coffee table in the center of her living room. Then she went back to bed.

Chapter Thirty-Nine

CHUY

COSTA RICA, 1994

THE BOAT, FILLED WITH PEOPLE FROM ALL OVER THE UNITED STATES, edged along the Costa Rican shoreline. Four cameramen walked back and forth across the deck. The fifth cameraman sat in a large spinning chair on the top deck with another camera in front of him; he steered the large thing around like he was spinning motorbike handles in front of him. Above us, a helicopter circled in the cloudless blue sky.

The boat stopped in front of a sandy, wide-open beach, and the handsome host of *CastAway* pulled up alongside us in a dingy. He yelled across the watery gap between the boats with a megaphone attached to his lips. This man with thick arms and a sharp jawline was no stranger. He had been a regular visitor to our apartment over the years.

I wanted to jump into the water, swim to him, and hug him, but I resisted the urge and wore a serious game-on grin (the director's words, not mine) as we had all been instructed to do. I gritted and ground my teeth and pursed my lips to look like a deadpan Chuy, not the Chuy I could barely hold inside, the Chuy who felt so giddy that I peed myself a little at every stage of the interview, the casting, and the filming process. It was my biggest adventure yet, and my shot at a million dollars.

They told us to wait on the boat until the host waved us in, but I couldn't handle it. I jumped immediately. The warm water of the Pacific Ocean off the western coastline of Costa Rica surrounded me. I climbed up onto the dingy, the director of the show yelling at me from the larger boat, and hugged the host.

The host hugged me back, and said into his megaphone, "I think someone is excited to be here. What's your name, son?"

I let go of him.

"Are you a big fan of the show?"

He threw his arm around me and pointed the both of us toward the cameraman that spun in the big chair on the other side of the water.

"I want to bring my family back to Utah," I said.

The host smiled and talked into the megaphone, "Well, a million dollars can change anyone's life."

He smiled and tapped me on the back. Another dingy had pulled up beside his, and he nudged me toward it. The cameras kept rolling while I climbed the ladder up the deck of the boat with the rest of the contestants.

I found my spot again, and the director pointed to the ground, implying that I should stay put for the rest of the scene.

"I know Chuy is ready to get started," the host said. "Who else is ready?"

The other contestants broke into a cheer.

"When the gun goes off, you will jump into the water, swim to the shore, and stand on the giant mat at the edge of the forest." The lush green rainforest lined the beach like a wall, and howler monkeys screeched from within the thick brush that climbed up from the water to the sky.

"Here's the twist this season. The last person to stand on the mat will not be divided into a tribe and will not even make it to their camp, because the last person on the mat will be sent home today, eliminating their chance at a million dollars," he said.

The contestants quickly sized each other up, but he gave no pause for them to plan or prepare.

"On your mark, get set, go!" he said.

The gun went off.

I'd already felt the water. It was warm. I jumped in headfirst, a shallow dive, and swam as hard as I could to the beach. Once my feet touched the wet sand beneath the water, I stood up and ran as fast as I could. I stood on the mat before any other contestant and turned around to see where the rest of the competitors were. No one was within thirty feet of me, their feet struggling to catch hold of the sand beneath them.

The rolling garbage can practice had paid off. I'd made it.

When the next person came close to the mat, I reached out my hand and pulled her in close for a hug. I did the same thing to every other contestant, pulling them in, hugging them, and thanking them for being on *CastAway* with me.

It seemed like everything happened on the show so quickly, but in reality, things happened so slowly, with multiple takes of us contestants acting shocked and surprised, and frustrated and fearful, and then happy and jubilant, before we were even divided up into teams and sent to our camp. What looked on TV to be spontaneous was anything but, so by the time we were divided up and sent walking toward our camp, everyone was flat-out exhausted. A lot of people wanted to lay on the beach instead of building a shelter, starting a fire, or cooking rice, so I did it all, since I was the youngest contestant by at least six or seven years. I felt bad for the old people, so I cooked their rice and handed it to them with spoons I had made out of sticks, much like how Hector and I made things to sell along with our lizard tails back in Chelem when we were kids. The pale people on *CastAway* reminded me of the pale people from my childhood in Utah, who got so red so quickly in the sun that it looked like their skin might burn right off their bodies. I boiled water for them and gave it to them in cups made from strung-together leaves the same way Veronica used to bundle up tamales before putting them in the oven. By the end of the first day, five of my team members, all over the age of forty-five, had referred to me as their 'dear son.' I made sure everyone was fed and had water to drink.

My parents and Tia Veronica would have killed me if they watched the show and saw me neglecting my elders. I did a lot of the work out of pure love for the wrinkly, pale people. But I have to admit, I also did a lot of it out of pure fear of my family.

The days on the beach went slowly, mostly filled with conversations repeated over and over so the cameraman could get the right shot. There were definitely fun times though. The challenges were great, and my team always won because I kept them fed. Some of them even gained weight while there. In the jungle, I found mounds of plantains and coconuts, so, how my mom and Veronica used to cook, I made patacones, fried plantains, for everyone every day. They tasted like potato chips. I would drain the oils from the coconuts and fry up the plantains with the salt we got from winning the second challenge on day four of the game.

We ate, ran, jumped, and did puzzles well, unlike other teams who struggled to even stay on their feet half the time.

On the seventeenth day, the last day that my team would be a team, the last day before we all had to play for ourselves because we had knocked everyone else out of the game, the handsome host stood in front of us. He held his megaphone in his hand. He looked so clean and groomed compared to us. We had grown beards and back hair and pubic hair, and, to my disappointment, I realized after all these years that the camera wasn't blurring out things that were sexy. It blurred out things that weren't—hair and bug bites in places no one at home would want to see.

"Today, we have a very special reward. Want to know what you're playing for?" he asked.

It had to be special because my team had won all the hot dogs, all the pizza, and all the cooking supplies we needed. Everyone cheered, knowing that we had all made it far enough to really get a shot at the million dollars.

"But you won't be doing this challenge alone," he said. "You will have the help of someone very close to you. If you win the challenge, your loved one will hand-deliver letters from friends and family who miss you and could not make the trip."

Most contestants started crying with the mention that they got to see someone they loved. I prayed that it would be my dad. I don't know why, but I wanted to see him more than any other person I knew. I closed my eyes and held in the tears. One of the other contestants shook me from behind to hopefully raise my excitement level.

One by one, the host brought out family members, first asking if the contestant knew who might be joining them. Everyone got their wish. If they yelled out, "My wife," their wife would come running out of the trees of the rainforest. If they yelled out, "My husband," their husband would run out. If they yelled out, "My mom," sure enough, their mom would run out, tears flowing from her eyes, and it went on that way until I stood very last on the mat, alone.

"Chuy, who would you like to see come out of there?" the host asked.

"My dad!" I yelled.

For the first time, the host shook his head back and forth, "Sorry, Chuy, but we couldn't make that happen."

"Okay, my mom!" I yelled.

"We couldn't do that either," he said. "I have to tell you that we tried. Let's bring your special someone out!"

Hans ran from the trees in a pair of the bright yellow, red, and green Mexican flag shorts he had worn four years earlier, when we first started to train to beat that bigot, Billy. Everyone gasped at the white young man who ran onto the beach with barely any clothes on.

I laughed so hard that I tumbled forward off the mat.

Hans gave me a hug.

The host explained the challenge, and we began.

We had to navigate a maze while tied together and blindfolded. Then we had to swing a ball around the pole that it had been tethered to until it landed in a basket at the top. Once we finished that, we had to eat a pile of earthworms without throwing up.

I have to say, Hans and I dominated that challenge. We made it through the maze by speaking German to each other so that the other teams couldn't understand what we were saying. We slapped that ball so hard, jumping up and over it as it swung over and beneath us, and we laughed when we challenged each other to a contest to see who could eat the worms the fastest. We beat the next team by four full minutes and the last team by nearly an hour. With the cameras off us, we talked about the dorms and our room. It was the best day on the island.

And it became the worst.

"Chuy and his friend Hans won the challenge decidedly. Hans, it's time to give Chuy his letters and say goodbye," the host said.

The host took a singular letter from a table next to him.

Hans stopped smiling. He stopped laughing.

He hugged me, handed me the letter, and told me that he couldn't wait until I returned. Then he ran into the jungle with all the other family members.

"Chuy, you can choose to read your letter now, or you can wait until you are back at camp. Which do you choose?" the host asked.

I don't know why, but I decided to read the letter. I couldn't wait.

I opened up the envelope. Inside there were two letters, one wrapped around the outside of another. I read the outside one first.

It was from my father, and it read:

Dear, Chuy,
Veronica left this letter for you.
We love you and miss you,
Mom, Dad, and Hector

I first looked at the outside of Veronica's letter. On the back, it read:

If you are reading this, do not let Chuy know until he can hear it directly from me, through this letter.

The tears began to swell up in my eyes before I even opened the letter to see what was on the inside. I wiped them away.

"Chuy, is it something you'd like to share with us?" the host asked. Everyone gathered around me and placed their hands on my back to give me comfort. I didn't answer him.

The letter read:

Dear Chuy,

You came into my life when I needed you most. I was meant to take care of you, but you took care of me. I love you, you idioto, more than you know.

I now feel like it is time for me to go home.

I want you to take me there.

If everyone has done as I have asked them to do, please take my ashes to the Gulf of Mexico, take my father's boat into the waves, and cast away, Chuy, cast away.

All my love to you, Jesús.

Tia Veronica

I collapsed to the ground. The words in the letter tore through me. My older friends gathered around me and shielded me from the cameras, even though the producers and directors yelled for them to move. They did not move. And neither did I.

Chapter Forty

CHUY

CHELEM, YUCATÁN 1994

IN NOVEMBER 1994, ONE WEEK AFTER THE FILMING OF CASTAWAY wrapped up, I yanked hard on the starter rope of a very, very old Evinrude outboard motor. It hung over the back of an even older aluminum boat. Both had been preserved behind our house in Chelem for nearly one hundred years, covered in a canvas, untouched before we dug it out to clean it up and get it ready for the ocean.

My dad, Hector, and I had spent two days welding together the cracked areas of the aluminum, Dad bringing in materials from work and Hector borrowing tools from his welding lab at the university. Those were two of the best days I could remember.

We spent the morning sitting at the table, talking about life. Hector, nearing twenty-one-years-old, had shed the skin of the older brother and looked me in the eye, listening to me when I talked to him about how Angela broke my heart and about how Veronica saved me when I came home from Mexico without Mom. He talked about school and the girls he had been dating and how he never planned on marrying, but instead planned to get a job on the giant cruise ships that pulled into port at Progresso and Cancun.

"They hire the highest-skilled underwater welders and mechanics on those ships, and the tradesmen, like me, get to sail all over the world and fix little things beneath the sea while the boat is at sail. But, from what I hear, I could go on a whole cruise and get to eat the food and hang out on deck, as long as I appear to be cruising. Also, they want English and Spanish speakers. Hell, Chuy, when you're done with college, you could join me," he said. "I've been trying to get Dad to apply, but he says he can never be away from Mom again."

My dad shook his head. He nodded toward my mom on the couch. "It's true," my dad said. "Those were the hardest six years of my life. I missed you boys que horrible, too."

Maybe I didn't need to go back to school, to go back to Utah. I could go to school where Hector went to school. I could stay home in Chelem, and my father and mother wouldn't miss me. We could spend our mornings how we did during those two days, talking and drinking coffee and eating warmed sopapillas with butter and jam.

My father tapped the table with his knuckles, and we all stood up at once and headed into the shop to work on the boat. Hector still hit me on the shoulder, but the whole tone of the slug had changed. My father still lectured me and bossed me around, but he did this in a way that he would talk to any apprentice. The shed smelled like men, burnt metal, and, toward the end of the day, breath filled with hints of cerveza.

"So, Chuy, are you a millionaire?" my father asked me. "Are we fixing a boat we don't need to fix?"

He laughed and told me to hand him a very thin sheet of metal I had cut.

I had signed a paper saying that I couldn't say a word about *Cast-Away* until the entire cast returned for the season finale in New York City, one month after filming on the beach wrapped. And, the truth was, I didn't know. I'd made it to the final four contestants, so I would find out like everyone else.

That day on the beach, when I read Veronica's letter, I rose from my knees and walked out from within my barrier of friends as the director threatened all of us with the contract we signed stating that we could never avoid the camera. I shoved the letter in the back pocket of my shorts and played the rest of the game as hard as I could, and in a way of which my father would be proud. Kind. Resourceful. Giving. Strong.

—

We ended those days in Chelem with food that we all cooked together, the four of us weaving around each other in the kitchen. Hot grease popping from the stovetop. The smells of home leaking from the oven. Open beer bottles on the counter. Mom and Dad gave random hugs to me and Hector and to each other. And, somehow, I missed them so much when we were together like that. Even though my dad had told me I could stay and that I had fulfilled his dream and made it worth it for him to leave us for four years, Utah had become my home.

I yanked on the pull cord of the Evinrude. The boat sat sturdy in the small swells of the Gulf of Mexico on the edge of Chelem. Giant cruise ships sat thirty miles away in the Port of Progresso. The smell of gas rose toward me with each pull. Veronica sat in an ornate urn at the front of the boat. My mother had wrapped the urn in a blanket and set the blanket into a small cardboard box so it wouldn't shift and break when the front of the boat hit the crashing waves on the way to the sea.

The motor kicked in, and I twisted the throttle on the steering handle. The little boat motored out through the first batch of crashing waves and its nose fell into the calm swells beyond the break. I slowed the throttle. The boat felt calm beneath me. The sun rose directly above me. It got hot very quickly in the center of the water with no shade and the sun's rays reflecting up to me from the green and blue waters.

I stripped down to my shorts and jumped in. I swam a few feet from the boat and let the swells lift me up and down above the great tectonic shelf beneath, above the remnants of the biggest graveyard in our earth's history, above the crater of the meteor that changed the face of our planet.

My arms grew tired, so I climbed back into the boat.

I picked up the urn. I took off its lid. I shook Veronica's ashes into the ocean. Her ashes floated in the breeze and settled on the rolling waves of the Caribbean Sea.

"Cast away, Veronica, cast away."

Acknowledgments

I am beyond grateful to the people who helped bring *Cast Away* to the page. This book would not exist without the belief and love of Chuy and Veronica of my agent and friend, Elizabeth Copps, who saw what this book aims to do from the very beginning and who was this book's first mega-fan. I am grateful for everyone at Torrey House Press, but especially Kirsten Johanna Allen who spent so much time with Chuy and Veronica and loved them too.

I want to say thank you to my grandma Chavez Cordova for all of those days in her kitchen. While she cooked beans, tortillas, and bunuelos, I ran around at her feet and laughed with her—and this is how *Cast Away* began. She was my first best friend.

I want thank my wife and son, as always, for their support and my mom for her love.

About the Author

Kase Johnstun is an award-winning novelist, memoirist, and essayist. He is the author of the medical memoir *Beyond the Grip of Craniosynostosis* and the novel *Let The Wild Grasses Grow*, which was a finalist for the High Plains Book Awards and Reading the West, and named a 2022 Women's National Book Association Great Group Read. His work has also been published widely by literary journals and trade magazines. Johnstun lives in Ogden, Utah.

TORREY HOUSE PRESS

Torrey House Press publishes books at the intersection of the literary arts and environmental advocacy. THP authors explore the diversity of human experiences and relationships with place. THP books create conversations about issues that concern the American West, landscape, literature, and the future of our ever-changing planet, inspiring action toward a more just world.

We believe that lively, contemporary literature is at the cutting edge of social change. We seek to inform, expand, and reshape the dialogue on environmental justice and stewardship for the natural world by elevating literary excellence from diverse voices.

Visit www.torreyhouse.org for reading group discussion guides, author interviews, and more.

As a 501(c)(3) nonprofit publisher, our work is made possible by generous donations from readers like you.

Join the Torrey House Press family and give today at
www.torreyhouse.org/give.

Torrey House Press is supported by the King's English Bookshop, Maria's Bookshop, the Jeffrey S. & Helen H. Cardon Foundation, the Sam & Diane Stewart Family Foundation, the Barker Foundation, the George S. and Dolores Doré Eccles Foundation, Diana Allison, Klaus Bielefeldt, Joe Breddan, Karen Edgley, Laurie Hilyer, Susan Markley, Marion S. Robinson, Kitty Swenson, Shelby Tisdale, Kirtly Parker Jones, Robert Aagard & Camille Bailey Aagard, Kif Augustine Adams & Stirling Adams, Rose Chilcoat & Mark Franklin, Jerome Cooney & Laura Storjohann, Linc Cornell & Lois Cornell, Susan Cushman & Charlie Quimby, Kathleen Metcalf & Peter Metcalf, Betsy Gaines Quammen & David Quammen, the Utah Division of Arts & Museums, Utah Humanities, the National Endowment for the Humanities, the National Endowment for the Arts, the Salt Lake City Arts Council, the Utah Governor's Office of Economic Development, and Salt Lake County Zoo, Arts & Parks. Our thanks to our readers, donors, members, and the Torrey House Press Board of Directors for their valued support.

Printed in the USA
CPSIA information can be obtained
at www.ICGtesting.com
JSHW080214290524
63872JS00019B/50